*Nicky Edwards*

Nicky Edwards was born in 1958. A lesbian feminist and ex-peace camper, she contributed to *Greenham Common: Women at the Wire* edited by Barbara Harford and Sarah Hopkins (The Women's Press, 1984). She is currently at work on a second novel.

NICKY EDWARDS

# Mud

The Women's Press

For Elizabeth

With thanks to Kim Smith, Maria
Jastrzebska and the woman who lent me the
room with the typewriter

First published by The Women's Press Limited 1986
A member of the Namara Group
124 Shoreditch High Street, London E1 6JE

British Library Cataloguing in Publication Data

Edwards, Nicky
    Mud.
    I. Title
    823'.914[F]        PR6055.D9/

    ISBN 0–7043–2882–8
    ISBN 0–7043–3999–4 Pbk

Typeset by M C Typeset, Chatham, Kent
Printed in Great Britain by Nene Litho
and bound by Woolnough Bookbinding,
both of Wellingborough, Northants

# One

I think I am allergic to Horatio Bottomley. Sitting with a heavy bound collection of a popular magazine (June 1915 to April 1916) in front of me, trying to read one of his editorials, my nose begins to itch. Municipal hush in library reading room threatened by imminent sneezing fit, shock, horror. Grasping the bridge of my nose firmly between thumb and index finger, like illustrated life-saving, eyes watering.

Not all the old fossils here are in glass cases round the wall. Some of them are glaring at me, daring me to make a noise. Retired colonels to a man. The 'silence' notice hangs on chains above my head, ready to fall on my neck. I slam the dry and yellow pages of the old magazines between their solid cover. A little mushroom cloud of dust and mouldering paper puffs up around my head. I collapse, exploding sneezes echoing round the high-roofed, otherwise deathly quiet room. Everyone turns to stare, the air is thick with glares, tutting and the heavy frown of sprouting eyebrows.

I drop my basket full of books and tat. On hands and knees, gasping and coughing, I search under the table for stray biros and furry old throat lozenges. A row of bronze heads, dead aldermen, got by a shrewd ways and means committee in a bulk purchase from a Victorian jobbing sculptor, glower down at me, enplinthed.

Bits and pieces all retrieved, crammed back into the overflowing basket, still sneezing helplessly, I walk out. Down the whole length of that echoing room, with my shoes squeaking on the lino. Out of the marbled hall into the sticky roar of rush-hour West London traffic, lorries crashing over badly fitting man-hole covers and planes droning into Heathrow.

Since it doesn't matter any more, of course, I stop sneezing. Despite the fact that it's summertime and the smog is rising, pollen count high.

Unchain the bicycle, load up with lights and spares, pump, map, waterproofs and gloves. I remember when once it snowed in June, and I'm not planning on being caught out again. 1975, it was. Ride off into the sunset, or where it would be if there was one. Freewheeling down the long hill at the slummy end of Ladbroke Grove, hoping the lights don't change at the bottom, wasting all that free velocity.

Home by the motorway, where the town foxes and scraggy moggies roam among the dustbins. Pavements gummy with trodden-in plane leaves and the black sticky tracks of roller-skate convoys. Inside the house, it's cool and quiet. No breeding colony of bicycles in the hall. Only the gentle thump of bean bags hitting the ceiling of the basement flat tells me it's juggling practice time downstairs. I throw my collection of books, papers and carefully researched trivia for the play on to the desk in the front room and go through to the kitchen to make a cup of coffee. A gentle cloud of stinking fumes curls in through the open window. My next door neighbour, having one of her garden bonfires. It smells like tractor tyres this time. Where does she get them from? This isn't what you would call a heavily agricultural district. I wouldn't like to ask, though. She has a forbidding presence, and I've seen her burn odder things out there, before now. I drink my coffee and stare out of the window through the clouds of smoke, minding my own business and saying nothing.

There's a good-sized row developing out back. Neighbour opposite has been watching the bonfire from his stripped-pine castle. I've seen the curtains twitching. He's stormed out to remonstrate with neighbour next door. He is upwardly socially mobile, and knows his clean-air legislation. 'Go on, then,' she laughs at him, 'call the fire brigade. I don't give a fuck.' That's the trouble with 'or else' threats. Mr Public Spirit has no choice but to go in and make a 999, feeling like a prize twit.

I go through to the front room to watch for the arrival of our gallant emergency services. Flashing lights, but no sirens, here they are. Two very large firemen in helmets and plastic trousers march through the house next door with their axes bumping on their hips. The rest of the crew roll up cigarettes and try to look bored but faintly heroic. The next-doors are all falling about laughing in the front yard. Return of the two gallant leaders looking sheepish. Ticking off for next door about bonfires, she still doesn't give a fuck.

2

The last time I met any firemen was when we overstoked the boiler and set the chimney off. They took it very seriously. We all sat in a corner of the living room and watched them stride purposefully, bark terse orders and pour water down from the roof. I don't think they were comfortable with an audience of drunken women in pyjamas. When they had finished, the youngest of them, who was called Nigel, rolled up the mats they had put down to protect our grotty old carpet from their manly boots and they sped off into the night. Flushed under their tans, every one.

The excitement over, I decide to go down the pensioners' one o'clock club and pin up a notice. I assume they will have a noticeboard, it's run by the kind of right-on young people who probably believe that a noticeboard is structurally necessary to prop up the walls of a community centre. Somewhere, in the heap of paper and things-to-do lists on the desk, is the appeal for help with the play which I typed out yesterday. If the senior citizens' club doesn't produce any results, I'll have to put an ad in the local paper, though I have this feeling that only dedicated cranks answer ads in the local rag.

The club is tucked behind the motorway. None of the senior citizens is visible when I breeze in, although I hear the sound of bingo calling from the main hall. Years of flyposting and pinning political leaflets on forbidden boards, chased by outraged porters, have given me a very furtive way with a drawing pin. I find the board, quickly clear a space and pin up a pink card with the message: 'WRITER WISHES TO TALK TO MEN AND WOMEN ABOUT THEIR EXPERIENCES DURING WW 1 FOR NEW PLAY. CONTACT JO WHEELAN, 19 SEBASTOPOL ROAD.'

I had agonised over the wording for a long time, finally deciding that 'Researcher' sounded too official and 'Playwright' too pretentious. I didn't hold out great hope of any response. Only the most senior of the senior citizens would have been adults at the time, and there can't be too many of them left. Still, it was worth a try. I went home to see what would come of it.

Next morning, the daily dilemma. Shall I leap out of bed, stand on my head for ten minutes and jog down to the corner shop for a *Guardian*? Or pile all the bedclothes round my ears and go back to sleep? If I concentrated hard on all the things that aren't particularly right with me, I could probably feel ill enough to spend a day pandering to myself. No, save that for the next time it's raining. Shoddy compromise, crawl out of bed into a bath, play with the clockwork frogs and don't read any of the overseas news. I may lack intellectual rigour, but I don't turn straight to the cartoons, like some people I know.

About a mile from the house, on my way to the library, I start wondering whether it wouldn't have been better to have written this morning off and gone to the launderette, or cleaned out the goldfish. Some suitable activity for tense and gloomy days. Every pedestrian in London is loitering on the pavement just so they can hurl themselves into the road under my front wheel. The lorry drivers are exercising their Boadicea fantasies and the lights at the bottom of every hill go red when they see me coming. People who travel by tube think this is a healthy way to get about. What a joke. Aerobics in a coal-mine, poor lungs working so efficiently in a stream of pure carbon monoxide. And the stress. I'm sure that dicing with death, manic cabbies and coach-loads of jay-walking tourists is character-forming. Frankly, I sometimes wonder if having too much moral fibre doesn't make the personality rather constipated.

Still, I think, as I collapse in a sweaty jittering heap by my favourite lamp-post, this may be killing me by centimetres, but it keeps me smug in the meanwhile. Self-satisfied bike-bores against longevity.

Upstairs in the reference reading room, I stake my claim to my accustomed place, putting down little territorial markers. File, pens, coat and bag form square around me. The others, being British, understand these 'Keep Out' notices perfectly.

Base camp established, it's off to find the books I was working from yesterday. There's always a moment of anxiety that someone else might be using them, but I resist the temptation to put them back on the wrong shelves, so they're safely hidden from any poor sap who thinks the catalogue system works. Military history (1900–1918) does have a surprising number of reference works from the botany section in it today. I suppose that means a journalist working on a herbicide scoop.

For an hour or so I crib notes from a file of contemporary newspaper articles. It's meant to be 'real people' research. It's still mostly about generals and great battles, leading politicians and affairs of state. Not a lot of 'Fred Bloggs, 22, says he hasn't had a clean pair of socks since Christmas and he's fed up with the lice'. In all these cuttings Fred is a gallant Tommy, with an occasional waggish quip about the roughness of life, but generally mucking in.

Cheer-oh.

Up on the roof for a cigarette break, I can see half the town sweating in an irritable summer haze. It is strictly forbidden to be up here of course, but there is nowhere else in this building. I only found out about it by accident, the door is inconspicuous, up a small flight of back stairs. I followed the maintenance man up here once, because he had the look of someone sneaking off work for an unofficial smoke break. We pass on the stairs sometimes, and have a conspiracy of silence about these few square feet on the leads.

I don't like summer. But then, I don't like London either, so this is the only time of the year I'm happy to be here. In winter, my favourite season, I can't bear the squalor of no proper snow-drifts, only piles of gritted slush on the pavements. It never gets decently cold. Summer, I have no rural fantasies about. All those acres of green are a burden on the eye, like having to smile too long at a party full of strangers. Summer in the country makes my mental smile-muscles ache. So I am quite happy to be in the city now, even though the water tastes like it's been filtered through old face flannels. When every woman I know seems to have taken off for a Greek island, to get away from it. Lesbos and Chia must be like Upper Street on a Saturday afternoon just now.

It would be pleasant to be bronzed and lissome. Make a bargain with myself. If I get enough done today, I'll spend some of the weekend by the pond on the Heath. If it keeps fine. If my ear isn't still full of weeds and tadpoles from the last time I swam there. I can't go and not swim. Us closet narcissists pretend a suntan is an irrelevant side-effect of stupendously wholesome outdoor lives. Like body-builders who say they only do it for the exercise.

This play I am meant to be writing nags at me. I am not comfortable with it. I am not at all sure that it will work. The two characters, a modern woman pacifist and the dead First World War infantryman haunt me as much as they're supposed to haunt each other. I have always been fascinated by that war, more than by any other: I wonder why the ordinary people who got involved did it. Why would anyone stand in a muddy ditch in a Belgian winter being shot at? How could they put up with it, not just say 'this is silly, I'm going home'?

I started to understand how it might have felt when I was living at a peace camp last winter. I know that sounds funny. It makes it very difficult to explain to my friends what I'm working on. At the camp we used to joke about being in the trenches. Living out of doors, in make-shift shelters. Standing about in the mud in ponchos, with leg-warmers for puttees, we probably even looked the part.

Living for the next arrival of cigarettes, hot drinks and sweet things. Long periods of tedium, interspersed with the excitement of action. Over the wire into the base, never quite knowing what would happen to you as a result. The occasional breaks to get a warm bath and a bit of the pressure off. Most of all, what we had in common was the feeling of remoteness from the rest of the world 'back home'. The folks at home thought they knew what it was like, they read in the papers about us, but they didn't have a clue how it really felt. It became more and more difficult to talk to people who weren't part of it, and going back to that other world for a visit was a strain. We were strange, uncomfortable, displaced persons in our former lives.

Still, everyone back there had an opinion. They read the papers. Sometimes they thought we were heroes and martyrs, when fashion changed we were naive or mad, bad and dangerous to know. We carried on anyway. But cheering us on or despising us, they still didn't know what it was really like.

The great thing about smoking roll-ups, is that it is always easy to tell when you've been talking too much, or thinking too much. They go out. I relit the mangled stub, which I had been chewing absent-mindedly through a five-minute brood, and watched the pigeons start creeping up on me like a game of grandmother's footsteps. Reclaiming their territory. Time to get back to work.

# Two

What I like about fiction is the way the heroine, taking herself off to await events, is always followed almost immediately by something Very Significant happening. Usually within a couple of paragraphs.

Since real life chugs along in a more rambling way, it was a week, at least, before Mrs Prince turned up on my doorstep.

It was mid-morning on a bad day. I'd been to sign on, and that always leaves me feeling like a reused tea-bag. I was sitting at the desk trying to blow the dust of a thousand unfiled forms from my sinuses when she rang the doorbell. Without much expectation of it being anything good, I went to answer it.

'Morning.' She had a hat and a brisk manner on. 'I've come to see Mr Wheelan. He put up a notice. My name's Prince. Ada Prince. Mrs.'

I tried to look unflappable.

'Not Mr Wheelan. It's me. I'm Jo Wheelan. Won't you come in?' I stepped back, but still she stood looking at me with her head tilted to one side.

'Well, I don't know, I thought you'd be a bloke. Not that it matters.' She tipped her head to the other side. 'And older. You look a bit young to be a writer.'

'We've all got to start somewhere.' She decided to risk my gender and youth, because she crossed the threshold and followed me into the flat.

'Tea?' I offered.

'That would be nice, dear.'

I saw her settled in the only armchair in the living room and went off to make the brew.

It was all very well, casually casting about for suppliers of oral history, but I wasn't at all sure that I knew how to go about it in a professional manner. It's hard to be gimlet-eyed and systematic with someone who looks like the granny who used to pour rose-hip syrup down my childish throat and check that I'd washed behind my ears. Perhaps she would turn out to be chronically chatty, and I could sit and take notes.

My hopes on that score faded when I walked back into the front room. She was sitting there, self-possessed, examining the contents of the room like a time-served burglar casing a joint. She was a very short woman, stoutish and strong-looking. Her hair was white and thin at the top, but carefully curled. Bunion-shaped feet, but she looked to be in very good nick for someone of seventy-odd.

I poured her a mug of tea and handed it to her.

'There you go, then,' I wish I could stop this jollyness. I sounded like a doctor.

'Ta, love.' She smiled at me, putting me at my ease. I can see I'll have zero credibility as an interviewer.

'Nice flat.'

'Thanks.' I try to be businesslike. 'Now you will know that I'm working on a play about the First War?'

'I saw your card in the club.' She was not to be herded. 'Seems like a funny thing for a young girl like you to want to write about. Still. You live here alone?'

'Yes.' The worst thing about granny lookalikes is that you can't snap 'woman' at them when they call you 'girl'.

'Well, I daresay there's others in the house. Do you get on?'

'Yes thank you.' I was trying not to grit my teeth too audibly.

'That's nice. Always nice to get on with your neighbours. Her next door hasn't spoken to me these forty years gone. Before they put her in the home, that is.'

'Why?'

'She was senile, they said. The council took her off. Well, her youngest put them up to it. Wanted the house, he did. I thought she still had most of her marbles. Just naturally cantankerous.'

'No, why wouldn't she speak to you for so long?'

Mrs Prince frowned for a moment.

'You know, it's a funny thing, but I can't for the life of me remember. I know it had something to do with her Ted. She thought we'd been carrying on. But we never had words about it. Just stopped talking to me from one day to the next.'

'Were you?' I realised what I was asking and hesitated. 'Er, carrying on. With Ted?' She smiled at me. It's a shock to get a

8

knowing lascivious grin from a little old lady.

'That'd be telling wouldn't it? Anyway, Ted's been dead these twenty years, so least said.'

'I'm sorry. I didn't mean to pry.'

'That's all right dear, there's plenty that have, and not asked me to my face either. He was a handsome-looking man. Cup Final took him off.'

'Sorry?' I had lost her again.

'Sixty-six. England won the world cup final. Excitement of it give him a heart attack.'

'How sad.'

'Oh no, dear, he lasted through the extra time. He would have been mad if he'd gone before the final whistle.'

There didn't seem a lot I could say to that, so I picked up my notebook and tried to look businesslike again. Put my glasses on, they make me feel purposeful.

'About this research I'm doing. . .'

'I thought you were writing a play?'

Yes, it's research for a play. What I was looking for. . .'

'Ever been on the telly, any of your plays?'

'No, actually, I don't write for the television. Too difficult to do what one wants in a commercial medium.'

'Never mind, ducks,' she consoled. 'Keep trying. I'm sure you'll make it one day.'

'No, it's not that. I write mostly for the stage.'

'That's nice. I used to like a good theatre. Haven't been for years, mind. Used to go up town to a show when I was courting Prince. If we were flush.' For a moment I thought Prince must be a dog, then I realised she was talking of her husband. 'Last time I was in the theatre was *The Mousetrap* on my sixty-fifth birthday. Or thereabouts. You write anything like that?'

'No, the stuff I do is mostly for radical groups. They tend to perform in rather smaller venues.'

'Never mind, we can't all be Agatha Christie, can we? Not that I like her books so much.'

Recognising that I was not going to get Mrs Prince to the point before she was good and ready, I put down my notebook and poured us both some more tea. That seemed to signal to her that she had established the right to do things at her own pace. Satisfied, perversely, she folded her hands and said briskly, 'What do you want to know then? For this research or whatever?'

9

I tried to recollect the little speech I had failed to deliver three times already.

'What I was looking for was a man who fought in the First World War or the wife of someone who did. Really, I had thought someone older perhaps. . .' I worked out she must have been all of six years old on armistice day.

'I would say I'd buried two husbands, only Gower, that was my first, never had a funeral. Didn't come back from third Ypres,' she pronounced it 'Wipers'. She saw my look of surprise. 'I'll be eighty-three next month.'

Now it must be brattish arrogance which made me think that vanity ended at forty, because no one over that age would have anything to preen themselves about. But Mrs Prince managed to look delighted and a little bit arch when I said she didn't look a day over seventy to me.

'How well do you remember back then?' I asked.

'Like it was yesterday. You know what they say about my time of life. Longer ago something happened the more you remember it. Never believed it myself,' she puffed out her chest. 'Me, I can still remember what happened yesterday as well. Not lost all my faculties, I can tell you.'

'I can see that,' I was getting to like Mrs P. 'Tell me about your first husband then.'

'He was a daft bugger to join. I told him so at the time. Got drunk with a bunch of his mates from when he was a kid and went down the recruiting office. Silly so and so. They were all off work, of course, end of the summer. It was a lark for them. But he had a good steady job. Didn't need to go at all.'

'What did he do?'

'His job?'

I nodded.

'He was a counter assistant in one of the big shops. There's a lot would have given their back teeth for his place. Work all the year round and nothing rough. He'd done well to get that far at his age. Worked up from a delivery boy. Bright, he was, not like those good-for-nothing friends of his. Couldn't hardly read, some of his best pals. Still, he stuck with them. Soft about the old days, he was.'

'Did he regret joining? If he was drunk when he did it?' It didn't seem that simple.

'No, dear, I don't know as he did.' She sighed. 'Got any smokes?'

'Only roll-ups. Shall I do you one?'

'Please. I'd do my own, but I'm sure you've quicker hands.'

She waited while I made her a cigarette, got it lit and started again.

'For a while I thought he'd see sense after a bit and get himself out. Don't know how I thought he'd do that, just stroll out of the training barracks when he got bored. I didn't know much about the army then. But, of course, I should have known John wouldn't give up on it that easy. He may have taken a few drinks and gone along in a rush with the old gang of his, but he would have joined sooner or later anyway.'

'Why was that?'

'He was a proud lad. Not stupid. I mean he wasn't taken in by all that hurrahing about the empire and the Germans. He read a lot, you see. Newspapers, books, pamphlets. All sorts. He always had his nose in something. He knew there was a war coming. Well, we all did, but he knew a bit about why. Used to get quite cross about it. But off he went, almost to spite himself, I thought.'

'Was that his pride?'

'Yes, I always thought so. You see, he was always having to prove that he was tougher than the next man. Ever since he was a little lad. Being bright at school he wasn't that popular. Always having to get into fights to prove he was just like the others. His mum brought him up, you see, after his old man died, on her own. She was always trying to give him better things than the kids round our way were used to.'

'Like what?'

'Oh, you know. Books. She taught him to play the piano. She used to talk to him like he was full grown. She must have been lonely after his dad died. Treated him more like a friend than a kid. She kept them with her sewing, and sometimes singing lessons for the children further up the hill. It wasn't much, but she always managed to treat him a bit special. So of course all the other kids thought he was a cissy.'

'You knew him when you were children, then?'

'Oh yes, we all went to the same school. I didn't think much of him then. Always getting duffed up on the way home. The bigger boys used to wait for him. Then he'd be off round the backs for a bit of a cry and clean himself up so as his mum wouldn't know he'd been scrapping. We used to follow him sometimes.'

'It seems a bit cruel.'

'Yes, it was. You know what kids are like with anything different.

11

You don't get tolerant till you're my age.' I felt well put in my place.

'Anyway,' she went back to her story (and I'd worried about getting her started), 'somewhere along the ways he learnt how to fight a bit, stopped being such a walk-over for the other lads. So they stopped laying into him. He even started to make some friends. He got up to all sorts of mischief in school. And, of course, the naughtier he was, the more the others looked up to him. So he was getting his jacket dusted by the teacher all the time, instead of being roughed up by the other lads. But he didn't seem to mind. And he still managed to keep up with his lessons, without anyone really noticing, like. He was always near the top of the form. But no one baited him for being a know-all, not after he learned how to scrap.'

'What happened after you all finished school?' I started a new subheading in my notes.

'Well, he left before me, being a bit older. He started off sweeping up in a tailor's cutting room, then he got taken on as a round boy. That's where he was when he joined the army. Working his way up. He had it all planned.' Even at the distance of seventy years, her exasperation was obvious. 'He was going to work his way up there for a while, save a bit of money and start his own shop maybe, when he knew the trade. I think his mother had something put by to start him up when he knew for sure what he wanted to do. He would have made a go of it as well. And we were going to get married, when he was ready to start out on his own.'

'You'd already decided that?' She must have been in her early teens.

'We didn't start courting till I'd been working a few months. But we'd an understanding.'

'What was your work?'

'Maid of all work.' She looked as though she was going to spit on the floor. 'Slavey was a better name for it. That's what we was called, and that's what I was. Bleeding slave.' She asked me to 'pardon her French' and went on. 'We had to wait, of course, till he left the store. And I was saving as well for us to get married. Only 'cos I never got time to go and spend any money. Not that I got that much.'

'Why did you have to wait?'

'Well even if I'd been really old enough for his mum and mine to be happy with it, which I wasn't then (not that mine would have worried that much, she was married younger) the store wouldn't have let him.'

'What did it have to do with them?'

'The junior assistants weren't allowed to marry. Their lives weren't their own really. They were told how they had to dress, and how to behave, and if they didn't like it, there were always plenty willing to take their jobs. They were like gentlemen, you see. Very respectable. The clothes they had to wear for work. Gower always looked like he was off to a funeral while he was there. That was another reason why he still had to keep on proving he wasn't a cissy to his mates.'

'What were they all doing?' I had rather forgotten about John Gower's peer group.

'Odds and sods. Albert, his best friend, did have a place as a messenger at an office in the city for a few weeks, but they threw him out for cheeking the boss. Mostly it was what they could pick up on building sites, which wasn't much. The whole gang of them had just come back from the hops before they joined. Which is how they had the money to be getting drunk and making fools of themselves.'

'Did their opinion of him matter so much to your husband?'

'No, it wasn't just that. Don't get me wrong about John, he wasn't so weak that he cared about what the others thought of him more than anything. But he wanted to prove things to himself. I think he was afraid of going, so that was all the more reason for him to go. He was very hard on himself. And he was swept along a bit. They all were. It was just something to do, because all the other lads were doing it. They made it all sound exciting and there were a lot who didn't want to miss out. And going abroad, too. Silly beggars, thought they'd all be home by Christmas.'

'Did he ever try and explain to you why he was going?'

'Not so as you'd notice. He got a bit of leave before they put him on a boat for France. That's when we were wed. The last night he tried to explain, but he ended up just kind of shrugging and saying, "Well you know, I've got to be off, girl, don't ask me why, or what for." But I think he still believed some of that stuff about poor little Belgium then. He couldn't be sure at first whether it all needed doing, or if it was just a great big stupid cock-up. He soon found out. But even then it was a bit like the song. You know, "We're here because we're here because we're here because we're here." ' She sang it to the tune of 'Auld Lang Syne' with some gusto.

There was a pause. She didn't seem lost in her memories exactly, just a bit distant. She picked up the tobacco from the desk, looking

13

for my permission. I nodded, and she rolled herself a cigarette. Not quickly, but neatly, as though her hands had gone through the motions often enough not to need any conscious direction. She sat smoking and looking out of the window for a few minutes. Her eyes were the palest blue I'd ever seen, almost grey. Strange that she managed to look so acute. Definitely a twinkle there. She gave her shoulders a little shake and smiled apologetically at me.

'You must think I'm a daft old woman, gone off in a daze like this.'

'If you only knew how many hours I spend gawping out of that window with a blank sheet of paper in front of me, you wouldn't worry about a few minutes wool-gathering.'

'Yes, I'm sure I spent more time day-dreaming when I was your age.' She smiled, wrinkling up her face to take any offence from her words. 'And now I've all the time I want to be silly in, I'm more practical than ever I used to be.'

'You make me feel like an infant.'

'That's what you are, my love, a real babe yet.'

'And here was I thinking I might just about count as a grown-up now.'

'Grown-up?' Mrs Prince nearly fell off her chair laughing this time. Her whole body shook gently. 'You never get there, girl, not till you've got kids of your own one day and they think you know all there is to know. And you still thinking you're young and wanting a bit of fun. Come into your life and don't imagine you was ever a kid yourself, they don't. Think you were put there ready-made just to run after them. Born with all your wrinkles and grey hair.'

Although she had more than her fair share of both, I decided to show her that I was no spring chicken myself.

'Look,' I said, bending my head towards her. 'Grey hair. Several of them.'

'Where?'

'There.' I jabbed what I thought was the spot. She peered at it.

'Well, maybe you have. Don't know why, though. What've you ever had to worry about?'

'This and that. I'm getting an early start on growing old gracefully.'

'I wouldn't bother about that if I were you. My eldest is always on at me not to be out down the pub till all hours "at my age". What's my age got to do with it, I'd like to know? I've always gone down the pub, and I'm not going to make my last years miserable just to

14

satisfy his idea of what's a proper way for a grandmother to behave.'

I stopped trying to attach my braces together with a paper clip and got back to the subject.

'Look, I was wondering if you had any letters or anything like that from your husband?' I realised how intrusive that might sound. 'I mean, if you didn't mind, perhaps I could see them.'

'Well, you're welcome to see what there is. Not that it's much.' She twisted the gold band on her ring finger. It was her only fidget, otherwise she was a very calm-sitting woman.

'Why's that?'

'Well to start with, he didn't write too much about what he thought, because he couldn't bear the idea of it being read. Their letters out had to be censored by an officer, you know.' I nodded. 'Some twit fresh from Eton reading his letters to me. He was sensitive about that. At first he was.'

'And later?'

'Later he didn't give that for who knew what he thought, but it was like he couldn't tell me that much. Didn't think I'd understand, maybe. So it was all about the food and the weather, and the things that he'd be missing at home, maybe what one of his mates said. Nothing really, he didn't have nothing he could say that mattered.'

'Did that hurt you?'

'Well I wasn't stupid. I knew there were things he wasn't telling me. Of course I was hurt. When he came home, the one time he got leave after he went over there, then he couldn't hide that there was a lot he wasn't talking about. And he used to tell me everything, before he went. Not like most blokes, used to treat me like I had something between my ears. Proud of it, he used to be. Said I was the brightest girl he ever met.'

'Was it unusual in those days? Having a man that listened to you?'

'I don't know about those days,' her laugh was a rasping at the base of her throat, 'I reckon it's bloody rare any time. Not that we were puritans or anything. Just that we always used to spend a lot of time talking, when we were courting. And not just all that lovey-dovey stuff, either. We were like good pals.'

'How much did you know about what was going on during the war?'

'If you had a bit of sense you took all that was in the papers about how our lads was all doing really well with a shovelful of salt. And I could tell a lot by the things that John wasn't talking about, if you see what I mean.' I nodded again. 'There was these great big silences that used to make me sit up and think something's going on. But mostly it was our Vicky's Jack coming back with his legs blown off. He'd been in John's company too. I used to sit with him of an evening, while she was working round the corner. He used to tell me all about it. No stopping him there wasn't, sometimes I don't think he even knew whether I was there or not. He was that bitter. Well, you could understand. Fine-looking man he was, before that shell took his legs off. Nearly signed professional with the Arsenal. Died soon after, didn't really have any fight left. Just slipped off.'

'Was he your brother-in-law?'

'That's right. Jack and Vicky married on his leave. Very sudden it was, though there was a lot hurrying things then. Funny that, us both marrying a man with the same name. Of course my John was never called Jack, not even when he was a nipper. His mother wouldn't let anyone call him anything but his given name. She was a bit funny like that. Thought it was common.'

There was another long pause. I realised we had been talking for over an hour. My visitor (I still couldn't think of her as Ada, and Mrs Prince didn't seem right any more) must be tired. I was wiped myself and needed a break.

'Shall we meet again? I don't know about you, but I need to stop there, have a bit of time to take all this in.'

'Yes, dear, I suppose I have been rabbiting on a bit.'

'No, no, it's not that.'

'Well anyway, it's time I was getting off. My meals on wheels woman gets in a real tizzy if I'm not in when she calls. Thinks I've lost me marbles and gone for a walk on the Westway.' She stood up slowly, enjoying making a performance of her solidity. She gathered her possessions and put on her hat, standing in front of the mirror over the fire to check its angle. Patting it, satisfied.

'Why don't you come round to my flat next time you want to know anything? Just pop in. That is if you haven't had enough already.' She told me the address, a block of flats a few streets away.

'That would be great.' I was a bit apprehensive about being on her territory, but I supposed it made sense. 'If it's less bother for you.'

'Yes, I think it would be best.' She regarded the room with interest but no fondness. 'When you get to my age, you're allowed to prefer the comfort of your own armchair. Although it's been a nice little outing for me.'

I showed her to the door and stood watching her as she descended the steps.

'What's a good time to call?'

'Any time during the day, dear. Not Thursdays, though. I go down the club Thursdays. And late afternoon I sometimes take a nap.'

'So do I.' I didn't tell many people that. 'Early next week perhaps?'

'I'll see you then. First floor I'm on.' She turned and started walking down the path.

'Bye. And thanks for coming.' She reached the gate, smiled briefly back at me and set off. I watched her walking along for a bit, a square, slow-moving figure, looking only in front of her.

# Three

     When I used to be a respectable working woman, I would have to invent important meetings at siesta time, so I could lock myself in my office and snooze undisturbed for the slack hours in the afternoon when my body tells me I have some Mediterranean blood way back somewhere.

Now I'm a self-employed, state-subsidised disgrace, I can make myself a present of some time off whenever I feel like it.

There's only one place to go when I feel self-indulgent and want a quiet think, and that's the weight room. Down the gym with all the sweaty white boys in union jack shorts, the boils on their necks glowing purple with the effort of not noticing the teenage Dreads lifting more kilos than they could manage in a month of hernias. In training to beat the shit out of each other, this is an area of armed truce. But everyone pretends they're alone in the gym.

I used to think that a well-ordered world would include women only multi-gym rooms. The smelly muscle cupboard upstairs from the swimming pool isn't exactly a women's space. But part of me enjoys breezing in there doing a bit of reclaiming, making the trainee sand-kickers squirm. Like strolling through a stock exchange dinner in your Doc Martens.

This afternoon, though, it was quiet. The woman on the pay desk always tells me who's in. She knows the regulars.

'The other girl's not in today.' She presumes we stick together.

I've seen that woman so many times in here. She's the only other one who uses the weight room regularly. We've never spoken, though. I don't even know her name, or she mine. We smile politely at each other, but I avoid watching her too closely when she's lifting. That would be bad manners.

Maybe she'll be in later. Warming up, I clock one of the clones who use this place a lot. I think he irons his running vests. Maybe his moustache too. He has a way of concentrating, as he works on his body beautiful, that reminds me of five-year-olds doing hard sums. Wrinkled brow, little grunts, tongue sticking out and oblivious to all around him.

This place is always full of small noises, although no one speaks. The clank of metal weights settling; the squeaking of a frayed cable on one of the pulleys; squelchy track shoes.

On my second circuit, the good point between the effort of getting going and starting to collapse. Trying not to skip the bits of equipment I don't enjoy and linger on the ones which are fun. Lying on the bench, pushing up the bar above my head, straight up from the shoulder. Feeling the blood pouring down the big arteries in my body all the way from brain to toes and back in seconds. Maybe it's not that far. Impossible to feel gloomy with all your corpuscles rushing about inside you like kids in a playground.

I was hanging upside down on the sloping bench, thinking about life, art and a dozen sit-ups. I felt my options narrowed by Ada's collaboration. Obliged to take it seriously on her behalf. Nothing for it but to press on with the play and hope she wouldn't be too disappointed if it isn't a box-office smash by Christmas. Or even finished. Maybe I should give up starting things which involve other people.

Uncurling from a half-hearted sit-up, I saw the knees of the only other woman who uses the gym go past at my eye-level. The rest of her must have gone past as well, but out of my upside-down field of vision. I unhooked my feet from the bar and slithered down the bench to land in a heap on my head.

I glanced over at her where she was nonchalantly swinging a dumb-bell round her head. She's very small and graceful. Tons of poise. Pointed nose and ears, a distant manner. I guess she's a serious dancer. I tend to think anyone with pink leg-warmers is a serious dancer.

She met my gaze and looked faintly friendly. More acknowledging than inviting. I could go and say hello. But if you embarrass someone in a small place, there's always going to be awkwardness between you. Conscious of each other. Somewhere like this, you need obliviousness, otherwise you start being aware of how silly you must look, red-faced and bug-eyed with the strain. So I would go on not speaking to her, and she not speaking to me, otherwise one of us would have to find somewhere else to workout, and that would be a shame. I understand commuters, not speaking on the same train with each other for thirty years.

It's time I fell in love again, I thought as I left the gym and made my way, pink and self-righteous-looking, out on to the unhealthy street. I had toyed with the idea of telling my friends that I was politically celibate, to cover up the fact that I was quite enjoying sleeping in my own bed and not having to make drastic compromises about breakfast cereal. The trouble with making political stands, though, you usually end up at a conference having to justify them.

I got back to the flat and lay in the hot green cliché of a Radox bath, watching the clockwork whale chug up and down, spouting water out of the top of its head, crashing into the frogs. I never had bath toys when I was a kid. My mother gave me three rubber ducks on my twenty-first birthday to make up for it.

I was going to have a night on the razzle, I decided, climbing out of the tub. It meant putting on my best socks and matching ear-rings, otherwise you might not have noticed the difference. Nearly ready to go. Only the right frame of mind to get into now. I did a little soft-shoe round the flat, checking the windows were shut, generally fussing. I wondered if I could ever persuade my hair to stand on end and look radically rumpled. Passing the mirror I grabbed a handful of it hopefully and tried for a street-wise look. I could hear the follicles heave a sigh of exasperation, humour me for a micro-second, then slump back to their normal, sensible flat-top heap. Ho hum.

I turned out all the lights in the flat. Thought about burglars and put the hall light back on. Thought about the electricity bill and turned it off again.

Got as far as the door, ran through the pre-launch check, with one foot keeping the door open in case I'd forgotton the keys. Patted each one of the eight pockets I had to lose things in. Keys; money; bit of paper with my phone number on it, in case I forgot; tissues; tobacco; papers; matches. My concession to not taking a lot of clutter was leaving my notebook and penknife behind. What would I do if I was struck by inspiration or found a boy-scout trapped in a horse's hoof?

I got to the bar about ten. Already the place was full of women, smoke and noise. As I stood in the short queue by the door, I had a look at the crowd. My eyes weren't used to the dimness yet, all I could make out was a sea of bodies in Marks and Spencer vests (it was a hot summer) with a lot of cropped bleached heads bobbing about on top.

I reached the pay desk. 'Unwaged,' I said, handing over a pocketful of change that looked like I'd robbed the kids' piggy bank for a night out. She gave me the disillusioned stare of someone who hasn't seen anybody come out as a wage-earner all evening, and a ticket. I fell into the gently heaving scrum by the bar, and caught the eye of the rudest barperson in the place. She walked off and served someone else. Came back eventually and condescended to pull me a pint. Slid it across from the pumps in the best wild west style, threw my change into a puddle of lager on the bar and stomped off. I used to work in a pub myself, so I know how she feels. A guy came up to me the other day and said I'd thrown him out of a pub six years ago, when he was a student. I used to throw a lot of students out of my pub. It comes of growing up in a university town. You get to be a bit prejudiced. This turkey said I was the rudest barmaid he'd ever met. Shook me by the hand. Obviously one of the happy memories of his wild youth.

I made my way over to the pool table. There was some cut-throat competition going on, and a stack of coins on the edge which would keep it running till closing time. As I stood watching the players, I felt someone prodding me in the side and looked down.

'Jo.' We hugged. I couldn't remember her name.

'Hi.' I covered up with another exuberant hug and hoped I wouldn't be found out. 'How are you?'

'Fine. Are you living in London now?'

'Yes, since the beginning of the summer.'

'You've left the camp?'

'Yes.' I hunkered down on the floor, beside where she was sitting.

'For good?' She looked distressed.

'You know how it is, It was time for me to leave.'

'Why?' She looked as though I'd just put her goldfish in the oven.

'I had enough of being dragged around by oafish policemen. I don't believe in non-violence any more. Not for myself. And I wanted some time to do other things that matter to me. Like writing.'

'But non-violence is the whole point of the camp. It would never have achieved anything without it.'

'Yes I know it's important.' I wished I could remember her name. 'And any woman who wants to carry on with the non-violent direct action has my support. It's a useful tactic. But I find it personally damaging, putting myself in that position. So I've stopped doing it. Simple.'

'But if everyone thought like that . . .' she bellowed. We were both yelling. Even in this far corner of the bar the noise of the disco was pretty deafening. It's hard to explain the finer points of your personal philosophy at full volume.

'Not everyone does though,' I interrupted her. 'There are still plenty of women there. It's just that some of us had enough of it. New women can come, us burnt-out cases can go off and recharge our batteries. There's no reason why we should all be there all the time.'

'It makes me sad to see women who were there a long time leaving.' Funny how it's the people who never lived at the camp who try and make you feel a sell-out for leaving. Maybe she read the thought, because she changed the subject.

'So what are you doing now?'

'Oh, this and that. Writing a play.'

'That's interesting. You in touch with any of the women's theatre groups?'

I grunted. 'How about you? How's work?' I'm so polite.

'Fine. Things are fine.' She glanced at one of the women who was playing pool a few feet from us. I'd noticed her doing that several times while we talked. Not gloating so much as glowing. The woman she was watching looked neat and self-confident, played a mean game of pool.

'Apart from work, what're you up to?'

'I'm in love,' she said, unnecessarily, still watching the pool player.

'Is she nice?' God, that's the sort of thing your mother might ask. Well, almost.

'Yes. It's like being a kid again. I haven't been in love for years.'

'Enjoy it then.' I prised myself to a standing position. Both my feet had pins and needles. 'Nothing wrong with being a kid.'

'You off?'

'Got to go for a pee. You know what the queues are like here. Have to plan a week in advance.' She laughed, clutched my elbow gently and gave my arm a little shake. She's a lapsed British non-touchist, gradually working her way up to being a big hug and cuddler.

I walked off through the crowd. Now we could avoid talking to each other again all evening without causing any offence. I still

22

wished I could remember her name.

There was no good new graffiti in the toilets. One of the long running ideological debates which had started off intense and concerned last week in about three different hands, had got down to ya boo sucks a foot from the floor.

Back at the noisiest end of the bar, I got another drink, said hello to a few women who didn't know me well enough to ask me what I was doing in London, and thought about having a bop. Twelve-inch singles are a real problem for us ageing teeny-boppers, with our stamina gone to pot. This DJ never plays anything else. There's no way I could hop through the entire length of one of the synthesiser marathons. When I was little, singles were still two minutes fifty. Anything longer had a ten-minute guitar solo in it. This DJ's taste for what sounded like disco-mix versions of men digging up the road left me cold. Maybe it's time to find another night spot.

Turning to go, the flash of reflected light from a giant pair of plastic earrings caught my notice. It must be Leah. No one else would have the brass neck to wear anything as outrageously tasteless as that any more. I stared into the alcove where she was sitting. Difficult to make out who else was there. But I knew if one of the gang was here, they all would be. The whole Brixton squat, out on one of their sprees.

I fought my way over to the corner they had colonised. Freda was sitting by Leah, and Rosie, in her pyjamas. Blue, sharing a stool with a woman I didn't recognise and Nasha (or was it Gnasher?) who was giving Leah a foot massage.

I couldn't see Sal. She must be there, surely, with that lot. My stomach still tightened at the thought of seeing her again, even after all these months of nothing between us. I took a step closer to the table, and recognised the shape of her head. She was sitting with her back to me. At the same moment Leah looked up and saw me standing there.

'Jo!' She swayed to her feet and kissed me. 'How are you?'

'Fine, thanks.' I was hugging each of them in turn, watching Sal. She was giving me a very enigmatic look. Not making things easy. I worked my way round to her.

'Hullo, my love.' Her smile only moved the corners of her eyes, her voice was as husky as I remembered it. Like an old blues singer taken to drinking bathtub gin, that's how she always sounded.

'Hullo,' I said, perching on the arm of her chair. Leah got up and picked her glass up from the table.

'Who's got the money?' There was a pause while some of the women rummaged in their hats and leg-warmers for cash. Sal asked me to get her a drink. Pint of bitter, as ever. I gave Leah the money. She got back with the round, and there was a general shuffling of drinks and change and space on the cluttered table-top.

'How's the house?'

'It's OK. The council know we're there, but we don't think they'll try and evict us just yet.'

'It's freezing, though,' said Rosie. 'Even in this weather. We all stayed in bed the whole of yesterday, 'cos it was too cold to get up, and there was no money to go out with.'

'Is that why you're wearing your jim-jams?'

'She didn't wake up till eight o'clock this evening.' Leah tweaked Rosie's ear affectionately. She did look very like Alice's door-mouse.

'They said they weren't going to hang around any longer while I thought about getting up and dressing,' Rosie explained to me. 'So I just put on a coat and came out. I couldn't decide what to wear.'

'Good thing they're warm.' They were too, winceyette pyjamas with a paisley pattern.

'We're going to have to go and do a shop tomorrow. I can't face any more lentil stew,' Blue said, taking the cigarette out of my hand, having a drag then passing it back.

'We did a wholefood store for a couple of sacks last week. Didn't have time to check what was in them.' Nasha said, going directly to source and taking the tobacco out of my pocket to roll herself one. She knew me better. 'One was lentils, the other was Afghan raisins.' She pulled a face.

Being soberish and as much in possession of my faculties as usual, I was having difficulty with the conversation. They were all smashed. It wasn't a big problem, a bit of dissonance. Like when sound and vision get ever so slightly out of synch at all those showings by amateur projectionists of films the BBC banned, for concerned audiences. Leah was the most together of them. Blue and her friend appeared to have passed out. It was Leah (most social poise) who remembered to ask me what I was doing.

'Oh, writing, you know. Getting away from the camp.' They didn't give me any shit about lacking commitment because I didn't want to get dragged around by policemen and soldiers any more. They'd all been there. In fact we'd all stopped living at the camp around the same time.

24

We swopped information for a few minutes more, but I knew the gap between us was too great. They were thinking about doing a bank, I was thinking of going home for an Ovaltine and an early night. I stood up.

'I'm off.' Leah had written the address of their squat on the back of a beer mat. She handed it to me.

'Call round sometime. If we're not there, we'll be in the pub.'

'Sure.' I didn't volunteer my address, and none of them asked for it. Leah got up and moved round to take the seat next to Sal which I had left. I'd stopped wondering whether they were lovers a while ago. I hugged both of them.

'See you, then.' Leah pecked me on the cheek.

As I walked towards the tube, chin resting on my chest, half an eye out for dodging the closing-time drunks driving home along the pavement, I thought I saw a woman I knew follow me out of the bar. Out of the corner of my eye, I saw her outline reflected in a plate-glass window from the glare of street lights. She was small and walked with a graceful bounce. I couldn't see her face but her shape was familiar. I turned, but she'd taken a step towards the road, with her back to me. A bus slowed down for the lights and she jumped on it as it pulled away.

# Four

Next morning, early, half waking up, I thought I'd dislocated my thumb. Listen. Click. It went out. Click. Back again. Can you dislocate your thumb in your sleep? Pull yourself together, Jo. It would have woken you up. Panic. What's that lump of bone then? Check. One on the other hand as well. It's meant to be there. Don't panic. Just never noticed it before. Don't know the front of my own hand.

Coming fully awake then, I sat up and looked at my fist. OK, I decided, just rheumatism. I've never had it in my thumb before. Maybe I shouldn't do any typing today. I got up and pottered about the flat. My head a bit thick from last night. Smoke-filled rooms hung me over. And I hadn't been able to get to sleep for a while after I got home. Sat staring at the unlit gas fire and thought about the past in an unproductive sort of way.

Eventually, morning routines couldn't be spun out any longer. I went over to the desk to see what I'd put down on my things-to-do list. I had a whole notebook of them. The current list said 'IWM, check Prince bkgrnd'. I must have decided to go down to Lambeth Road and do a bit of digging about Ada's first husband. Well, if that's what it said I was doing, that's what I'd better do.

Half an hour later, I was peddling dutifully south. Through the West End, looking for monopoly finance capitalists to run over. I never did, too soft-hearted. I made up for it, thinking blood-curdling thoughts while I was weaving between the bankermobiles.

It was a beautiful day. Again. This summer was getting tedious beyond words. The first few weeks, when everyone had come out in shorts and singlets, a lot of bashful pale and knobbly bodies around. Then another week of unrelieved ultra-violet and a bit of swagger started to materialise. Bronzed and scorched limbs being flaunted, ghastly torsos uncovered on any pretext. Now, weeks into a heatwave that was statistically the hottest since the last one when the sun shone, it was all sweat and irritability and a semi-permanent headache. Moving through a sea of hot, slightly rancid suntan oil, I felt a lot of sympathy for the average chip in a low turnover fish shop.

I knew I must be getting old when I realised that no summer, however hot, even if I holidayed in the Gobi, would seem hotter than the summer I did my 'O'-levels. My mum swears the hottest summer was in nineteen forty-something when she was doing her school cert. Then I saw that it had nothing to do with the temperature, the met office may as well junk all their thermometers now. Obviously, the summer of everyone's seventeenth year is the hottest of all time. It grows in memory, defying all comparison. How can reality compete with that?

I stopped on Westminister Bridge and squinted east along the river, uptown. The only bit of London I felt at all fond of, this smelly old waterway. I always routed myself along the embankment if I could. While I still had my rose-tinted spectacles on, I thought about the river I had been beside, that never-to-be-beaten summer when I was sixteen. All those long afternoons lying in the pollen trap of Grantchester Meadows with a stack of exercise books and a bottle of cider. Even the kindness of hazy memory couldn't make me think that the Cam had been anything short of disgusting that year. The most polluted river in Britain, we told each other with a morbid pride, swimming banned and rumours of meningitis after an accidental mouthful. Poor sappy hoorays still thought it was part of the fun of punting to fall in. We sat on the bank and pitied them.

The Thames didn't look so great today, either. I never believed the stories about salmon swimming in Putney. Stinky or not, I always stopped to say hello in passing. Kept my running away to sea fantasies alive.

Hang about on any of the bridges gazing at the view and some eager young born-again Christian always manages to come up and ask you if you're all right, ready to cop the spiritual brownie badge for saving a soul in torment from topping itself in a public waterway.

I pushed off from the kerb and wobbled into the warm wall of grimy traffic fumes. The air wrapped itself around me like a gritty blanket. Over to the other side of the river, the other side of town. South London was another world to me, although I'd lived there. I still half expected to have to show my papers and state the reason for my visit at the other end of the bridge. South London was a lot of cats and no bars and oddities like the Imperial War Museum. I was always glad when I'd left my bicycle and got inside, past the welcoming display of military hardware, without being spotted by anyone I knew.

Inside the high-roofed building at least it was cool, though the air felt as though it had been hanging around for weeks and was getting bored with seeing the insides of the same lungs all the time.

In the section where all the museum's books and papers were kept, I slipped into my library routine and marked out a little territory. The same atmosphere of dusty preoccupation and self-motivating folk staring at their fingernails, wondering if they were ever going to finish their great work. It was a bit more rarefied than the book-barn in which I normally mouldered. Gentlemanly librarians (and ladylike ones too) kept a polite grip on the memorabilia of countless wars, scraps and engagements. Last time I told a friend I was spending a day in the archives, she thought I was off climbing in an obscure Scottish mountain range.

Checking the records of the movements of John Gower's battalion, I found Ada's memory of dates and places was spot on, after all this time. He had 'gone over' in early 1915, after training in England. Arrived at Ypres on May Day, with the first-time novelty of poison-gas clouds barely cleared away. For most of the next year, John and his pals seem to have stood around in that small patch of Belgium slime. As far as I could make out, the greatest distance forward his lot had ever managed to advance was five hundred yards or so. And that was in a good month.

I scribbled down a list of places and dates as quickly as I could. I wanted to fix time and place in my mind before I went on. The official history of the regiment was a bland catalogue of battles and decorations, not much use to me. The casualty lists I skipped through. Normally lists have a hypnotic effect on me. I could read bus timetables from cover to cover. But I didn't have time to boggle over the pages of names and dates of decease. How could a few square miles of northern Europe have room for so many dead Smiths?

What I was really after were the letters and diaries of guys who had been there at the same time. At a pinch, memoirs written afterwards, although there were a lot of those which sounded sanitised by survival and the distance of time. Most of the what-I-did-in-the-war books were by officers and gents anyway, not what I was looking for.

I was working through the diary of a machine-gunner who had been attached to Ada's John's (I must find a shorter way of thinking of him) company. He was half-way between cynicism and pride about 'his' war, a strange mixture. In between pages and pages about lousy food and trench mouth and boils on his bum which made sitting down a misery, there were small occasional bursts of action. For him, that seemed to involve lying in a puddle, trying not to catch his fingers in the belts of bullets he was feeding into the gun and feeling certain that the barrel was going to melt just as the Germans came out to play. In a wet shell-hole, a little forward of the line, fear and discomfort at being isolated from the larger group competed with pride in his small gang's efficiency and what sounded like hero-worship of his number one gunner. And when it was all over for that bit of the slugging match, and nobody had gone anywhere very much, he'd crawl back to the trench and write about how the ASC had managed to drop all the jam off the back of a mule into a mud-filled crater, so it was dry biscuits, and the stupidity of being ordered to polish up his tunic buttons to make nice shiny targets for snipers.

I had been sitting there for hours, hunched up with interest, the pile of scribbled notes spreading all round me. The late afternoon chill hit me, and I pulled on a sweat-shirt as I finished reading the gunner's diary. Putting that to one side, I opened the last of the books that I had stacked in front of me.

It was some contrast from the diary. A gung-ho staff captain turned military historian's account of the war. No sitting around in mucky ditches for this chap. It was all top-level descisions, bold strokes and blunders, great movements of men. Large complicated maps, with big arrows sweeping hither and yon. Black arrows for the British going hither, grey arrows for the enemy briskly counter-attacking yon. A cross-hatched blodge in the bottom left-hand corner indicated that the author thought the French were probably sitting about doing nothing very much, in that demoralised way foreigners have.

I was about to sling the good captain's pompous tome, when I got the feeling that someone was standing behind me. Half turning, I saw a tall, pale young man reading over my shoulder. The skin between my shoulder blades crawled.

'You don't want to take any notice of that,' he said conversationally, nodding at the book I had been about to put down.

'How long have you been standing there?' He took no notice. I felt at a disadvantage sitting down.

'He's all right,' he reached for the diary I had been working from earlier. His hands were long and bloodless-looking. 'Bit pious, mind, but not bad.'

'Look, piss off will you?' I turned around in my chair to give him the full benefit of my space-defending glare. He looked like an American, with his short hair parted in the middle and his little moustache, but sounded like a Londoner. Early twenties, I would have said, except for the lines of strain around his eyes. Not quite all there.

'I'm sorry,' he looked more puzzled than hurt. The permanent comprehension gap of the unwanted male.

'This may be difficult for you to understand,' I said with heavy patience, 'but I am quite capable of deciding a book's crap without some strange man sneaking up to give unasked-for lit. crit.'

'I'm sorry. I just wanted to save you wasting your time. I saw you reading that armchair general's book. It's no good. He didn't know anything about it. I could help you with what you're doing. There are things you don't know about.'

'I'm the best judge of what's a waste of my time, thank you very much.' I gave him a withering sneer. 'And just now, it's you.' With that I turned pointedly back to my work, even though I'd finished. I wasn't going to be driven away by discomfort. The pale man said nothing more, and I waited for the sounds of him taking the hint and walking away. Bloody hell, why did they always think you needed their opinion on everything? There was no sound from my unwanted assistant. After a few minutes of staring fixedly at the papers in front of me, while all the hairs on my neck jumped up and down on the spot, I turned to tell him to stop hanging about and leave me alone. He had gone. Completely silently. I looked around the room, but there was no sign of him. He must have left straight away.

I could pack up then. Sorting my things out, I wondered if men would ever be able to see women doing things on their own without wanting to interfere. I doubted it. Fear of women's independence disguised as helpful interest.

Returning all the papers, books and bits and pieces I had been using to one of the librarians, I fumed about my unwelcome helper. It wasn't just being snuck up on that gave me goose pimples. The bloke was weird. His skin looked kind of damp and he had less colour in him than a fish which spends all its life in a cave. Oddest of all he had no smell. Not just unstinky, he hadn't smelled of anything. What was usually my sharpest sense had failed to register him.

Walking out I detoured through the exhibition hall, passing the boys' toys through the ages at a rate of ten years a yard. Boer hunting; the world wars; Korea; the fallout protection suit in its display case. A relief to be out of there and heading home again. I had been living in seventy years ago for a whole afternoon, there was nothing to drag me home to the present. These back streets of terraces didn't look much different now from then, I imagined. My skin felt like a cold wet overcoat and an army of ghosts were still tangoing slowly over my grave.

Now I wasn't even sure if that strange man had really been there. I remembered him in faded sepia, like one of the sad khaki photographs I had been looking at all afternoon. No, he had been there. But he could have just as easily fitted into one of those books about the young dead, long-forgotten first warriors.

Home again, alone again. If I weren't allergic to them I'd keep a cat, to have some warm-blooded thing to say hello to, tell what I'd been doing. I don't think most cat-owners have adjusted to coming in from the school bus and having their mum say, 'What did you do today?' Not that there's any reason why they should get over it. Telling things puts them at one remove and makes them safe. The world isn't less strange and alarming just because you're older.

So I chatted gently to the house plants while I waited for the kettle to boil. The plants didn't answer, or even strop themselves against my shin demanding to be fed. Well, you can't have everything, at least they don't make me sneeze.

The phone rang. 'Who's this?' I asked the ceiling. No answer. About as chatty as the house plants. The phone carried on ringing. I'd have to find out the hard way. I was prolonging the time I could think it might be someone I wanted to talk to, before I picked up the receiver and found out for sure that it wasn't. I couldn't leave it too long, though, in case they rang off. Another juggling act.

'Hello.' I had taken the plunge.

'Jo?' it was my best buddy, Kate.

'Hiya, toots, how you doing?' I clamped the phone to my shoulder with the muscular force of my right ear, and started to roll a cigarette. I hadn't spoken to her for weeks, so it seemed worth settling down for a chat.

'Fine. How're you? How's the flat?'

'It's fine. Though why people keep asking after it as though it had measles, I don't know.'

'You know what I mean. Manner of speech. Politeness, you remember it?'

'Don't you polite me, ratbag.' My number-one endearment. 'Tell me what you're up to.'

'Nothing you'd approve of. Since you moved to town and became respectable.'

'Listen, I've just been nicked for riding my bike with no hands on the bars. Even if I wanted to be a model citizen, I don't think they'd have me.'

'My heart bleeds.' Kate was a friend from the camp. We'd spent a lot of time getting arrested together. She still did.

'No, really, what are you doing? I haven't heard from you for donkey's.'

'Oh, this and that.' She sounded suspiciously nonchalant. 'Your phone tapped?'

'In a separatist house, packed to the rafters with socially deviant dykes and militant cat-owners? Probably. Or I'll want my taxes back, 'cos they're not up to their job.'

'I'll be all discreet and conspiratorial then.'

'Oh, Kate, leave it out. You know even if they're bothering to listen, they're too stupid to know what you're talking about.' We took routine phone-tapping for granted. It was a nuisance, and made for shouted conversations over a storm of electric crackling, but that was about it.

'I'll give you the edited highlights then.' I heard her strike a match and take a drag on her cigarette.

'When did you get back from Geneva?' I'd just remembered that a vanload of them had zoomed off to sort out the arms negotiators.

'Last week.'

'How was it?'

'OK. We broke into the Russian embassy. They didn't know what to make of it at all. We were all singing this Russian kids' song to the guards. Great big babies.'

'You didn't get carted off to the cantonal slammer, then?'

'No, it was fine. We stayed with some brilliant women. They had this huge house in the middle of town.'

'How did you find them?' I didn't know any Swiss women, brilliant or otherwise.

'They found us.'

'Don't they always?'

'Yes. They came down to the park where we were camping and swept us off away from all the official Christians and the well-meaning beards with anarchists attached to them.'

We carried on chatting for five minutes, slipping easily back into our personal shorthand. When we spent a lot of time together, we often both said the same thing at the same moment. We joked about sharing a brain cell and constantly got called by each other's name. Even her lover used to call her Jo sometimes, by mistake.

In a roundabout way, between all the gossip and catching up on what we'd both been doing, I got the point of what she wanted. There was something on, some action or other and she wanted me to come down to the camp and take part. Not putting a lot of pressure on. Just letting me know. Reminding me how well we used to work together as a team. Hinting that London was making me dull and staid. Or even worse, trendy. I didn't think there was much fear of that, but I knew what she was getting at. I was surrounded by women for whom sneering at the camp had a kind of counter-radical chic.

I was evasive. Said I didn't know whether I'd be able to get away for a while. Didn't commit myself one way or the other. Dammit, I'd only just managed to wrench myself away. I didn't know whether I could or would go.

'Well, it'd be nice if you could come down to see us,' she was leaving it up to me.

'Yeah. maybe. I don't know.' I was doing stretching exercises to ease the tension, so my words came out as a series of grunts.

'You doing leg stretches?'

'Uh huh.'

'Go and make some Horlicks and think about it. We miss you, you know.'

'Yes. I miss you all. A lot.'

'Why don't you come, then?'

'I don't think I want to be involved in any action. And I couldn't stand around and watch you all doing one.'

'But you still think it's necessary?'

'You know I never stopped believing in the camp. Most of the women who matter to me are still there. It's just not the right thing for me to be doing any more.'

'Personal responsibility?'

'That's it.'

'It's not easy.' She sighed.

'You know, if it wasn't for the base, the camp'd be the perfect place to live.' An old joke. She laughed and said good night, I sent my love to everyone and hung up.

# Five

Mud everywhere, my first day at the camp. Deep brown, ankle-clutching gluey carpet of the stuff. Getting off the bus from town, rustling in new waterproofs. Wished off well, with love, admiration and warm vests by my friends.

It had been raining then, steady cold January soaking. Solidly for the first three days I was there. From the bus stop, I'd squelched up to the centre of the camp outside the main gates of the airbase. Fences and searchlights; barbed-wire rolls in the background. Four or five women standing around a smoking camp-fire burning in a pit.

I'd got to the fire, stepping over the plastic-covered straw bale ring which did for sitting on, stood there feeling a bit lost, trying to get my bearings. A woman with ginger hair and a heavy rucksack on her back took in my arrival.

'Hello. You come to stay?'

'Yes. For a couple of weeks.'

'That's nice.' She sounded as though she meant it. 'My name's Ann.'

'I'm Jo. You live here?'

'Yes.' She looked a bit glazed at the question, the response came from stock. 'I'm off for a week or so.'

'Oh.' I felt on my own again, all of a sudden. She had shown me where to put my rucksack out of the rain, under one of the tent-shaped, tunnel-length plastic structures made from sheets of polythene slung between two of the trees that surrounded the fireplace. Then she had given me a cheerful grin and tramped off through the dark ooze in a welter of goodbyes and 'see you Ann's and 'give my love to Ruth's.

I'd watched all this going on and worked out who were camp women from the ones who spoke. There were a couple of them. The rest stood looking as unfamiliar as I did. One came up and asked me how long I'd been at the camp. When I told her about five minutes, she wandered off again. I realised she was looking for a bona fide camp woman to talk to. I was doing the same myself.

The rest of that dark sodden afternoon had passed in a confusing daze. The rain had turned from steady to vicious, with a mean wind pushing sheets of grey chilling water down on that flat Berkshire common. At some point Maddy had shoved a large enamel mug into my freezing hands. The mug was chipped and muddy on the outside, the coffee throat-bitingly strong and hot. It was the best drink I'd ever had.

Maddy had taken me under her wing, without me noticing it. Very fair and English-looking, in her thirties, straight hair under a pom-pom hat. Sensible mittens and rosy cheeks. While I watched, during those last few hours of daylight, she received three carloads of visitors with all the courtesy of a rural housewife welcoming neighbours into an impeccable front room. She answered the same half-dozen questions each time with patience (and the first one was always 'How long have you lived here?'). She swore a good deal, but in a very demure tone of voice.

I had wandered off, exploring the camp. Up to the wire to look at the military men going about their business inside. The MOD policeman in his sentry box stared balefully at me as I stood with my nose to the wire. Trying to look warm and dry, he just managed to look stuffed. I already knew that women are more waterproof.

Away from the fence, the camp spread through low bushes by a series of quagmire paths. I picked my way over the trail of duckboards and sawn-up pallets that reinforced the swampier bits. They tilted and settled with the weight of passing footsteps. When I lurched off one and landed beside it, the mud came almost to my knee. All around were tents and more plastic and tarpaulin structures, standing on straw and blankets, keeping dry(ish) by an act of faith.

The pattern of the days, I found, fitted in with my own. Mid to late afternoon was the low, slow time, when everyone thought about being somewhere else. The morning was filled with purposeful bounce, if you wanted it that way. But it was when darkness fell and the evening meal was being cooked that the camp came properly alive. The last of the well-meaning men who came to be supportive and get reassurance were shooed away. The women re-emerged from town and tents where they had passed the dog hours.

That first evening I had sat in the circle at the fire watching the camp's most flamboyant cook racing round the hearth, throwing handfuls of rice into one black and massive cauldron, piling logs under another so the flames leapt and melted the soles of the boots of the women drying their feet on the other side. The cook was cooking because she had felt like it. There was no rota and no sense of ought. Chaos, but functional.

'Can someone find a tin of tomatoes?' Mo asked, as she bounced round the fire seasoning and tasting. I was still feeling like a guest, trying to be useful, so off to the storage dustbins I'd lumbered to rummage through the one with 'Tins' painted on its lid. All the labels had come off in the damp. I picked up one which was the right size and shape and shook it. Too little squelch. It sounded like baked beans. Tried another one. Too sloshy. Probably soup. The next one sounded plausible. Opened it to see, finding the tin-opener by touch in the dark, from a jumble of cutlery on the trestle table by the row of dustbins. It was peaches. Oh well. Eventually I found some tomatoes and took them back to the fire. Handed them to Mo. She took them and smiled, preoccupied. I went back to the sodden straw bale on which I had perched. Two more women had arrived while I was away, both small and bright-looking in the reflected light. They made room for me and I sat down again.

'You're Jo, aren't you?' one of the newcomers turned and stared at me.

'Yes.'

'We met at the women's conference in Manchester last year. I'm Mary. This is Liz.' She indicated the woman next to her.

'Hi.' It had been a comforting feeling, not being the only one who didn't know everyone else.

We'd talked with ease, on the basis of one meeting months ago. She told me that she'd been at the camp a week and was on her way back to Bristol the next day. Food came round on tin plates, in plastic bowls. Curried pulses with rice and a stir-fry. Afterwards, feeling warm for the first time that day I propped my feet on the rocks around the fireplace with the others and happily ignored the smell of molten vibrams as a dozen pairs of walking boots glowed in the heat.

It had almost stopped raining. We sat over coffee, talking and smoking. Just like regular folks. Maddy and another woman collected up the plates and stacked them on one of the trestles to be washed in daylight. A few yards away groups of airmen started leaving the base for the night. Home to their families in the American compound a few miles away. Their enormous cars with sunshine state plates rumbled past unnoticed, the other side of the low hedge dividing the road into the base from the anarchy the other side. Privet. Very suburban. Every now and then a shouted obscenity, or a gesture out of the smoked glass interior of a cadillac. But mostly they stared straight ahead and pretended we weren't there. Well, that's how they're taught to deal with bogeys and witches.

There was some singing. One very small woman, absurdly cuddly in five layers of wool and looking like Paddington Bear was pressed to sing a song about a big strong woman and a mountain. She must have a special voice, I thought, as the others teased and cajoled her to sing.

'Not sober,' she said. 'I can't sing sober.'

'Go on,' they said, 'sing it for us. We can't wait till closing time before you feel like singing. Some of us go to bed before midnight.'

The woman was adamant. She pulled her floppy Paddington hat over her eyes and stood up. She was going to the pub. She'd feel like singing when she got back. Sure to. She felt like a drink, though, and since they'd finished off the crate of scotch which had been brought as a Christmas present, and all the assorted home-made wines and supporters' spirits, there was nothing for it but a trip into town.

Really like regular folks. The disreputable element off to the local while the staider members of the family settled down for an evening of domesticity and making their own entertainment. I felt a lot of sympathy for the singer who wouldn't give voice without a bit of liquid encouragement. She was only half as big again as her moon boots. I stood up and joined the five who looked as though they intended making the journey to the pub with her.

That got to be a habit. Evenings in the one pub in town that would serve us. The Irish pub. Being called Kippers in town, because of the smell of woodsmoke that always clung to us. And other, more insulting, things too, of course. We were the alternative to the established order walking about on two muddy feet. 'All women' was more threatening than 'anti-military'.

But in the pub we were tolerated. Sitting with our damp outer clothes steaming dry on the radiators, running up high scores on the galaxians machine. Hand-jiving like crazy in that strange pub with a

Saturday night disco and no dance licence. We could only dance if we stayed seated. Piling into the car at closing time, struggling back into all the discarded scarves and ponchos. And after the first rainy days a succession of clear, freezing, beautiful late nights back at the fire afterwards, when I found out that the Paddington really did have a voice worth waiting for, and the sound of women singing in the night was enough to be out in the snow for at midnight even without the world to save.

I'd gone to the camp, intending to stay up to a fortnight. Carefully judged time off from my other commitments in London. On my third day, Sal came into the pub to a shower of hugs from the others. She'd been away since before I arrived. We were introduced.

'You come to live at the camp?' she asked casually.

'Yes,' I said, surprising myself, 'I have.' Although I hadn't known it till then.

The next day I built myself a bender. Low, whale-shaped, womb-shaped structure like an upturned boat. Called a bender because of the bent-over branches which formed the roof beam and supports. Covered in plastic, camouflaged with bracken, hidden in the gorse bushes. Long enough for me and my boots. Wide enough for me and my rucksack. High enough to sit up in, with morning sunlight breaking through the opaque roofing. A tunnel entrance and only my good night vision to get me there, after dark and well away from the light of the fire and the base. Two pallets and straw for a floor. Sleeping bag for a bed. I built it in an afternoon. When I went back a year later, it was still standing, still hidden. Grown over by gorse bushes now, but still weatherproof. The only person I ever shared it with was a discreet fieldmouse. My bender mouse.

I'd gone for maybe a couple of weeks (if I could stand it) and stayed the best part of a year.

I remembered a conversation I'd had with Kate one night to pass the time while we waited to break into the base to hang a banner on the radar tower. It was a full moon, too bright for invisibility. We were crouched in the shadow of the fence waiting for a snow-filled cloud that was zipping across the sky to block out some of the light. We lay on our backs in a shallow ditch in the woodland that had hidden our approach, waiting on the weather.

'What are you going to do when this is over?' she'd asked.

'When what's over?' I shifted uncomfortably. With a pair of boltcutters hidden up your jumper, uncomfortably is how you mostly shift.

'When we've saved the world. What will you do then?'

'I don't know.' I thought about it. 'Go back to writing plays, I suppose.'

'Where will you live?' she was keeping a wary eye on the headlights of the patrol cars on the runway as we talked.

'I don't want to go back to London. In fact I don't want to go back to anywhere indoors. I'm allergic to indoors.'

'Where will you build your bender "Duncruising?" Somewhere scenic?' She lowered her head below the rim of the dip in which we lay and pulled a face. Still too many police about.

'No. Scenery's damp and boring. I'm going somewhere rugged and dour.'

'Sounds revolting. Setting up home in Arbroath.'

'Is Arbroath dour?'

'I don't know,' Kate admitted. 'But it sounds pretty dour.'

'Racist scumbag.' I tried to tickle her through her waxed cotton motorcycle jacket. She hardly noticed. 'Some bits of Scotland are very cuddly and twee.'

'Where?'

'Don't know. But there must be some.'

The headlights of one of the police patrols inside the base came towards our corner and stopped. We both slithered lower down in the leaf mould and stared up at the light sweeping slowly a few feet over our heads, the pattern of the beam broken up by the mesh fence through which it was shining. I slid the boltcutters out from under my clothes and hid them in a pile of leaves by my hand. Who wants to be done for going equipped before you've had a chance to do any damage?

For a few minutes the patrolman turned his headlights our way and stared down the beam. We were safe so long as they never learned to look without lights. What existed for them was framed by the car's windscreen. If you were above or below or to one side of that, they couldn't see you. If I'd heard the sound of a car door, I would have worried. But they were frightened of the dark, and didn't venture out into it if they could help it.

The sound of gears being crunched and wheels churning wet gravel came to us over the distance of a hundred yards which separated us from the patrol. He was going. Kate looked at me, and with our efficient telepathy, we decided to give it another couple of minutes, then move. I took up where we'd left off.

'What about you? What are you doing when we've saved the world?'

'Sail round the globe. Go and grow sheep in Cornwall. Retire to the admiring applause of a grateful populace.'

'Ha bloody ha.'

'Yes, well, have a rest at any rate. Never see another uniform in my life, if I had the choice.'

'You won't go back to what you were doing before?'

'No. I've done that number. Though I could quite get into a rural idyll again. So soothing.'

'Me too.' I was feeling for the cutters. 'But I guess we're pretty much dyed-in-the-wool social pariahs now.'

'Dedicated to a life of subversion and disruption until we're a handful of toothless and wrinkly old threats to the state.' She had risen to a crouch as she spoke. We looked at each other, and as the cloud finally approached the face of the moon, started to walk towards the fence. I swarmed up it and stood with one boot on Kate's shoulder, cutting through the three strands of barbed wire leaning out from the top. The strands parted and whipped away under their own tension. One caught the side of my head in passing, and I felt a drop of blood start to make its way down my face.

We shinned over the fence and made our way to the unhealthy white tower which was the object of the night's excursion. There was traffic on the runway, beside which it stood. We flattened ourselves against the wall of the building at the base of the tower and waited for a car-free interval. When it came, without saying a word, Kate moved to the smooth metal pillar and started climbing. Past the danger notice, past the sign about this radar installation being an official secret, and none of our business. I followed.

She stopped underneath the catwalk platform which ran round the tower. Silently she pointed at a yard-long microphone which was hung from the underside of the platform. I nodded and clambered back down again to ground level. If they were awake in the control room and had heard us clomping our way up their precious bit of hardware a quick exit might be necessary. Two get down a ladder a lot slower than one.

Standing by the runway again, waiting for Kate to finish, I kept half an eye out for plods and thought about our chances of being rehabilitated into polite society. It would be difficult to go back to normal life. Even if I'd wanted to, I didn't think we qualified as respectable citizens any longer. But saving the world was too all-absorbing. It didn't leave time or energy for anything else. A very demanding hobby.

The patrol car came back. Kate was still up the tower. They must have picked up something on their sound alarms. I leant against the far wall of the old airforce hut and looked at the moon, thinking resigned thoughts about a night in the nick and concentrating on being invisible. The MOD policeman sat in his oversized Dodge Ram, with the roof spots on the radar tower. I could see Kate, small and immobile, frozen on her way down from the top.

He didn't see her. Stupid bastard didn't think to look up. Ten feet above his head, in plain view, with the moon out again, bright in the freezing winter sky and he didn't see her.

Off he drove, all correct and nothing to report. What a turkey. Glory be, and thanks for turkeys.

Mission accomplished, beating a hasty retreat, trying to save our laughter for the other side of the fence, we got back to the woods and walked away. With no need to restrain ourselves any longer, we cackled our way through the undergrowth the mile back to the camp. So what if we didn't have any personal space, and were stifling all the things we wanted to do with our lives for the sake of a largely uncaring human race? On its good days, like the song said, saving the world could be really fun.

# Six

Wet West London Wednesday morning. Fun, who needs it? Head heavy with a night of reverie prompted by Kate's call, I woke and stared out at the grey damped-down dust of the end of the heatwave. Knowing I wouldn't go and join my friend in whatever she was planning. Not trusting myself to resist the lure of purpose and action, the certainty that stopping the bomb is a worthwhile thing to be doing.

I heaved myself out of bed and stared with more than usual resentment at the hideous decor. Nymphs and bloody shepherds prancing up the walls in pastel shades, I could do without this morning. I had to go and see Ada Prince again, on her own ground. She had pushed me around enough in my own territory, so god knew what she would be like on hers. Facing up to another alienating day in this unsuitable town, knowing that I could live where and how I wanted, or do what I wanted to do, but not both. Living in a plastic bag in the middle of Berkshire, I'd never sneezed and had glowed with health, but string two words together on paper, I could not. Here I was a sullen wreck, but productive.

Two hours and a pint of coffee later, I was standing on Ada's doorstep, feeling if not human, at least resigned, waiting for her to answer the bell. I had knocked as well, never expecting bells to work. Too many friends in squats.

I heard her firmly planted footsteps approaching me down the hall. Through the frosted glass, I could make out her shape and something vaguely floral about her person. She opened the door without suspicion, but slowly, as though expecting Jehovah's Witnesses rather than teenage muggers.

'Hullo, Ada.' I tried using her first name. It came out well enough. The floral print turned out to be a wrapover pinny, like my gran wore.

'Hullo. I didn't think I'd be seeing you again so soon. Come in, won't you?'

'I hope it's not an inconvenient time.'

'Suits me fine.' She held the door of the living room open for me. 'Thought you might have decided you didn't need any more notes about my John, that's all.'

'Not at all, why should I?' I sat down in the chair she offered. 'In fact, I've been doing some more work around his battalion.'

'Where would you be doing that?'

'Down at the Imperial War Museum.'

'Oh. Seems like a funny place for you to be working. Can't see it somehow. But then, I never did care much for museums. Too quiet for me. Too many things you're not supposed to do.'

'It's OK.' I relaxed enough to take off my coat and put it on the floor beside my chair.

'You'd like a cup of tea?' She took it for granted, no hostessly fussing for her.

'If it's no bother.'

'I was making myself a pot anyway. Mid-morning's a good time to come visiting me.'

She went out and I heard her moving about in the kitchen, behind the room in which I was sitting. All the rooms in the flat opened off the hall, I guessed her bedroom was opposite, with the bathroom behind it. I looked around and unlaced my boots. She kept the room tidy, but not obsessively neat. The furniture was heavy and oldish, except for a modern high armchair by the television. It looked like the sort of thing that people's children buy them when getting up starts to be a bit of an effort. Not that Ada had ever struck me as being at all tottery.

In front of the gas fire was a set of fire irons, brought with her, I guessed, from her old coal-burning house. No use now, but not the sort of thing that could be thrown away. Along half the length of one wall was a large old sideboard, dark wood and Victorian-looking. It was covered with ornaments, photos, a heavy noisy old clock which chimed the quarter hours. I got up and walked over to take a closer look. Most of the photos were of her children at various stages of their growing. Thirties school kids, last war in uniforms, one of the daughters in a group of women, laughing on a farm. Land army? Wedding groups and then a burst of colour, grandchildren. Stiff posed school annual pictures. Grey jumpers and shirts. The same as their parents at that age. The colour film

44

showed up their eyes and the bright blue photographer's backcloth.

No pictures of Ada herself. One out of focus snap of a man who I presumed to be her second husband, standing in a garden, squinting in bright sunlight at the lens. A short, cheerful-looking middle-aged chap. Not much of a heart-throb to look at. Still, I was no judge. But the one photograph I had been looking for wasn't there. No portrait of her first husband, her John. Strange, I would have expected it to have pride of place in this family collection.

I heard the rattle of a tray in the hall. I went to open the door for her, not wanting to be found snooping. Before I could get there, she had kicked the door open herself with one carpet-slippered foot. Years of practice carrying things and not expecting any help. I stood in the middle of the room and felt awkward, while she carried the tray over to the table and poured the tea.

'Here we are then.' She handed me a cup. I sat down again.

'Thanks. I've been looking at your photographs.'

'Oh yes.' She glanced over at the sideboard. 'They're not all there, of course. Those are just the ones the kids expect to see when they come round. Dead traditional, they are. Sometimes wonder how I came to have such a dull lot.'

'I was wondering if you had a photo of John?'

'Yes. I've got pictures of him.' She had an inward-looking expression on her face. 'Not in here, though. I don't keep them out.'

There was a pause. I wanted to see a picture of the guy, but only if she suggested it. She looked at me in a considering way. She shifted in her chair, as though about to get up, and then appeared to change her mind. Instead she folded her hands on her lap and sat looking at them. I found myself following her gaze. Tendons knotted and lumpy, like the mess of ropes on the deck of a barge. Patches of brown age-spots running into the red of her inflamed knuckles. A lifetime of hard work ingrained in cracked skin and callouses. But the nails were beautiful, flawless and straight. The fingers short and strong, only slightly twisted. I thought that maybe it was Ada's story I should be writing, if she would have let me.

'I don't think I'll show you his picture just yet, dear,' she spoke at last, not seeming to notice the length of her silence. 'You don't know him well enough yet.'

What did she mean by that? I was using this man as background, a minor bit of local authenticity. She sounded as though she was carefully weighing the making of a boxing match.

45

'As you like.' I sounded stiff. 'I don't want to intrude.'

'You're not doing that,' she looked at me slyly, from the corner of her eye, 'or not that I don't choose to let you.'

'But you don't want to show me his picture?'

'Maybe I will. But not yet. You can tell me, when you've done a bit more of your research,' she gave the word an emphasis that sounded ironic, 'whether he looks like what you would have thought.'

'But I don't have any idea what he looks like.' A dark rather skinny bloke, probably a bit intense-looking, I'd expect. Don't know why though.

'We'll see.'

'Yes, well it's not important. I don't need to know what he looked like. I just thought it might be interesting. But I'm not writing about him, as such. Getting a general picture of the experience of people like him.' Ada snorted. 'I'm sorry, I didn't mean to sound as though what you're telling me isn't important. Of course it is.' I looked round for an ashtray.

'Over there.' She pointed to the sideboard where there was a collection of presents from Margate and Clacton for stubbing out cigarettes in. 'And while you're about it you can do me one if you like.'

'Sure.' I was glad to make the peace offering.

'Well, then,' she was restored to her normal brisk good humour. 'There's some things you might like to see. Stuff he sent. Letters and that. Not much, but it might be useful to you. I'll get them.' She left the room.

Well, she'd offered, I hadn't pushed her. Couldn't be anything too private. I got up and went over to the window. Still raining out. Through the net curtains I looked out at the road and the shopping precinct opposite. Not many people about. Those that were, heads down and scurrying, distaste at the unaccustomed cold and nobody sure it was going to last long enough to make it worth looking out warmer autumn clothes.

One man, directly opposite, stood still, tolerating the rain sluicing over his head. Like a horse in a field, not comfortable but putting up with it. At least he had a waterproof, one of those old army surplus mackintoshes, and what looked like khaki leg-warmers. A Notting Hill trendy. He looked like someone waiting for a bus. I didn't know there was a stop there, and couldn't see any sign.

He looked up at the window where I stood. I felt he was staring straight at me, although I knew I was hidden by the nets. His face turned towards me was pale in the half-light of a thundery morning. The rain made a steady stream down both sides of his head from the watershed of his parting, as though his hair was oiled. I recognised the man from the reading room of the museum. He looked preoccupied and had an air of belonging round here. Must live locally. If I'd thought he'd been trailing me around, I'd have gone out and pulped him on the spot for his pains. I didn't think I rated an MI5 tail yet. So he's just some sad little man standing in the rain looking as though he doesn't expect anything better of life than cold water down his collar, and whoever he's waiting for failing to show up.

Ada came back with a bundle of papers in her hand, and I turned away from the window.

'Still raining, is it?' she handed me the bundle, letters mostly.

'Yes, it's foul. Thanks.' I took them over to the chair and sat down, started taking letters out of envelopes at random. 'Are they in any sort of order?'

'No. I keep them by me to read every now and then, so they're all a jumble. But the letters are mostly dated, so you can sort them out for yourself if you want to.'

The first thing I read was the official war office telegram announcing John's death. The standard formula. 'Killed in action' it said. Ada saw me handle the faded yellow form.

'Knew what it was as soon as the boy came to the door with it. That's all you ever got a telegram for. My youngest sent me one on my birthday once. Silly sod. Should've known I'd think it was bad news.'

'Even now?'

'Well they don't have them now, do they? But if they did I wouldn't want one. They always meant a death, during both wars. You don't forget that in a hurry. And all the neighbours would know. You'd see the delivery boy and know. It's all right if you're one as needs people around you, times like that, but myself, I just wanted to be let alone.'

Under the telegram was a letter from a friend of John's saying how sorry he was, and Ada wasn't to worry, 'I'm sure he didn't suffer, or know much about it.' Consoling thoughts. Ada was to let him know if she needed any help, as he'd promised his pal to give her a hand if she needed it. Not that he could do much till he got back himself, god willing, but she was to let him know if there was

47

anything he could do.

'This guy,' I peered at the scrawled signature, 'Albert, was John's best friend?'

'From when they were kids. Those two joined together. Bert lived next to us for years. Still does now, he's got a place just round the corner of here.'

I boggled at the idea of living near someone for the best part of a century and picked up the next document from the pile on my knee. It was a citation. John had been awarded the military medal for showing conspicuous bravery and presence of mind in leading a raiding party of which he was a member back from no man's land after the death of the officer in charge and both NCOs.

'You didn't tell me about this.' I waved the stiff citation. 'It's quite a big thing, isn't it? The military medal?'

'John didn't reckon much to it. I think it embarrassed him, getting it. The whole thing was a shambles, he said. They were ordered out there to keep everybody on their toes. That's what he said. Pointless. Half of them was killed, to maintain the offensive spirit, and he got a medal for having the sense to skedaddle.'

'Keep who on their toes?'

'Who knows? The men. The gerries. Doesn't really matter. Their CO thought it was bad for morale if they all sat around keeping their heads down and out of trouble for no better reason than there was nothing more useful they could do. So he'd make them go out on little sorties of a night time. Wear the other side down. Stop them getting soft. John was very scathing about his CO. Well, about most of them really.'

'The officers?'

'Yes. Bunch of schoolboys, he reckoned.'

I turned back to the rest of the papers. A couple of field postcards. Pre-printed messages with delete-where-not-appropriate phrases. I am well/slightly wounded/in hospital. I have got your letter/parcel/have not heard from you. Fill in name of sender and recipient. No alterations permitted. As issued to the troops before going into battle to save them the time it took them to write a whole letter.

All the rest of the bundle was made up of letters from John to Ada. I started sorting them into order by date. The writing was a cramped copperplate, stiff and controlled, the ink surprisingly black still, even after all these years. I took each folded sheet out of its envelope and smoothed it flat, careful not to pull at the edges. The creases in the letters were almost worn through in some places with decades of rereading. I wondered at the persistence of her feeling for her first husband. She wasn't a romantic. Definitely a pragmatist. But she spoke of him as though he were a good friend who'd gone out of the neighbourhood for a short while, not a long dead, made perfect in the memory, lover.

I was still laying the letters out in order when the doorbell rang and Ada stomped off the answer it. When she came back it was with an impossibly wrinkled man of about her age and half her size. His false teeth were uniformly dazzling white, his hair grew in snowy tufts like the last stubborn pockets in the face of a thaw. The overall effect of brightness was completed by a still bright pair of eyes, small and hazel coloured. He made his way to the second most comfortable armchair with the ease of long familiarity and sat down.

'Bert, where are your manners?' Ada scolded him. 'I haven't introduced you to Jo yet.'

Looking sheepish, he started to unfold himself from the chair.

'Please don't bother getting up again.' I went over and held out my hand. He stood up anyway and we shook hands. His grip was weak and dry, the opposite of Ada's firm warm grasp when we had first met.

'Jo, this is Albert. Him I told you about. Bert, this is Jo.'

'I've heard about you too.' Bert settled himself again. 'Writing a play about John Gower, aren't you?'

'Sort of. About people like him, at any rate.' I sat myself down again too. Ada picked up the teapot and slapped its side in a temperature-taking gesture.

'You'll be wanting a cup too, I suppose?'

'Wouldn't say no.' Bert was rummaging in the pockets of his cardigan for cigarettes and matches. 'If you've got a pot on the go.'

'I'll freshen it up a bit,' Ada set off for the kitchen, shouting through, 'and I thought the doctor said you were to stop smoking?'

'She did, she did,' Bert grumbled to himself, lighting up. 'As though there was any point stopping at my age. Been smoking since I was fourteen. Number of times I've been told to pack it in or I won't last a year, you wouldn't believe.'

'You got a bad chest?'

'Bronchitis. In the winter.'

'Me too,' I sympathised.

'At your age?' He sounded indignant, as though his illness was a prerogative of his age.

'Mm.'

'Anyway,' he went straight back to our previous line of conversation. 'I don't know what you mean by people like John. There weren't that many like him. Bit of a law to his own self, he was.'

'I thought he was quite typical. What I know of him.'

Bert shook his head vigorously. 'No. John was a rum bugger. I don't mean that nasty. I was his best mate and all that.'

'How rum?'

'Well you'd have to have known him to have said. He was a smart lad, for one thing. Too damn smart for his own good, half the time. Never learnt to take things quiet. Not like the rest of us.'

'The rest of you?' I wished I could take notes again.

'All the lads. The old gang from round here. All went out together.'

'Ada told me.'

'I know most of them didn't make it back. Or in one piece, at any rate. But they got by all right, while they had to. Not John. Not one for getting by, him. Always sticking his neck out. Always asking why and what for. Bleeding stupid, that was. For all his brains, he didn't know when to keep his head down and shut his lip.'

Bert sat back looking quite cross. I tried to press him further, but Ada had come back into the room and he clammed up. We talked more generally about how the area had changed in the time they had both been living there. I went back to John's letters.

Ada and Bert chatted in a companionable way about their health, their families, the telly, normal friendly gossip with as many silences as statements. I took myself back to the late summer of 1914 and John's first letter from his training barracks.

My dearest Ada,

I hope you are not too angry with me for having joined up in such a rush, and without having told you what I was up to. To tell you the truth, it was a bit of a surprise to me, although as you know I had been expecting that there would be a war for some time, and that I would have to go, so I suppose that must be my excuse, that it had unsettled me.

We are kept pretty hard at it here. A lot of drill and cleaning things that were clean to start with, and being shouted at. We have not actually been allowed to handle a rifle yet, or fire a shot in anger, or otherwise. Maybe they have got to make us learn to walk like clockwork toys first. I am enjoying the chance to be out of doors in this weather, though, and am feeling very well on it.

Maybe you would not recognise me now, as we have all been barbered today. We are so shorn it looks like a company of old men, with not a hair on our heads. The uniform too, is very prickly, as well as hot, we have been running around in a muck sweat.

I am kept too busy to think much, but I miss you already. We should get leave when we finish training, so I look forward to seeing you then. In the meantime, I shall carry on being cursed and shouted at, tripping over my two left feet and polishing everything that does not move. The rest we salute.

Your affectionate,

John.


That was about the longest letter he'd written her in the whole time. The next was also from the training barracks. He thanked her for her letter and apologised for not having had time to reply sooner. He'd not had a free moment having been disciplined for being improperly dressed – he'd taken off his cap to mop his forehead while on the drill square. He didn't specify his punishment, but it sounded like a week of cleaning out the latrines, reading between the lines. The last letter he'd written from Aldershot was mainly about the arrangements for his pre-embarkation leave. His world was narrowing to encompass nothing more than immediate concerns and discomforts.

Ada was pottering about the flat, Bert sat and watched me as I read. The low rumble of their talk had stopped.

John wrote an amusing account of the troopship crossing the channel. He had been seasick despite the nearly flat conditions. Ada would be glad to know that they had not run into the German High Sea Fleet, and had arrived safely. He was excited about being abroad for the first time, although he didn't say so. He had spent fourteen hours standing on a train from somewhere in France to somewhere else in France. He wasn't allowed to say where. He was well, apart from a sore neck which he had given himself picking up his pack too quickly when he was half asleep at the railhead. They could hear the artillery at the front.

In his second letter from abroad, dated March 1915, he wrote:

We have got on trains and got off them again and marched

around a bit and got back on another train to return to where we started from. I feel like one of the grand old Duke of York's men in the nursery rhyme. No one seems quite sure what to do with us now that we have got over here. They hurry us to one place where there is a panic on, but we hurry so slowly that by the time we get there, no one can remember why they asked for us in the first place. The latest rumour is that the whole battalion is to be sent off for some more training. I don't think any of the generals much care for us as we are, soft and straight from home. I can't tell you where this place is, of course, but the lads who have been here before call it the Bull Ring and tell blood-curdling stories about the sort of reception we can expect. More frightening than the Germans.

He signed off quite jauntily, promising to let her know how he got on at the Bull Ring. He must mean the training camp at Étaples. I would have to check my notes when I got home. Anyway, he never did describe it to Ada, the next letter on route to Ypres was terse and uninformative.

We have left the last place and are being sent to the next. I do not expect it to be any better, but I doubt if it could be much worse. But it is not for the likes of me to expect much, there is probably some article of the King's Regulations which forbids private soldiers to expect anything at all. Stupidity is the only defence. I miss you, of course. Do keep on writing to me, although I know I have not answered you as quick as I should. Your last letter followed me all around for weeks and I finally read it nearly a month after you wrote.

Then another big chronological pause, during which John must have had his first wallow in the poisoned wastes of Ypres. One of the field postcards dated from around then. I paused to stretch my stiff shoulders and saw Ada and Bert, their chairs pulled close together, playing cards by the window.

'You got enough light to read by?' she asked at a pause in the play.

'Mm.' It was still a very dark day, and the gloom had been creeping into the room without me noticing.

'Best put the light on. You don't want to strain your eyes. Give yourself a headache.' I got up and turned on the overhead light. The room seemed smaller, the murk outside stepped back a pace or two.

'Perhaps I ought to be going. I hadn't realised I'd been here so long.' It was afternoon. I had got used to the old clock's musical performance and stopped noticing the passing quarters.

'Suit yourself, of course.' She sorted her hand with the dexterity of long practice. 'But you're welcome to stay. Don't take much entertaining.'

'Well, I would quite like to finish these letters. And I don't suppose you want me to take them away to read.'

'No. You stop here and finish them. Me and Bert won't take any notice of you. Will we?'

Bert was counting furiously, silently moving his lips to aid his calculations. They were playing for pennies and Ada was giving him a thorough thrashing.

'No,' he said, preoccupied. 'I don't mind you there at all.' They went back to their game, I to my war.

I had been hoping that he would have written about his first bit of real fighting, but the letter was heavily censored. Infuriating half sentences with the point lopped off them, whole paragraphs buried under the clumsy blocking out. Dark lines through what may have been place names or adverse comments. It hadn't been a long letter to start with, and what was left were the endearments at the end, a comment on the dreariness of the weather and the polite greeting.

I felt cut off, and wondered how Ada must have taken the intrusion of some strange officer into her correspondence, deciding what she was allowed to know.

There was another spate of short, not-much-happening letters in the late autumn and winter of that year. He had written during slack times and took to mentioning death and fighting in asides. 'Davey went west in that one, as you will have heard at home by now.' Or 'Sorry I have not had time to write, these last few weeks, but we have been a bit busy. I have collected a shrapnel cut on the face. Not serious, unfortunately. Jack got his blighty from the same bursting shell that spoiled my good looks. Last I saw of him he was on his way to the dressing station with one of his legs off and the other one a bit of a mess. I heard he is pulling through, though, and will be shipped home. He left his leg in our trench and I have given it a decent burial in a shell-hole.'

Normally John was careful to avoid things that might disgust or frighten. Did he take clearing up the blown-off limbs of his friends so much for granted that he didn't realise how it read? Private about his horrors, was John. Maybe he was shocked himself, for such a casual admission to have slipped past the internal censor who tried to stop her seeing what it was really like for him.

It was an aberration. The rest of the communications that winter were in his normal tone of studied distance and safe subjects. A good part of every letter was a repeat of his formula enquiries after her. How was she, and everyone they knew? Had she seen his mother lately? Thanks for her last letter. He missed her. He loved her (not that he sounded comfortable with writing it, as though he couldn't do justice to his feelings). And for the rest, the trivia of his life: 'Today we played "A" coy. at football and I am very badly hacked on the shins'; 'Could you send me any lice powder out? The stuff I have is useless, and they are eating so much of me there will be nothing left for the other lot to shoot at soon.'

Mostly he talked about the weather: the lethal seas of mud when it rained; sleeping in a dug-out while snow filled the bottom of the trench. Spring upset him, the touches of normality, stray birds and flowers who didn't know that there was a war on and that everything was being laid waste around them. He preferred it unrelentingly bleak, nothing to remind him of the abnormality of total ugliness and desolation, no painful contrasts. In every letter he mentioned some small ailment or hurt: bleeding gums; rotting feet; a rash on his neck; heavy colds. Always something.

I saw what Ada meant about him not telling her anything. The longer he was out, the less informative his letters were. After a year, they were almost straight formula notes, with very little of himself coming through, as if he was in another world from which he could not make the mental effort to drag himself back and would not drag her into. He thought he was trying to protect her from distress, but it seemed all of a piece with him not being able to bear hearing a bird singing in the one blasted tree left standing in their hundred square yards of nothingness. No part of him could be spared for another life. So he talked about the weather and grumbled about the food and kept the woman he used to talk to 'not like most blokes would' at arms' length, for fear that she would make him realise that not all the world was a muddy ditch in the middle of a war.

I felt angry for her sake, as I put the last of the say-nothing, don't-risk-a-feeling letters down. What a real man. How bloody British. 'There, there, dear, don't you worry about me. I'm fine.' Of course he wasn't. Making endurance possible, by putting whatever unmanly feelings made him able to talk to her aside for the duration. Making killing possible. And Ada rereading these letters all down the years, trying to wring out some scraps of meaning or caring that he hadn't been able to put in, for fear that he'd see the emperor's new uniform for what it was.

I looked over at her, still living with her ghost cheerfully enough, playing crib with his best mate. She didn't need my pity for sure, probably not my anger either. I got up and put on my coat, left the letters on the sideboard. She looked up from her cards.

'You off, love?'

'Yes. Thanks a lot. Don't stop your game, I'll show myself out.'

'Sure?' She laid a card.

'Yes.' I hesitated.

'You'll come again, will you?'

'If that's OK with you.'

'I'll want to know why if you don't. Well don't stand there gawking all day. Haven't you got a play to write, or something?'

'Sure.' I walked to the door. 'Goodbye, Bert.'

'I'll see you again.' A statement, not a politeness. He was busy sulking that Ada was still beating him at cards.

'Goodbye, Ada. And thanks again.'

'For nothing. Off you go, pet. No ceremony here.'

Before I'd got the door closed, they were absorbed in their game again. I heard the triumphant slap of another of Ada's winning hands being thrown down. Bert groaned. I let myself out.

# Seven

I trudged back down the Golborne Road, skipping over the yellow and purple oil-filmed puddles. This season's colours. Made a huge effort and didn't go into the Portuguese coffee-shop with the wrought-iron chairs and pictures of the sea. There I could end up sitting for an hour over a cappuccino, pretending that I was abroad again, somewhere warm, with nothing better to do than sit over a long coffee and talk about the meaning of life with Kate. In between learning essential phrases like, 'I am hysterical, give me cammomile' and 'The police are coming.' We had a whole Italian phrase-book from our last jaunt to Sicily which we were thinking of marketing as a sort of radical Berlitz – Languages for Peace-Keepers. Illustrating such indispensable lines as: 'You are breaking my arm'; 'I want to phone my lawyer'; 'This is a women's space, go away'; and 'When is the last bus from Comiso?' We'd decided not to bother with things like 'Let's do it now' and 'When is it due?' so as not to raise false hopes in poor time-anxious northern Europeans.

Today I resisted that inviting day-dream, contenting myself with muttering 'Grosso Porco' at the policeman at the crossroads, just to keep in practice.

I stopped at the newsagents to buy some typing paper. Maybe it would be worth working in an office for a few weeks again, to stock up on necessaries like paper and Tipp-Ex.

While I was trying to work out whether one hundred foolscap pages at 99p worked out a better bet than a hundred and fifty A4 for £1.35, the woman from the weight room walked in and started rifling through the typewriter ribbons. Should I say hello? She hadn't seen me. But I was never any good at standing next to people I know pretending they weren't there, so I cleared my throat, prepared to be embarrassed and spoke.

'Hello.' Innocuous enough. She turned, spent half a second

taking in who I was.

'Hello.'

'I can't really say anything else. We haven't been introduced.'

'I'm Beryl.'

'Jo.' We didn't shake hands. Just as well, my palms were sweating. There was a lump in my throat, too. Strange. 'Did they used to call you the Peril, when you were little?'

'Of course. I spent years trying to live it down.'

'And now?' I looked at the way she stood, revelling in her smallness and strength, like a spring about to bounce.

'Now I try to live up to it,' she grinned.

We both suddenly remembered that we were in a shop and looked around for the pay desk. I took one of the pads at random, she picked out a ribbon. We walked over to the checkout together.

'Um, do you feel like going for a quick drink?' I muttered through gritted teeth, as we left the shop.

'OK.' Cool enough. I knew I was blushing. I felt thirteen again. My stomach tied itself in a knot, and I felt like I'd swallowed a pair of castanets.

We asked each other which pub, then which bar, what would you like to drink and I'll get them, and no, it's all right, let me. I sat down exhausted by all the politeness, while she went to the bar. I looked at her properly for the first time. She was sharp. Very blonde, short hair, tousled at the top. Art or a stiff breeze, I couldn't tell. Shocking green eyes and bright pink trousers. Canary-coloured T-shirt, and when she'd taken her jacket off, very white arms, a few freckles. Delicate, but the muscles well defined.

'There you go,' she set two pints on the table and sat down opposite me. The pub was half empty, with the serious relaxation of afternoon drinkers.

'Thanks.' I drank a quarter of it in one go, nervously. Rolled a cigarette. She reached for my tobacco.

'May I?'

'Sure. Go ahead.'

Both of us keeping displacement activities going. Did this mean she was nervous too? If so, of what? No, she was probably being sociable. Going to the pub with someone's not such a big deal. Anyway, she was most likely a remedial netball teacher, or something, and a member of the rotary club.

'You writing the definitive novel, too?'

'Huh?'

'I just assumed.' She pointed to the typing paper.

'No. A play.'

'What about?' I gave her a sketchy outline. 'Sounds like a feminist rewrite of *Journey's End*.' How dare she tease me, we'd only known each other half an hour.

'How about you?' I decided to change the subject. 'I presume you're writing the definitive novel?'

'My dear,' she struck a pose, 'name me a dyke in West 10 who isn't.'

I choked slightly on my beer. Did I have to answer in kind?

'Well, there's me.' I addressed the bottom of my glass. When I looked up again, she seemed perfectly poised, except for the very tips of her little pointed ears, which had gone pink.

'It's the same thing. You being a lady dramatist and all that.'

We skated on, enough said.

'What's it about?'

'I can tell you, because you're not likely to pinch the idea for your own definitive etcetera.' She leaned forward, as though the pub was full of aspiring novelists, notebooks in hand, ready to eavesdrop on her plot then rush off home and pirate it. 'The central characters are three women and a duck-billed platypus, which they've saved from a fur farm.'

'I've never heard of platypus fur.'

'That's because it's so fiendishly exclusive. Platipi die in their thousands to make mittens for the smart set on the slopes of Gstaad.'

As she talked, she waved her hands and tapped her feet a lot. I'd noticed the general pointedness of her shape: head; face and ears; but now took in her eyebrows as well. Very mobile, rising to an angle of sixty degrees like a circumflex accent over her eyes. Her voice came from somewhere on the top of her tonsils, smoky, but insistent. A trace of a west-country accent, overlaid with general-purpose London.

She was telling me about the crimes this gang of women and mammal would commit, each one wilder than the last, mammoth heists and the loot always going to a good cause, like keeping the women's centre open in the face of villainous landlords. That sort of thing.

'Robyn Hood,' I suggested. She stopped and grinned at me. 'A radical alternative to jumble sales and sponsored walks.'

'Sort of. The good guys rip off the baddies and spread the

ill-gottens among the deserving poor. Anyway, they have a lot of fun. Trouble is, every time I think up a really neat crime plot, I want to go out and do it.'

'Why not?' I asked lazily. 'Go out and do it first then write it up. If anyone asks, you're fictionalising real crimes.'

'You can't have your cake and eat it.'

'Why not? I've always wanted to know why not.'

'Because. That's why.'

'Not good enough. I demand a woman's right to have her cake and eat it too.'

'You can if you insist. But it'll end in tears.'

'What doesn't? And I do insist.' I stood up and picked my empty glass from the table, looked at hers. 'Meanwhile how about having your beer and drinking it too?'

'OK, thanks.'

We talked again desultorily, when I got back. Neither of us so nervous now. A hovering cloud of tension settling down to solar plexus level was keeping me alert. My head started to swim slightly. I felt as though my middle ear had been packed with cotton wool, or porridge. A bit distant.

'If I have any more to drink, you'll have to carry me out.'

'No problem,' she gave me a sizing up look, 'except that I'd be asleep myself by then.'

'Mm.'

'I don't normally drink in the daytime.'

'Me neither.'

'Bit of a shock to the constitution.'

'I used to. But I'm out of practice.'

The barman had called time and now came out and started ostentatiously clearing glasses off tables and emptying ashtrays. We still sat, neither of us sure what to do next.

'Come along now,' the barman bellowed at the emptying room, 'haven't you lot got homes to go to?'

'Have you?' Beryl asked.

'Have I what?'

'Got a home to go to?'

'Yes, of course.'

'Well,' she said 'Where is it? I'm giving up this convoluted way of trying to find out where you live, incidentally.'

'Oh, I see.' I told her.

We were the last punters left in the pub and, even preoccupied as we were, the barman's impatience to be gone was hard to ignore. We walked out. I started off for home, she ambled beside me.

'Would you like to come in for a coffee?' Damn euphemisms.

She laughed and said wasn't it strange how much social rituals depended on pouring things down your throat.

'I'd like to. But I have to go to a meeting.'

'Oh.' I thought, that means she doesn't want to and she's too polite to say. We drifted on. She poked me in the ribs.

'Why the long face?' I would have made a lousy poker player.

'I'm not being polite, you know. I really do have to go to a meeting. In fact I've been playing truant from it this last half-hour, and they'll probably make me go and stand in the corner in disgrace as it is.'

My rib tingled.

'OK. Shall I see you again?'

'If you like.'

'I'll give you my phone number.' She took out her diary and I told her the number. 'Give us a bell if you want to meet.'

'Neatly done.' She looked at me from under a raised eyebrow. 'Puts the ping-pong ball firmly on my half of the table.'

'Of course.'

'So, to even things up, I'll give you my number.' She did, lending me her biro to scrawl it on the back of my hand. 'So I don't have a monopoly responsibility for what happens next, if anything.' Her qualification habit wasn't doing my paranoia any good, but the knot behind my belly-button wouldn't be convinced that this was all one-sided.

We got to the corner of my street.

'I'll give you a ring.'

'Have fun at your meeting. Whatever it is.'

'It's about countering the euphoria of Greenham incorporated,' she said. 'We're organising a feminist alternative to saving the world to bring up babies in.' She waved airily. 'See you.' Walked off.

I wanted to call after her 'Hang on a minute.' I wanted to shout down Portobello, 'But we've just stumbled over a major ideological incompatibility, and I think we should discuss it.' Instead I went home, feeling slightly sick.

I knew that there were feminists who thought that the women's peace camps were divisive and misguided and filled with wallies and old hippies. But they'd never been women who I minded avoiding.

Damn, dammit and blast. I stamped up the steps to the house. Just my luck to fall in with a woman whose teeth were set on edge

60

by what I'd spent my recent life wrapped up in. Obviously no suspicion that I had been one of those she was so busy conferring against. Probably didn't recognise me without a woolly hat on. I'd been saving the world for babies to romp in? I didn't care about future generations' birthright, not being a member of the breeding colony. I wanted to save the world for myself and my friends and my mum, and days when you felt like singing for no particular reason. Future generations could look out for themselves.

The rest of the day, I stomped around the flat, fidgeting and irritable, dealing with politics and the squeezed head and slimy tongue after-effects of afternoon drinking. By the time the window, out of which I had been staring, began to fill in with the early night-time darkness I was still feeling confused and hung-over.

I could do without all this. I propped my feet on the desk and considered the state of my social life. I had enjoyed being celibate and nursing a broken heart, these last few months. Very undemanding it had been. And increasingly socially acceptable. Lots of women I knew had taken to political celibacy lately. Something to do with the fact that theories of right-on relationships had got stuck in their heads too firmly to be shifted and turned out to be unworkable in practice. When you're not allowed by your inner politbureau to be monogamous or jealous, giving up altogether has its attractions.

I hadn't exactly been celibate with a capital C. It had just worked out that way, and suited me fine. Not like Danu, when she'd discovered the letters 'LA' on her personal file in prison. They stood for 'Lesbian: Active'. She'd demanded they change it to 'LC' for 'Lesbian: Celibate'. They weren't really equipped to deal with a woman of such principle.

Beryl should have stayed a mystery woman. I should have run out of the shop instead of accosting her. Whatever happened now would rumple my calm. If nothing worked out I'd be left with a dent in my social competence. If anything did happen, it would disrupt my well-ordered life something chronic. Either way, I'd have to find a new gym.

This was no good. I threw a woolly round my shoulders against the night chill and went out for a walk. This felt like a two-mile trauma. A really big tizzy could take me half-way across London before I'd walked it off.

The air was damp and cool, as I headed up towards Westbourne Park, but pleasant after the weeks of gritty heat. Not many people about. A dark blue transit driving at my side, walking speed, a well-practised sort of harassment. The police, keeping the streets safe for respectable folk. The sergeant in the passenger seat pulled back his window and stared me up and down, as I walked on, four miles an hour, ignoring them. That's the theory, anyway. He looked in silence, I walked in silence. One of us was going to collide with a lamp-post at this rate. Satisfied that I wasn't going to do anything exciting (Evening, officer, I'm having a riot, how about you?) he spat his chewing-gum on to the pavement in front of my feet and waved his hand at the driver to speed up. A vanful of very bored men, cruising around looking for some action. Four lads in a Cortina wouldn't have been any different.

I walked on, faster now, head down, hands in pockets, talking silently to myself. And occasionally out loud, it must be admitted. A long-term trainee eccentric old lady, that's me. I'm quite looking forward to being a disreputable crone, frightening boring middle-aged pillars of the community as I shuffle by. I didn't really see where I was going, my sense of direction was taking me east. I kept half an eye, two ears and the hair on the back of my neck out for trouble. Footsteps following me. Large groups of youths coming towards me, making a point of hustling everyone in their way off the pavement. Routine little things like that.

The night had darkened up a lot, with a new set of rain clouds hurrying to fill the blue-black sky. I felt comforted by the closeness of the thickening air, wrapped it around me and felt invisible. Turned north and crossed the canal, stinking and sluggish, reflecting the street lights from its greasy surface. A barge, laid up for the night, bumped against the side of the bridge. Who'd go on that industrial drain for pleasure? The beer garden patches of concrete scattered with stacking chairs out back of canalside pubs were empty. A week ago they would have been full of smart young people drinking vodka and reliving their continental holidays. Maybe one month a year, England gets a bit of sunshine, loosens up, thinks it's in Europe. Then it's back to vests and early bedtime.

By the time I was half way up Sutherland Avenue, my head had cleared and my shoulders unhunched. I stopped rerunning obsessively the conversation in the pub with Beryl. Stopped plotting all the 'what if?' scenarios of how things might turn out with her. 'Que sera sera', I sang quietly to the empty street, in a way that would have Doris Day spitting on the sidewalk.

Maida Vale is not the sort of place you expect to find knee deep in agonised poets and artists having their dark night of the soul. Tonight was no exception as I scooted briskly up it, feeling relaxed, giving my legs a treat, getting up some steam to tackle the hill up to the park. Passing the cricket ground, with a few late-dining taverners bumbling towards their cars, purple-flushed faces glowing dully in a tasteless clash with their stripey tribal neckware.

Into the park, back with the smelly old canal, hiya pal, you still here? Running now, with a slow, bouncy inefficient stride. Just for the hell of it, forgetting why I came out anyway. Ahead of me the exotic birds in their elegant award-winning cages, their wings folded for the night, didn't raise a scaly eyelid at my approach. They must get used to all sorts, living in the middle of a park. Sensible people don't go to parks at night time. They're full of weirdos, it's a well-known fact. I felt safer in the unambiguous odd-ball territory than I did walking down the street, with the illusion of safety. Fellow human beings who'd cross the road to avoid treading on you as you lay spitting blood and teeth into the gutter, but that's about as far as they would go.

Cutting across the road, heading for the dark interior of the park. Motorists speeding by like they were on safari, windows firmly closed, insulated against the wild beasts and crazed joggers. Do not stop, do not feed the animals. If they broke down, would they sit in their protective metal capsule and wait for a rugged ranger to tow them to the laager?

Slowing to a walk again, the tarry sludge in the bottom of my lungs not amused by all this agitation and *joie de vivre*. Don't make waves, my breathing apparatus tells me. I remember all those schools programme pictures of serious biologists in white coats measuring out beakers of the black stuff to represent the accumulation of a life-time's ignoring the Health Education Council.

Walking round the lakes, picking my way carefully so as not to tread on the dozing ducks who had settled themselves down on the lawns, wings and feet tucked up, semi-visible. Craning my neck to see the moon apparent every now and then between the dark bulk of the fast-moving rain clouds. As I headed back towards the outer circle, starting to think about getting home, I stopped on the footbridge over the neck of the lake. In one of the moments of light through a window in the clouds, I looked back towards the bandstand. Two people standing a hundred yards from me, unmoving and silent. I must have walked past them in the dark. A woman and a man, not speaking or touching. Standing close looking at each other. He was a dark shape, obscured by the woman, who had her back to me. I could see the top half of his face, where he was taller than her. He stared at her, with his body inclined towards her. Her outline was vague, I got no impression of her. She seemed distant from him, not physically. I had an idea that he was straining to keep her there, not able to do anything, making an effort of will to stop her vanishing altogether. He was losing. A large bank of cloud approached the moon, pushing a clear space in front of it. In a second of bright illumination, I saw the pale familiar face of the man I had met in the war museum. The woman too, I knew. Or if I had ever seen any of Ada's granddaughters, that's who I would have said she was. A seventy-year-younger version of Ada.

The cloud closed in, the light was gone, I strained my eyes towards the couple; they vanished from my sight. I took one step back to where they had been standing, then changed my mind. I didn't understand what was going on, but if I was to find out, it wouldn't be by chasing round Regent's Park in the dark. Either I would discover why this guy appeared, seeming more unreal every time, or decide that I was going off my box, seeing things. Either way, I would leave it for now.

I have no memory of the walk home. I think I must have put myself on auto pilot and dozed off. Late-night long walks home across any number of cities had given me the habit of marching in my sleep, as near as makes no odds. It was past one when I got in. Climbing into bed and starting to fall properly asleep, I decided tomorrow I'd do some more thinking. Tomorrow, the mystery man wouldn't seem so mysterious and the problem of Beryl not such a problem. Tomorrow, I would do my work and sort out my life. Tonight, I would curl up in a ball and pull the bedclothes over my head. Tonight – I was already asleep.

# Eight

Time passed, as it does, without any of the problematic areas of my life being resolved. While I was waiting for all to be revealed I carried on pottering about. Went back to the library a couple of times to check out the last of the boring factoids. Wrote the first draft of the first act. Binned it in disgust and rewrote. Second draft went the same way. By the third attempt, I was so sick of the sight of the damn thing, I decided that it would have to do. Probably no better than the efforts which I'd shredded.

In between times, catching the last days of summer as they popped up here and there, I did some serious last-minute lying-about practice at the women's pond. There were never whole days of summer any more. A golden morning or a sultry afternoon. Not very many balmy evenings. The holiday-makers started trickling back to find all their poor relations who'd stayed at home with the same depth of tan. Ostentatious consumption confounded.

Still I didn't call Beryl and she didn't call me. I'd stopped going to the gym and always kept an eye out, when I was around, to avoid bumping into her on the street. Then one day, she interrupted a restful few hours I'd been spending looking at a piece of paper with 'Act Three: Scene One' and nothing else on it, ringing up to ask if I wanted to come to dinner.

Poleaxed by the phone, and politeness and surprise, I said yes before I'd worked out how I could have said no. She sounded breezy and matter of fact, I was gruff and monosyllabic, but that's not so unusual.

'Sorry I didn't ring sooner,' she said, 'but I've been running around like a hamster on an exercise wheel these last couple of weeks.'

'That's OK.' I didn't want her to think I'd been pining for word of her. 'I've been pretty busy myself.'

'Tomorrow night, then? It's a house social evening, so there should be quite a lot of us in.'

'Fine.' It sounded ghastly, but I could hardly say so. 'House social evening' – the people's committee for social interaction, brackets theraputic, close brackets, non-optional. Oh well.

'You know the road?'

'I'll find it.' I'd never admit that I didn't know the way. It might involve being given directions.

The house was easy enough to spot anyway. Posters in the windows, stickers on the door.Brightly painted woodwork not even attempting to mask the fact that the house itself was falling down, and not slowly. One of a line of large Victorian terraced town houses, an indeterminate shade of London brick and soot-coloured.

I banged on the splitting panel of the front door, picking up a splinter in my knuckle. A woman I didn't recognise opened the door to find me trying to extract the chunk of timber from my hand at the same time as balancing my bicycle at the top of the steps. It was a losing battle.

'What happened to you?' She tried to help me with the bike, we juggled it between us for an awkward moment.

'I think your front door's got dutch-elm disease. Or a bit of it's trying to run away from home.' I showed her the splinter.

'It is a bit decrepit,' she said, as though she'd only just noticed it. 'Who are you, by the way? I'm Caroline.'

'Jo. This is the right house, isn't it?'

'Oh yes. Friend of Beryl's?'

I grunted and squeezed past the bike, which between us we'd managed to manoeuvre into the hall, along with the half-dozen that were already parked. There was a stained glass fanlight over the front door, which gave a faintly cathedral air. Up the stairs, a series of neatly ordered women's prints stuck to the wall. The layout was very stations-of-the-cross. Subliminal influences on a lapsed Catholic, I diagnosed.

I followed Caroline through to the back of the house. Her hair was cropped short, except for one long thin plait at the back. She opened the door into a large kitchen. Plaster mouldings on the ceiling still from when it was a sitting room in the better days of the family house. Three women at the table in the corner, drinking wine and making salad. Another woman standing at the sink washing vegetables. And Beryl sitting on the sill of the open french windows looking out into the long, overgrown, walled-in garden.

'Hullo,' I said, standing in the middle of the room not looking at anyone in particular. Beryl jumped up and made hostessly motions, taking the bottle I had brought, finding me a drink, doing the introductions.

'Avril, Connie, Zelda, Jess, Caroline,' she said rapidly, indicating the women from the sink anti-clockwise. 'This is Jo.' They all murmured 'Hi' and I said 'Hi' back and looked for a chair.

There wasn't one, so I perched on the other half of the french window sill and everyone got on with what they'd been doing before. Jess lounged at the table reading a newsletter. She was yards up and down, a few inches across. Occasionally she grunted with disapproval or support, calling the attention of other women to items that she found particularly outrageous. Avril's busy back-view expressed annoyance, as she shook slugs off the lettuce with an unnerving lack of frivolity. The one between Jess and Connie was trying to cut interlinked women's symbols out of tomatoes and beetroot. Connie took the lethally sharp vegetable knife from her.

'Griz, you'll do yourself an injury, waving it about like that.'

'Griz?' She looked the most cheerful of the lot to me.

'Christened Grizelda,' she smiled at me. 'Can you believe it? Would you do that to a helpless little baby? Most people call me Zelda because it sounds Slavic and romantic. Connie's just naturally cussed.'

Connie didn't look offended. 'If you don't stop doing goddam handicrafts with the tomatoes and fix the salad, I'll give you cussed.' She tried for a ferocious look, which must have come hard to someone with freckles all over and a very short nose. There was no bad humour in it. Zelda picked up the knife again and began whacking it down on a cucumber, pantomiming an Italian soap opera chef.

'You'll bruise it doing that,' Avril said from the sink, sharply. 'Or cut yourself.' Zelda subsided and Connie gave Avril a lifted eyebrow, flared nostril, 'what's bugging you?' look, although no one spoke. Beryl who had sat down opposite me at the window caught my eye and winked. The joys of communal living. There was quite a bit of tension in the room, but it saved me from the worse strain of being alone with Beryl. We made polite conversation for a while. How was my work going? Fine. And hers? Fine. Had she been to the gym lately? No, no time.

'It's ready,' announced Avril, hanging up her apron on the back of the kitchen door. I half expected to be sent off to wash my hands.

'I'm going down the offy to get another bottle of plonk.' Jess stood up. 'Does anyone else want anything?'

'You could have gone before.'

'It won't get cold.' Jess shrugged. I could see the temptation to play wilful kid to Avril's ostentatious adult. Not that she looked much older than several of the others. Mid to late twenties. When I asked Beryl later, she told me that Jess, whose age I couldn't have guessed, was the oldest, at thirty.

While the alcoholic reinforcements were coming up, the other women had a small argument of habit about whether to eat at the table or go out and sit in the garden. The mildness of the evening with the sun just starting to think about sloping off in a soft haze, and the shortage of chairs swung it in favour of the garden.

We carried an old check travelling rug and a blanket out to sit on. Zelda lay on her front, nose to nose with a tortoise who had lumbered out from under a hydrangea. The letters SAP were painted on her shell.

'What's the tortoise called?'

'Sappho, of course.' Beryl had joined Zelda eyeballing the little wrinkly face. 'Only she's just a baby of fifty or so, and there wasn't room for it all on her shell. Was there, darling?' she addressed the animal directly, from a distance of about two inches.

'Why paint her name on at all?'

'You have to identify them. For when they hibernate.' Avril answered too crisply. I guessed there had been arguments about it.

'Why?' I didn't mean to cause trouble, but Avril's tone implied that facts were facts and that was the end of it.

'Because that's what you do with tortoises. They all look the same, you see, when they're packed in straw.' Avril set the knives and forks, which had been put down in a heap, out properly.

'Don't you think that's rather speciesist?' Zelda asked muffledly, her chin crammed on to her chest, doing a shoulder stand.

'I still don't see that it matters,' I persisted, 'even if she does forget her name because she's been asleep for a few months, she's hardly going to be able to climb out of her shell and take a look at what it says on the back.'

'And you would have thought,' Beryl put in, 'that tortoises would have developed a strong enough sense of identity to still know who they are after a long period of not affirming it.'

Avril fussed around the supper things with little gestures of impatience, not wanting to acknowledge that she was being got at, not easy enough with the others to walk away from the subject. She made very little eye contact, seemed to regard it as an effort, bracing herself up for it, engaging in an eye lock like an arm wrestler, then breaking off with relief and too much abruptness.

'Avril's trouble,' Zelda fell gracefully away from the flower bed, 'is that she watched too much Blue Peter as a child.' Her tone of voice was smooth, the remark itself innocuous, but it was obviously not friendly banter. I wondered why they lived with Avril, or she lived with them, if it was always like this.

'What's Blue Peter?' Connie asked.

'A kid's programme for anal retentive trainee bank-managers,' Jess answered, walking out from the kitchen, holding a wine box. 'Don't tell me you've been waiting for me. The social polish round here is getting dazzling.' She sat down and the meal appeared to start.

'How can you not know Blue Peter?' I nudged Connie's attention away from the daisies she was adding to her salad sandwich.

'Grew up in the States mostly,' she grunted through a mouthful, as though surprised that anyone could not know her life-story. 'Didn't come over here till I was twelve or so. Guess I was past the age for that kind of stuff by then. Anyway, it sounds pretty creepy, if they were always painting up their pets.'

'Damn colonials don't know they're born,' Beryl jeered. 'Never learnt to build useful and acceptable gifts for grandparents.'

'Proton accelerators made out of toilet rolls and old squeezy bottles,' I remembered.

'With the brand names scrubbed off,' Zelda zoomed back to childhood too.

'I have here a proton accelerator I made earlier,' Beryl continued, with a passable imitation of Valerie Singleton. 'As you can see I have finished it off with a covering of sticky-backed plastic. Remember to ask a grown-up to cut this out for you, as you need *very* sharp scissors.'

The rest of the meal passed easily enough, reliving the kids' programmes we could all still recall better than what we had watched last night. Bill and Ben had been a favourite with us all, no one had cared for Camberwick Green. Even Avril loosened up enough to admit that she wished the Muppets had been around when she was little.

We sat smoking in the fading light, swatting lazily at the insects, finished the last of the wine. Zelda lay with her face in the tough unmown grass while Caroline gave her a shoulder rub. Connie had got up muttering something about rotas, and taken the plates in to wash up.

Beryl was sitting close to me, her back propped against a battered old walnut tree. Closer than a polite distance, not so close that my personal space was intruded upon. Very nicely judged. Every now and then we would bump into each other's territory, a hand brushing mine as she passed the matches, nothing more than warm and normal. No stray static crackling in the stuffy air of the garden. As if to make up for our lack of personal fireworks, the air pressure shot up, as darkness finally arrived, with a suggestion of the sky filling up with storm clouds again. There was a ripple of thunder from somewhere over Ealing.

'Thunder on the left,' Caroline looked up from Zelda's shoulders, sweating from the effort of her massaging, 'hadn't we better go and propitiate the odd deity?'

'I'm not bowing and scraping to any fucking godlet,' Connie came back out from the kitchen. 'The goddess can see them off if they start to get bumptious.'

Avril stood up. She expected everyone to be going in, the way she stood there. Reluctant to leave, maybe, a group in which she wasn't comfortable, in case they started talking about her when she was gone.

'Can you bring the rug in when it starts raining?' was all she said before going.

'Sure.' Caroline didn't look up again. Avril carefully shut the french windows behind her.

'Is she still looking for a place with Martha?' Connie asked, when Avril had been gone a few minutes.

'I guess so.'

'I think they blow hot and cold about it,' (Caroline's voice) 'depending on how keen they are on living happily ever after in monogomous bliss at the time.'

'But they've been a stable couple in inverted commas for years,' Zelda rolled over and looked up at Caroline, 'how come they're still agonising about living together?'

'There's no inverted commas about their couple,' Jess sounded impatient. 'But despite the fact we drive her nuts, Avril gets some things out of this communal living that she's going to miss when it's just two of them. I guess that's why she's hanging on here.'

'Best of both worlds,' Beryl agreed. 'When it's all too tough here she can go off to Martha for soul's balm, and when that gets stifling she can zip back here and be as communal as you like.'

'Is it always as tense as this with her?' I wondered.

'Not always,' Caroline thought for a minute. 'Me and her have lived here the longest. Five years it must be, near enough. It's worked well enough most of the time, I suppose. Just these last few months, though, she's rather taken on the role of senior matriarch. It causes problems.'

'She always treats women who've moved in more recently as though she had some kind of hidden seniority,' Zelda complained.

'The worst thing is,' Beryl followed on, 'that you can feel her doing it, but it's impossible to pin down. So you can never talk about it with her, or you end up sounding unfair.'

'Yes,' (Zelda again) 'she's so practical. She wants everything in really concrete terms. "What did I do?" She's perfectly prepared to talk about it of course, but it's not that easy.'

'She's too good at meetings,' Jess put in. 'She sets everythings up as though it was a formal meeting, and brings her impeccable logic to bear on it, so half the things that really piss women off never come up. We end up talking about the cleaning rotas a lot.'

'We were going to have all our house meetings in the nude,' Caroline said, 'so no one could take themselves too seriously. But it got to be too cold in winter, and a bit of a distraction in summer, so we gave up on the idea.'

'All politics and most meetings would grind to a halt if the people at them couldn't take themselves seriously any more,' Jess said.

'Politics with a big P would,' I agreed, 'being full of boys, and you know what they're like about their dignity. . .'

'No. All meetings,' Caroline interrupted, definite, 'would become an impossible concept if you deprived the participants of their sense of social standing.'

'Humph.' Beryl jumped into the argument, waving her hands. 'Women can have meetings that aren't meetings like men have meetings. A different kettle of fish.'

'When?' Connie joined in. 'Name me one damn meeting you've ever been to that you honestly think could have carried on without role-playing and pomposity.'

'Who needs it anyway?' Zelda didn't have the arguing tone that the others were using. 'Why bother trying to feminise meetings as a way of doing things? Why not just admit that they're a repressive patriarchal set-up and leave them to men to tinker about with?'

71

'Well, I think women can have meetings without doing all that sort of stuff.' Beryl was on the defensive. In one of the flash-bulb glimpses which I got of her in the more frequent lightning, I saw her hunch into herself, sticking her chin out. 'We can reclaim them as a way of getting things done.'

'But what "things" do you want to get done, poppet?' Caroline again, driving Beryl into a corner and trying to sound soothing with it. 'Patriarchal methods make for patriarchal results.'

'Women's anarchic revolution will not be organised by a committee, you know,' Jess said dryly.

'Well, if it did, I know I'd get stuck taking the bloody minutes,' Zelda grumbled.

'But I don't see that a group of women meeting together because they want to make something happen, like a benefit or a conference or something, is one step removed from a board of directors of General Motors.' Beryl wasn't giving up.

'Games still get played.'

'Never heard of collectives, you lot?' I tried to even things up a bit.

'Oh yeah?' Connie tried to sound worldly wise, it didn't suit her, 'you ever been in one that worked?'

'Yes.'

'Ha. Where was this paradise on earth?' Zelda was taking an interest.

'It wasn't that. Just that we got along most of the time without a structure to our name. It was a women's peace camp.'

There was a two-second ghastly pause, the kind that used to happen when someone had farted very loudly in church when I was a kid. One solitary heavy drop of rain fell on the end of my nose, and the thunder rolled overhead, as though even the sky was clearing its throat for a good row.

'What?' I could feel the whole of Beryl's attention snapped towards me. Oh well, we had to get here sooner or later.

'You lived at a women's peace camp?' There was an edge to Caroline's voice. I realised that she was trying not to laugh. At me or Beryl?

'Yes, until quite recently.'

'We're not terribly keen on the women's peace movement in this house,' Connie tried for studied neutrality. I wanted to laugh, she sounded so carefully Victorian. Must be nervous.

'So I gather.'

'Why didn't you tell me?' Beryl sounded hurt.

'You didn't ask. We haven't really had a chance to swop life-stories yet.' And probably never would now, I added to myself.

'Everyone should be introduced by a computer which matches up their prejudices and rules out this kind of nasty shock discovery.' Jess, ironic.

'Is it such a big deal?'

'We've never had one across the threshold before.'

'A real live peace woman,' Connie murmured. 'In probably the only right-on household in London that doesn't want to save the mother earth for generations of unborn little pink babies.'

'They come in other shades than pink, you know,' I snapped. There was a sense of gears changing, real disagreements about to come out. 'And why not save the world, anyway? You got a death wish?'

'Because it's full of shit. Here and now.' Jess was definitely not into keeping it civilised. 'It's a fucking awful world, full of women getting fucked over and you want to save it just as it is for men to carry on like they always have.'

'You don't know what I want.'

'The women's peace movement, then.' Caroline was smoother than Jess, but getting as angry. 'The point is, if we can't change the way women get treated in the world, frankly who cares if it all goes up in a mushroom cloud?'

'That's sounds pretty much like a fate-worse-than-death approach. Better radioactive than oppressed?'

'Not at all. But you must admit,' Caroline's reasonable tone got to me far more than Jess's anger, or Beryl's silent quivering disapproval, 'that the peace movement diverted the energy of a lot of women away from women's issues.'

'No.' I was baffled by so many things with which to disagree in one sentence. 'I don't believe in 'women's issues' or that the women's peace movement has been co-opted by men, which is what you're implying.'

'Indeed I am.'

'But all the women who come to the camp wouldn't necessarily be doing anything else.' I tried to sound calm, despite the tension I felt. It was catching. 'You know, the famous "ordinary woman" the women's movement is always going on about. The kind who never go near women's movement events and conferences which are meant to be for them, because they're so damn alienating.'

73

'Well, it's not surprising you did so well with "ordinary women" as you call them,' Jess was bitter, 'falling all over yourself to be respectable baby-loving nurturers like you do. What good wives and mothers! A nice little enclave of hets in a sea of dangerous threatening dyke feminists.'

'Bloody hell, Jess.' I couldn't believe what she was saying. 'Why do you think all those women chose to live together without men? As a heterosexual enclave? Come off it. It's the only separatist living situation I've ever been in that worked as that. Not like all the compromises you have to make in London.'

I slumped back against the apple tree and felt Beryl unexpectedly gripping the scruff of my neck. Was she about to shake me? Or trying to get me to relax. My shoulder muscles were like overcooked spaghetti. She passed me the cigarette which she had been smoking, and I decided to interpret the hand on my neck as personal support. In spite of herself, because she didn't agree with what I was saying.

'Why did you leave the camp then, if it's so great?' Connie had spotted one of my logical inconsistencies.

'Lots of reasons. Because I think there is a point in dealing with male violence by being non-violent, under certain circumstances. But it got to be personally damaging for me. I'd had enough of it. Starting to want to hit all those bastard policemen and soldiers who were kicking me around, more than I wanted to make a political point and win support by moral superiority.'

There had been no thunder or lightning for a few minutes, the dark was intense and the night closed in so close I felt there was darkness half-way down my throat. One last flash of lightning right overhead lit us all crouched on the grass like runners on the blocks. A smack of thunder and the storm properly hit us. Rain bucketed down. Beryl grabbed my arm and pulled me towards the shelter of the house, the others following. In the few seconds that it had taken us to register the onset of the rain and get indoors, we were all soaked.

I stood in the kitchen, dripping on to the floor, not cold, but exhilarated.

'How do you feel about skipping round two of this argument?' Beryl said quietly, so the others wouldn't hear.

'I'm a dedicated coward.' I felt good, that kind of scene is like beating your head on a brick wall. Nice when it stops. I didn't want it all to start again.

'Let's go and get dry then.' I followed her upstairs.

Beryl's room was like the woman herself, small and colourful, full of unexpected angles and sharp bits which I kept bumping up against. I asked her if she and it had grown to resemble each other like an old dog-owner and her pet. She laughed.

A cramped writing space underneath the raised platform bed, built from stolen railway sleepers; 'do it yourself design council' she called it disparagingly, but I could see she was fond of her arrangements.

'Here, catch.' She threw me a towel and I dried off the rain water roughly. The chairs were hi-tec, Scandinavian and clinical, so I sat on the floor and counted my toes waiting for something to happen.

'We could carry on thrashing out the peace question, if you like,' she hunkered down in front of me and took hold of one of my big toes, at which I happened to be staring.

'I thought this was a bit of running-away practice.'

'I said "if you like".'

'Can I at least go back to my corner and take out my gumshield for a few minutes between bouts?'

'You can do what you like,' she let go of my foot. 'I wasn't saying much down there. But there's a lot of stuff that I feel very strongly about that you won't agree with.'

'You assume.'

'It seems reasonable. And vice versa.'

'So?'

'So it's there,' she pointed to a spot on the floor between us, 'and we have to talk about it. If not now, then some other time.'

'Can't we just agree to differ? Because I feel quite strongly about it all too. Even though I've given up trying to save the world, I still have a lot of loyalty to my friends who haven't.'

'Sure.'

'And lapsed people are the most defensive. Just like converts are the most enthusiastic.'

'Hmph.'

'So the chances are we'd end up yelling at each other.'

'Not necessarily.' Soothing tone, fierce expression. I believed her face more than her words.

'But likely. You must admit.'

'Possibly. But we can't have a whole no-go area that matters to both of us where we're afraid to talk to each other in case we row. It's ridiculous.'

'Pretty right-off,' I agreed. 'But I'm a practical sort.'

'But if we can't be honest with each other,' she didn't finish her sentence, Can't what, I wondered? Can't be friends? Can't be close? Can't trust each other? Can't be lovers? I wasn't even sure what she wanted.

'What do you want?'

'Are you asking me my intentions?'

'Um.' I havered. 'Possibly.'

'Well, I don't know that I have any as such.' I reckoned that she had her fingers crossed behind her back. 'I just feel that ruling whole chunks of our experience as inadmissible subjects for discussion between us creates a lack of trust. And that prejudices any chance of a more than superficial relationship between us.' She looked at me, defensively, 'Of any kind.'

I stared at her amazed. I'd never met anyone who talked like that about the reasons why they didn't think it was a good idea to go to bed with you.

'Is that the most unbelievably pompous thing you've heard all evening?' she asked, eventually.

'Well, I wasn't going to say it, but . . .'

'I know, I know,' she curled herself up in a small ball and beat her forehead gently on the floor. 'I guess I'm feeling awkward. But you know what I'm getting at.'

'I suppose so.'

She sat up and looked at me again. I wanted to hug her. Stop it, I thought, we're having a serious agonise here. Her hair was standing on end. Was it the electricity in the air, or the tension in her? I felt as though we were tied together with strong elastic bands.

'OK,' she conceded, 'maybe this is all a bit daft and over-formal, and too much like an everyday story of right-on folk trying to decide if they're compatible.' She took a deep breath and put on a self-protecting 'you don't have to take this seriously' voice. 'But I don't just want you for your body, you know.'

I was flabbergasted, again.

'I'm flabbergasted,' I said.

'Don't be. It's not a heavy number.'

'No, but it's not very British, either.'

She disagreed. 'I think we're being exceptionally British. We should stop it at once.'

'Maybe we could call half-time?'

'I'll go and get the lemons.'

'Skip the lemons. Just make with the pep-talk.'

'OK team, it goes like this,' she got into a huddle with herself, inviting me in. 'We've taken a bit of a pounding in the first half. Our defence is solid, but we need to loosen up. I want to see less of the fancy footwork, Ron. And you should be getting forward more. Or getting more forward. I'll be sick as a parrot if we go ninety minutes without a result. Team talk over, let's go for it,' she unhuddled.

'I'm over the moon,' I said. 'Does this mean that we can agree that we've got to talk some more about the things that we've got to talk about, but that we don't have to talk about it any more right now?'

'Couldn't have put it worse myself.'

So that was pretty much the end of it, for the time being. We agreed to carry on disagreeing at a later date, and in the meantime – I got acrobatic butterflies, thinking about the meantime. She looked to be in the same state. Let's boldly go, I thought. There was an awkward pause, while we both looked at each other's feet and wondered how to begin. She started to speak, her voice squeaky, she coughed and tried again.

'Would you like a cup of tea?'

It's not that easy to give up being British.

# Nine

For days I did no work. The play sat on my desk going curly at the edges and my typewriter got an allergy to dust. I bopped about with a fatuous grin, wafted on a cloud of that natural anaesthetic which gets you through the first weeks of an affair.

Of course, things were a little precarious between me and Beryl. For all that we were both wallowing in pleasedness-with-ourselves, we still hadn't managed to have the definitive woman-to-woman exhange of views on peace (or the lack of it). A couple of times we'd started, usually with her making some dig at me about woolly hats, or hand-knitted crucifixes, but we'd always put the brakes on after a bit of snapping and bristling. 'No,' we'd say, 'this isn't the way to do it. We have to talk about this properly.' So we'd put it back on our things-to-do list and get on with the serious business of having a good time.

One morning Beryl was sitting on my desk kicking her heels, trying to persuade me to take the day off to go to Frinton with her.

'You know you'd enjoy it. You keep telling me how much you love the seaside.'

'Maybe I would,' I shuffled around grumpily, sorting my anger into neat piles of old folded newspapers, straightening the hearth rug. Waiting for her to go away.

'But you're not going to give up the chance to stare at your typewriter gloomily waiting for your muse, are you?'

'Probably not,' I grunted at the cheese plant whose leaves I was rearranging.

'You're a masochist. An old-fashioned moralist.'

'Humph.'

'Will you stop doing the bloody housework. I'm trying to provoke you.'

'I hadn't noticed. And why?'

'Because I think you're old before your time. Because there's something so damn reasonable about the way you organise your life and it irritates me. Because I don't think hard work and cold showers and virtue get rewarded.'

'Oh yes?' I banged the chair cushions together, raising clouds of dust.

'I don't know. But it's a beautiful day, which you're going to spend mouldering away indoors, and for some reason that makes me angry.' She picked up a sheaf of closely-typed pages from the desk and dropped them again with a thump. 'Look at this. It's indecent.'

'My play? It's a family show. I thought I'd mentioned.'

'Not the content, blockhead, the amount. Acres of the bloody thing. It's not right, you sitting in here day after day, while real life passes you by, writing such volumes of stuff.'

'Like Mr Lear?'

She threw a dictionary at my head. It was our first row. In the end we did go to Frinton, but not that day. I agreed to a date, so as not to appear unreasonable, and secretly hoped that it would rain. But the appointed morning came around sunny and settled, so I packed sandwiches, towels and a small grudge and set off to meet Beryl at Liverpool Street.

'You're late,' Beryl greeted me with a perfunctory kiss, trying not to gloat that I'd come at all. I bought a paper, so she could have the crossword and we wouldn't have to make polite conversation on the train. She had been cunning, picking this distraction of all those on offer. I did like the sea, and spent the last couple of miles with my head out of the corridor window, trying to get a sniff of the salt and ozone.

'God almighty, what a one-horse watering-hole this is,' Beryl gazed in mild horror at the dopy little town as we walked from the station to the beach.

'You never been here before?'

'Nope. Heard about it. Report didn't tell half of it though.'

'It's a family resort.'

'The last one, I should think. Before the divorce courts.'

'Family as in a euphemism for no sex and violence. Anyway the beach is worth the journey,' I said firmly. I wasn't having Beryl going into a sulk about Frinton when it was me who should have been aggrieved about being dragged out on a working day.

A swim seemed to improve her temper a bit. We lay on damp

79

towels in the sun, drinking warm shandy out of cans. I watched the children building sandcastles, thinking I could do better, and wishing we had an orange stripy wind-break to section off some territory.

'Glad you came?' she scooped up a fistful of sand and let it trickle slowly into my navel.

'Beryl! I'm covered in suntan oil! It'll take me weeks to get the sand out. Or are you trying to bury me?'

'I'll wait till you're asleep. And you didn't answer my question.'

'I'm having quite a good time,' I conceded, guardedly.

'But rather be fossiking about in your casualty lists and army regulations.'

'What have you got against it? You write yourself, it's not such an uncommon perversion.'

'It's the subject I find morbid.'

'That's not what you said last time. I distinctly remember you saying it was the quantity that upset you.'

'Oh don't be so bloody logical. Do you always remember things like that?'

'It's a bad habit.' I pulled a corner of towel over my eyes to shade them, hoping I'd look like I was going to sleep.

'It's an unhealthy obsession.'

'What is?' I was a bit muffled by the towel.

'Your refusal to acknowledge that the armistice was ever declared. You know, poppy days, wreath-laying, all that. The war's over, Jo.'

'It's a historical interest.'

'You're wasting your energy. Not living in the real world.'

'It happened in the real world.'

'Over sixty years ago.'

'Never heard of learning the lessons of history?'

'Don't give me that marxist claptrap. You're just obsessed with wars.'

'Their prevention maybe. Perhaps you don't think that's important?'

'Two sides of the same coin. You do them the compliment of taking their boys' games as seriously as they take themselves.'

'You must admit that you can't be neutral now. The next war will happen to us all. Even if the men start it.'

'And you're going to stop them?' She sat up and started digging angry little holes in the sand with her heel.

'Beryl, I'm writing a play which happens to be about a war. Maybe I think it's useful to understand how men can let that sort of fiasco happen, if you want to stop them doing it again. What's the big deal? And I used to live at a peace camp, which you don't like, but we all make our personal choices. Again, what's there to be angry about?'

She looked down at me with an expression I couldn't read, the sun full behind her. 'I've seen a lot of women making the personal choices you made. All siphoned off into the peace movement, thinking it's just down to them, their personal choice. But it adds up to an awful lot of women with no energy left to spare for women's things. Which the peace movement isn't.'

'There probably won't be a lot of feminist collectives around in the bunkers below the radioactive desert.' I found a pebble and threw it at the waves.

'What a wonderful excuse for not doing anything in the here and now.'

'No it isn't.'

'Of course it is. The peace movement is a great big, morally satisfying diversion. Unattainable, nebulous and never-bloody-ending. The powers that be must love the way it keeps potential trouble-makers safely locked in an unwinnable confrontation with the police and the army.'

'That's a very gloomy view.'

'It's a realistic one. Jaundiced, I grant you. I've seen too many feminists allowing themselves to be portrayed as naturally peace-making and family loving. Letting themselves be decoyed from all the hard and nasty struggles that confront them back in the hard and nasty real world.'

I sat up, feeling at a disadvantage with her looming over me. 'You can't blame us for the way we got portrayed in the media. And why put women down for thinking nuclear war's preventable? If you don't think that's the case you might as well jump under a bus tomorrow.'

'Do you think that sitting around in the mud holding hands wearing a beatific smile will stop the bomb? If you reckon that sort of thing will save the world why aren't you doing it any more? I don't believe you think it, or that most women pacifists think it. You all want to have a clear conscience when you're blown up, however futile your gestures in the meantime.'

I didn't answer. Got up and walked along the beach feeling hot and angry. Damn Beryl's sweeping generalisations. I swam out to the old wooden diving board perched on three legs in the sea. When Beryl hauled herself up the steps, like a seal on a rock, I was sitting on the board, trying to see Holland.

'Sorry,' she said, shaking water off the spikes of her hair. 'I wasn't trying to wind you up.'

'I don't understand why it matters to you so much. You seem to take the women's peace movement as a personal affront.'

'In a way I guess I do.' she sighed and made way for a small boy to run along the board, watched him plummet ten feet into the waves. 'All that wasted energy.'

'It's funny how feminists who don't approve of things regard any woman's energy which gets put into them as some kind of theft of their personal property. It sounds dangerously like you think there are duties that women ought to be undertaking.'

'I don't think that. It makes me sad to see so many women giving so much in what's basically a male-defined area. When there are other, more positive things to be done to get us the kind of lives we want immediately. Not just asking men politely not to blow us up, so everything can carry on in the lousy state it's in.'

'You generalise from the kind of Christian/hippy ethic of a few women in the peace movement and attribute those attitudes to all of us. What about all the stroppy dykes confronting the state and challenging traditional ways of living in peace camps?'

'What about them? They're largely invisible.'

'Invisibilised. By the media and the liberal public's desire only to see what they can understand.'

'And not wanting to rock the boat and risk alienating straight women?'

'As if that never happened elsewhere.' I stood up and flexed at the far end of the board. 'How many collectives do you know busily pretending not to be separatist organisations, for fear of offending straight feminists, where all the work is done by lesbians?'

'Dozens.'

'Well don't blame us if a lot of straight pacifists tried to pretend we didn't exist, when we took every opportunity to remind them that we did.' I dived in, touched sand and pulled up in time to see Beryl hitting the water behind me. We turned on our backs and floated.

'I'm glad we've started to talk about it,' she raised her feet from the surface of the waves to look at her toes. Wonderful stomach muscles the woman had.

'Umph.' I tried to do the same and got a mouthful of salt water as my head sank. 'Would it be very right off of me to confess that I'd rather lie in the sun and watch you being lithe and sinuous?'

'Yes it would.' She did a quick duck-dive and popped up on the other side of me. 'I only talk about these things because they matter to you and I want to get to know you properly.'

'How ominous that sounds. We could swim to Europe instead.'

'I know a wonderful bar in Amsterdam . . . '

In the end we compromised and went to sleep on the beach.

She took me to the theatre once to see a ballet (she *was* a dancer, the leg-warmers never lie). But there were no tutus, no pirouettes or graceful leapings. It was the modern dance group which Beryl most admired, and she sat entranced through the two-hour programme of writhings and limb-clutching, while I waited hopefully for the intermission. There was no popcorn.

'I suppose you'd rather have nice tunes and dying swans?' she hissed at me in a lull. They had lulls, rather than reassuring rests.

'They could be terminal poultry for all I know,' I whispered back. All around us lovers of modern dance were getting into the experience. 'What's it meant to be about?'

'They're improvising, dolt. On a theme of the soul of the industrial revolution.

'Is it in torment?' I asked politely.

'Philistine! Doesn't this communicate anything to you?'

'Rather less than Crossroads.' All around us people started making subdued shushing noises. 'I wouldn't mind, if you didn't have to be so reverential. Hushed awe makes me sneeze.'

'I thought you'd be interested.' She hunched a shoulder at me. 'I wish I hadn't brought you.'

'Don't mind me.' I started working my arms into the jacket on which I was sitting. 'I'll slide out the back and sneer vigorously in the foyer until the performance finishes. Then we can go to the pub, and you can despise my uncouthness over a pint.' She didn't answer so I oozed along the row of knees crammed into small, uncomfortable chairs and made my escape. At the end of the dance she stalked out of the hall and led the way disapprovingly to the theatre-goers' local.

I was getting used to Beryl's mercurial changes of mood. Quite often I found her picking rows with me, mostly about difficult abstract things. She'd work herself into a lather of indignation, and nine times out of ten abandon the subject in mid-froth, give me a big hug and suggest going out for a drink. All very disconcerting. I had a lowering feeling that it was her fascinating body which kept me persevering through the ructions.

We kept returning to the subject of peace, though not by my choosing. She seemed fascinated by my motives for having been involved, as the only tame ex-camper of her acquaintance. I began to feel like an endlessly examined specimen in a biology lab.

'Why did you go to live there in the first place?' she demanded when we were settled in the pub, at the end of our second pint and a short lecture from her on my yobbish tendencies.

'Sorry?'

'The camp. Why did you go to live there?'

'I don't know.'

'You must know,' she said sternly.

'An irresistible urge.' If she was stern, I would be frivolous.

'Don't be flippant. You can't have just woken up one morning and thought, I'll go and knit myself a women's community outside an airbase for the hell of it.'

'Not quite.'

'So why did you go?'

'Put it down to women's magnetism.'

'Which women?'

'Any women. All women. It doesn't matter. Things that a lot of women are involved in draw in others. Somebody's probably propounded a law of physics explaining it.'

'I can see I'm not going to get a sensible answer out of you.' The disapproving look reappeared, full force.

'How about the idea of being killed making me frightened and angry? Anger making me go there to try and stop it?'

'It's not enough, Jo.'

'It was enough for me.'

She was silent, not-understanding written on her face. I think I gave up trying to explain to her then.

Soon afterwards she went off to Devon for a fortnight's contact improvisation workshop. After the first day of misery I surprised myself with a big inward sigh of relief. A break from putting all my energy into being OK by someone else.

We talked on the phone every evening about how much I missed her and she missed me. It was true, we did miss each other, especially at the end of the day. Peak, standard and soppy is how the call bands split for us. But when we weren't having forlorn breathy pauses, we were talking double-four time to fit in an account of all the things we'd done during the day. Without each other. Because of being without each other. We both knew it. She'd given up as much as I had to play the part of a bright young lover and, like me, was enjoying reclaiming her own life.

At first it was the pleasure of always waking up in my own place, never having to wear the same shirt two days running, not starting the day with a brisk bike-ride home. Then I rediscovered the ability to be in a foul or boring mood without feeling guilty or trying to pretend that everything was fine. By the third day of her course, I was back into all my own routines, getting enough sleep and starting to think about rescuing the mouldering play from its Dead Sea scroll state.

It wasn't that easy to pick it up again. In one of the staring out of the window pauses the next morning, I wondered why being requited put the stoppers on anything else you might want to do. I spent the whole day wondering about it, and then it was evening already. Lying in front of the radio, a real old steam wireless, blowing smoke rings in the dark and listening to something modern for two oboes and piano, followed by an unspeakably dreary recital of songs by a tortured teutonic sub-semi genius. If it sounds like a hare being jugged and makes you thoroughly miserable, it must be art. I rolled onto my stomach and put my ear close to the music, turned down low, so it was me and the singer united in secret masochism. Surely no one else in the world could be listening to this? She sang on, and I was soothed, willing her to the end of the ghastly octet, but half hoping to hear her kick over the microphone and say, 'I'm not singing this rubbish any more. Bring me some real music.' But she didn't, of course; she struggled on to the end.

I had half dozed off, lying there pillowed on the music. The voice of the announcer seeped into my head, although I was never conscious of him starting to speak. There are many ways in which men intrude, I thought, taking my ear away from the radio.

'Webern,' he was saying, in slow, hushed tones issued from the Radio 3 sound archive cupboard under the stairs. Long pauses between clauses, almost impossible to sustain or believe in. Giving a little potted biog. of the worthless composer. Putting opus 22 in context. Explaining the particular combination of philosophical crisis and domestic trauma (were the baillifs after this one?) which informed the atmosphere of the piece.

Why didn't they do that for the singer? Why not those smooth and chilly tones announcing that the luckless soprano had had a hell of a morning, she's just split up with her lover, none of the 73s would stop for her on her way to rehearsals and the gas bill's come? Was none of it supposed to be significant until you'd been dead a hundred years? Or was she only the vehicle for the adolescent anxieties of the composer?

'. . . and the nature/spring imagery,' old magarine-tones slithered on, 'of course symbolising,' pause, 'new hope.'

Of course, silly me, how could I have not understood that. I turned off the man, sat up. How dare he say 'of course' like that? Casually including me in his cruddy obsessive desire not to be found outside the fold of straight European middle-class culture, with a capital C? If music needed a nerd to explain what it meant, then it wasn't going anywhere very much for me. And that tone. The assmption that, of course, it wasn't the music that was obscure, or the inadequate composer's intentions failing to come through. No, audience density is the problem here, but since we're all pretending to be gentlemen, let's speak as though we know the symbolic clichés by heart, as if we weren't going to an Open University summer school to learn how to allude to them casually in the correct order. New hope. Of course.

# Ten

Feeling guilty at having wasted a whole day, I sat down the next morning to work with more dutifulness than enthusiasm. So I didn't mind the interruption when there was a knock on the door. It was Dympna from upstairs, standing in the hall with Ada's friend Bert.

'Visitor for you,' she muttered, a thick head balanced precariously on her early day shoulders.

'I didn't know which bell to ring,' Bert apologised. 'Didn't bring me reading specs with me.' Dympna took herself off back upstairs and I showed Bert into the flat.

'How are you?' I sat him down and offered tea, which he refused.

'Not so bad. I won't stop though. Only popped in on the way back from the barbers.'

'The barbers?' I looked at his almost complete lack of hair. Maybe the tufts did look slightly neater than they had the last time I saw him. But there was hardly enough there to trouble a stylist.

'Always go on a Thursday. Cheap rate for pensioners. May not look like there's much there to bother with,' he said, pointedly, 'but I like to keep it neat. Such as it is. Don't want people thinking I'm the kind of old fool who won't admit he's going bald. You know, trying to make the one hair you've got grow over your whole head.'

'Yes. Sort of, if you haven't got it, flaunt it. I'm sorry I looked so surprised.'

'Think nothing of it.'

'What can I do for you, now you're here?'

'Couple of things. Ada says you're to call round again soon.' He ticked the first point off on his bright yellow/orange nicotine-stained finger. Mine would be like that if I lived so long.

'That's nice of her.' I didn't know if this was a firm invitation being conveyed, or just a passing politeness. 'But I don't actually need to do any more background with her for a little while. I'm still working through the stuff I already collected.'

'I wouldn't know about that,' he passed his hand smoothingly over the patches of stubble on his head. 'But she says to tell you that you're to come round anyways. Whether you need to do any more of whatever it is you're doing or not.' He struggled to give the full sense of the message. 'Social call, if you like.'

'That's very kind of her.'

'She's taken quite a shine to you.'

'I'd like to come. Tell her I'll certainly pop round in the next few days.'

'Don't feel you have to, mind,' he coughed, looking as though he would have spat if he'd been somewhere else, and then thought better of it. 'She'd understand if you were busy.'

'No, really. I'd like to.'

'That's all right, then. I'll tell her you're coming.' His coughing fit over, he lit a cigarette, unperturbed. 'She'll be pleased. Doesn't get out as much as she used to. Don't tell her I said so, she's touchy about it and all, but she's slowed down a lot, these last few years. Feeling her age, if you ask me.'

'What was the other thing?'

'Oh yes,' he leaned back in his chair, looking at me through a cloud of smoke, clicking his new dentures thoughtfully. 'Well, I thought, you know, there's a lot Ada could tell you about her John.'

'Yes?' I encouraged him.

'But then again, there's a lot she couldn't. Never having known it herself, you see.'

'I'm not sure what you're getting at.'

'You know me and him was best mates, as it were.' I nodded. 'We was always around together, joined up together. Same platoon, even.'

'Yes, Ada told me all that.'

'I know there's a lot of things he never told her about being in the army. Well, he told me so hisself. Used to piss him off something rotten, but he couldn't make her understand. Said he didn't want to try. You got to feeling like we was in a world of our own, same way for all of us, I reckon.'

'She knew that.' He wasn't telling me anything that justified his conspiratorial tone.

'I know she did.' He looked pleased with himself, as though he was manipulating the conversation the way he wanted to go. Didn't people ever stop playing games? Although why I supposed the over-eighties should be less devious than the rest of us, I don't know.

'But you think there are things you could tell me about being in the war that she couldn't. Is that it?'

'Not your facts and what do you call it – background? Though there's plenty I could say about what it was like for us PBI. Poor Bloody Infantry,' he added for my benefit, 'if I wanted to.'

'But you don't want to?' I was puzzled. I thought that was just what he did want. To get in on the act. To have the attention paid him I'd paid Ada.

'Not me.' He grimaced with a mixture of anger and disgust. 'I spent sixty and odd years trying to forget it. Damn stupidest thing I ever done, joining up like that. Bunch of kids, we were, clueless as all get out.' He stopped, wheezing and breathless, his anger robbing him of the power to go on. He smelled faintly of mentholated chest rub.

'You know,' he carried on more quietly, 'I've gone through three-quarters of me life with hardly any mates. All the blokes I grew up with was dead before they was twenty-five. Or head cases. I used to wish I'd gone with them, if truth be known. Couldn't bear spending the rest of me days with nothing but a bunch of women around.'

'Is that such a bad thing?' I bristled.

'It's not bad,' he thought for a minute. 'Ada's been the best pal I've had this long time.' He stopped again, picking his words. 'But it's not what you expect. Losing all the mates you had when you were a lad, you can't make new ones who shared that with you. Feels like something missing, you know.'

I said I did, although I found it hard to imagine. Did he feel guilty that he'd survived and they hadn't? It sounded like it.

'So you don't want to talk to me about the war? As it was for you?'

'No ta. I reckon you can get all that stuff out of books in the library. Lots of blokes made a living out of writing about it.'

'Do you resent people writing about the war who weren't in it?'

'Not *you*. It doesn't bother me now. If you can do it, good luck to you. I used to get mad with the know-alls sounding off about what we done wrong, and how stupid we were to go, or stay once we'd got there, and how Kitchener's army was full of rascals and not a patch on the old regulars, that sort of bull. Never take much notice of what they're saying now.'

'What do you want to tell me? About John?' I was getting more and more baffled.

'When I says there's a lot Ada don't know, it's not the blood and the lice and misery I'm talking about. She's a bright girl, she worked that out for herself. Even though John was so cagey about all that sort of thing.'

'What, then?'

'There's things that happened.'

'What sort of things?' I felt as though he were still deciding whether to trust me with something. Advancing and retreating. Making me chase him.

'I could tell you and you go straight off and tell Ada. I don't want her upset.'

'Things she doesn't know that would upset her to find out?'

'I promised John, you see,' he nodded, 'last thing he said to me before he was killed, near enough.'

'Promised him what?'

'I was with him, you see,' he leaned forward in his chair, clasping his knees with his elbows turned in, hugging himself, 'those last few weeks before he died.'

'Yes?'

'Like a lot of blokes would say "Take care of the missus" when they knew they were for it. Didn't mean that much by it, really. Comforting, it was, for them to think of it.'

'Did John say that to you?'

'In his own way,' he sniffed. 'We neither of us thought there was much chance I'd be going home myself. But it wasn't that he wanted, so much as to be sure I'd never tell her about, like him getting killed and all.' He sat back and folded his arms. Is that it? I thought. He saw the bloke blown away and had carried the importance of his promise not to distress Ada with the knowledge of how her husband had died around all these years. Not like a hero, I presumed.

'I see,' and I thought I did. I wasn't that interested. Of course, the details of the death would be distressing to the widow, but it was no big deal for me. I had plenty of descriptions of pointless manglings and agonising demises to go on, I didn't really need a blow-by-blow account of John Gower's wretched ending.

Bert looked at me speculatively. Maybe what I was thinking showed.

'I doubt if you do see,' he snapped. 'Unless you're clairvoyant or some such.'

'You're not making it that easy for me.'

'I'm saying I can help you. If you want to know what really happened to John.' He put heavy emphasis on the word 'if'. He's doubting my seriousness, I thought. I've never been accused of dilettantism by a geriatric ex-squaddy before.

'Of course I do.'

'And a lot like him, there's that too.'

'Of course I'm interested.'

'I can help you, like I said.' He chewed his lower lip and tried to come to a decision. 'If I reckon you're not going to run straight off to Ada and upset her.'

'I wouldn't do that.'

'Promise?'

'Cross my heart.'

'I mean it, you know, if you don't take it serious . . .'

'I'm sorry,' I soothed him. 'Of course I'll respect your confidence, if there's anything you want to tell me.'

'Show you.'

'Pardon?'

'Show you. Not tell you. There's something John left with me. Like a diary, sort of. Some things he wrote, anyway.'

'And he gave them to you?'

'Yes, before he got it. Knew his papers'd be sent back to Ada otherwise. Didn't want her to see it. Knew it would hurt her.'

'Why didn't he destroy it then?'

'Dunno. Too much of himself in it, maybe. Wanted the truth around somewhere, even if no one but me ever got to see it. Like, the record could be set straight, at least one place.'

'And you're prepared to let me see it?'

'Maybe.'

'If I promise not to tell Ada about it. Or write about what's in it in such a way that she finds out?'

'Yes.'

'Does she know that you've got it?' I looked him straight in the eye for the first time in minutes. 'This diary?'

'Do me a favour. She wouldn't give me a moment's peace if she'd known about it. I know her. Strong willed. "I'll be the best judge of that," she'd say if I told her there was things John didn't think she ought to find out about.'

'Can I see it?'

'It's at my house.' He was still evasive, still not sure I could be trusted.

'I'll come round and fetch it sometime, shall I?' I pushed him. He told me the address, but still didn't commit himself to saying I could see the journal. Both of us were hedging our bets. I wasn't that bothered about whether I got to see the diary, which was unlikely to be useful to me anyway. I suspected he had an inflated idea of its importance, having kept it in trust for so long. Special to him, maybe, and Ada.

I was stung by his lack of trust, though, as he was stung by my being unimpressed by his revelations.

'I'll be getting along,' he rose to go. As I thanked him politely for calling, I thought, we still haven't resolved anything. Irked by the untidiness of it, I showed him out.

# Eleven

Doesn't habit make for ingratitude, I thought the next morning, watching for the kettle to boil. And custom stale the infinite variety of the marvels of technology. All those mornings, not long ago, when getting up had involved such an effort, I'd sworn if I ever lived indoors again, and could make a cup of tea in five minutes, bath every day, I'd never cease to be amazed. Here I was, not amazed at all.

It had been something then, at the camp, to be an early riser. Waking with the first sunlight coming through the plastic of my bender. Shedding the sleeping bag, quickly covering each part of myself with clothes as it emerged into the freezing air. Getting dressed lying down, no room to stand. The early morning financial news on the radio, incongruous then as now. Slithering backwards out of my polythene tunnel. Boots on last to keep the mud at the doorstep, survival bag closed in case the mouse decided to sleep in there. Brushing through the gorse and bracken to the clearing, to the main gates, where the morning jam of cadillacs was already snarling, avoiding eye-contact like crazy. Sometimes a cheery hullo from the police. Stuff that for a lark. I always hated the game they wanted to make it.

The effort of lighting the fire, finding the kettle, finding the tea, finding the milk, with everything blown all over the place in the night's storms, or dropped anywhere in the dark of the late-night coffee-drinkers back from the pub. Washing in cold water out of the jerry cans, drying my face on my scarf. Using up ten times the energy these things would normally take, back there in the comfortable world of nothing being quite so serious as one's domestic arrangements. The real world, people who came from there call it, refusing the reality of self-denied conveniences.

So I never understood why I wasn't now presented with a store of surplus energy, released from the strenuousness of simple tasks. I could be up and dressed, washed and have boiling water with such speed and ease now, surely I should be bouncing around doing three times as much of everything else? But I'd got to take it for granted within weeks of coming back to town. Morning sloth rebroken. The truth was, I'd had more early sparkle out there despite all the difficulties. Maybe a moralistic upbringing made us thrive in the face of hardship. A peace camp fuelled by the Dunkirk spirit. Very droll.

I would go and see Ada today, since she was happy for me to go round without any carefully-made pretext. I wondered if I could think of anyone that much older than me as a friend. Funny, but I had only ever used that label about those my own age. Really, from school, when friends were things that occurred in your own class, or maybe at a pinch in the other classes of your year. And apart from an interlude at the camp, where no one seemed to have a particular age, not much had changed since then. Maybe a spread of five years or so between me and my best buddies. If that much. So we all lacked the mental equipment to deal with the idea of being friends across a generation or two.

There was no doubt that I liked Ada. She was robust and irreverent, a bit bossy maybe, but quite subversive in a pleasant sort of way. I have no practice at expressing liking for a woman who does not share many of my tribal clichés and experiences. Even with Beryl, and her household. We may be on different sides of a political fence, but we know the planks and concrete posts of its construction intimately.

There were all the assumptions I made about Ada because of her age, laid out in front of me. That she must be straight (it seemed a reasonable bet, from what she'd said about her two husbands). But from that I assumed on her part an inability to think in any other terms. Like Queen Victoria. Not necessarily fair, protecting her supposed ignorance by my studied neutrality. Maybe creating a no-go area that I assumed to be ignorance, reacting to it, reinforcing as I went.

Don't be a fool, I interrupted my own ramblings. You don't have to go round and bludgeon her to death with your world-view. Pay a social call, like she said. Be sociable. Not everything has to be difficult.

Luckily for Ada, this grim, cheerful determination to go and be jolly to her, in the interests of forging a new pidgin language for use with the Older Woman had time to wear off before I set out to see her that afternoon.

I enjoyed the feeling of time with no pretext of work attached to it. Idly walking towards her place, browsing the market stalls along the way. Not that many of them were out today, the road would be packed tomorrow. Lots of tat, delightful rubbish, undemandingly ghastly and not pretending to be much else. I find junk stalls very restful.

At the top of Ada's road, I looked out for that man. He wasn't there, although I half expected him to be. Not sure why. I remembered that I had to ask Ada if she had a granddaughter, the woman I had seen that night in the park.

Ada opened the door to me; seemed pleased that I had come.

'Bert gave you the message, then?' She led me into the sitting room, got me a cup of tea.

'Yes. I would have come again, of course. But I might have waited until I had some good work excuse, and come with my notebook and a serious attitude.'

'You don't want to do too much of that. Life's too short to be taking yourself seriously all the time.'

'I agree.'

'Especially at your age.'

'Does that mean I'm entitled to take myself seriously when I get to be your age?'

'You're entitled,' she snorted, 'if you want to. Me, I still think life's too short for that. Haven't managed to find time for it yet.'

We had a pleasant sort of an afternoon together. Chatted about general things, families and houses and our favourite time of year. I tried to get her talking about what it had been like for her being in domestic service. She made sure I wasn't in a note-taking mood before she'd let herself be drawn. None of the original bitterness with which she had spoken of being a 'slavey' had abated.

'Worst thing I ever done,' she snorted.

'Very hard, was it?'

'All the work I've done's been hard. But it wasn't that. It was the way you got treated like you weren't human.'

'How long did you do it for?'

'Few years. Don't know how I stuck it.'

'No choice?'

'No. Not till the war. That's when I got out. Never went back afterwards. No matter how bad things got, I could never choke down me pride enough.'

'How did you get out? What else was there to do?'

'There was the munition factories, but not straightaway. I didn't walk out of service so much as get kicked out.'

'How come?'

'It was the people I was working for.'

'Yes?'

'They got it into their heads that the war would be the ruin of them. That they'd go bust. They didn't have anyone in it to worry about losing. Oldish couple, they were. No kids. Anyway, they thought the Kaiser'd be over the Channel and marching up Whitehall before you could say knife. Decided to take themselves off to their place in Sussex and sit it out quietly. Turned us all off, of course.'

'Sorry?'

'Give us the push. Give notice to me and the other girl. Sent the butler to enlist. Kept on the cook, I seem to remember.'

'What did you do?'

'Not a lot I could do, really. Went back to me mum's to live. John's mum tried to get me a bit of work dressmaking, which was good of her, she didn't have enough to keep herself on hardly. Nobody seemed to be buying fancy things, there wasn't the demand. Seemed like the first year was the worst. Not knowing what was going to happen. After that I suppose things kind of sorted themselves out a bit.'

'And then you got into munitions work?'

'That's right. I wasn't dead keen. The pay wasn't brilliant then, and they weren't that set on having women in the factories either. It wasn't till later they found the need for us. And the men working there didn't half give you a rough time. If you went in looking like you meant to do any work, they'd call you a slag and worse. If you tried to keep yourself looking pretty, they despised you for being in the factory. Couldn't win. But Mary I was at school with and some of the others had started up there, so I thought I'd be all right, I could stick with them till I sorted out what's what. And I couldn't go on living off me mum, bringing nothing in. It was hard for her as well.'

'Was it difficult to get a job?'

'Not so as you'd notice. It wasn't skilled work, though the union tried to make out it was. All men, that was, running that. Worried about all us with no five-year apprenticeship keeping hold of men's

jobs after the war was finished. Some chance of that happening.
Anyway, they'd got some new machines in this factory, so it wasn't
like women doing the exact same jobs that men had before. Such
men as there were could still have all the skilled work. We were just
like bits of the machines.'

'Were you filling shells?'

'No, though I did later on. We were making the casings. Shells
and bullets and bombs. Bullets mostly. That's what I was on, time I
was there. Machine-gun bullets. The bottom half, you know the
blunt end. Used to see those blessed things in my sleep. Every time
I shut my eyes for the first month I was working. Thousands of
them, popping out the press like buttons off trousers.'

'It wasn't a big arsenal then?'

'No, just a couple of big sheds, really. But it wasn't too far off
that I couldn't carry on living at home. And I wanted to be round
here, in case John got leave, you see. So we could have a chance to
see each other.'

'What was it like in the factory?'

'Bloody murder,' she cracked her knuckles, not something I'd
ever seen her do before. 'You should have seen me on the first day.
No idea what I was letting myself in for, of course. There was about
ten of us starting off new that morning. Like a little flock of sheep
we were. All wide-eyed and innocent. Half of them thought they
were doing their patriotic duty or some such. But they took us
through the machine shop where they were pressing out the big
shell casings. And the noise. You can't imagine.'

'Loud, was it?'

'Are you trying to be funny? It was like nothing you've ever
heard. I thought we'd walked into the middle of an explosion, the
whole place was about to fall down. Till I saw the face of the woman
that was leading all us new ones along.'

'I bet she was laughing at you.'

'Pissing herself. Us all stood there with our mouths hanging open,
looking terrified. There was no need for us to go through that part
of the factory to get to where we'd be working. They always did it,
though, with the new workers. Did myself, when I'd been there a
bit.'

'Getting your own back?'

'I suppose,' she grinned apologetically. 'It was tradition, and we'd
all been through it. And it was funny, to see the look on their faces.'

I harrumphed a bit, disapprovingly. Ada caught my frown and

offered me a cigarette to disrupt it. Letting her get away with it, I thought it had been fun seeing her briefly sheepish.

'Anyway, we got to where we were going to be working, and the foreman sort of showed us how to feed the machines, though a child of four could've worked it out. But the foreman acted like royalty. One of the girls with us even curtseyed to him first time he came over. She never lived that down in a hurry.'

'And were you left to get on with it?'

'Really we were. There was an older girl meant to be keeping an eye on us. Training, it was called,' she snorted, 'but anyway, after a few weeks, Mary managed to get me shifted to a machine over by her. Which was a good thing, nobody took any liberties with her. Or me either, when they knew she was looking out for me.'

'Did they before?'

'Well, you know how it is,' she shifted a bit in her chair, setting her spine further to the back of it.

'No, I don't. Was there a lot of bother?'

'What do you want to know all this for? You don't come here to talk about me.'

'It's interesting. Go on, really,' I wheedled, trying to look harmless. 'I'd like to know.'

'You're too curious for your own good.' She folded her hands and pursed her lips a bit primly, though I didn't get the impression she minded being pushed, 'Used to get slapped for that when I was a child.'

'Sorry, I didn't mean to pry,' I lied, 'but I would like you to go on.'

She sniffed, satisfied that she had been asked.

'There was,' she picked her words, 'what you might call bother. Those first few weeks. I think you could say I had quite a bit of bother. Mostly from the men. Some of the older girls as well though.'

'What sort of bother?'

'Some of it was what all the new hands got. Teasing, it was. Well, some of the jokes seemed a bit cruel to me, but then it was tradition again. Like they used to send you to the storeman to ask for a long wait. You'd not work out they hadn't said weight till you'd been stood there half an hour. Then you'd catch it from the foreman when you got back. Putting metal filings down your neck, that kind of thing.'

'Sounds pretty childish.'

'Maybe. But it was so boring, the work, you could understand people'd do anything for a laugh. And you had to go along with it, or they'd say you were stuck-up and really give you a hard time.'

'But from what you were saying, there was more to it than that.'

'Yes, for me there was. For a lot of us, I suppose, I didn't notice much apart from myself.'

'A different kind of teasing?'

'If that's what you want to call it.' She glowered, not at me. 'You have to understand that I was very young then. Thought I knew how to take care of myself, but still a bit wet behind the ears, really. Though if anyone came straight out and gave me any cheek, I'd soon enough put them right. Could look after myself that way. But I wasn't really used to how sly some people are. Me, I always said what I meant, showed people what I thought of them to their face and all that. Very friendly, I was. That was half the trouble.'

'How come?'

'I didn't act all shy and little girlish with the men. Well, I thought, why should I, being a married woman, like I was. Don't get me wrong, I wasn't looking to do anything John wouldn't have liked. But I'd always got on well with the lads. Comes of having brothers.'

'And was that a problem? Your being relaxed around men?'

'You're right, it was. Those blokes were like peacocks. Knew they'd never have to go and fight so long as the war lasted, they had a nice safe job. Plus they're all in the best-paid jobs, fitters and foremen and blacksmiths, you know. And all of a sudden they've got these hundreds of women around the place, all bored witless with the work they were doing, mostly with no husbands at home. You could see them strutting about like they were god's gift. Just insufferable, mostly.'

'But I thought you said the men weren't keen on women coming into what they regarded as man's work?'

'That's the trouble. They'd resent you being there, not think you were good enough to do the job, and at the same time they'd reckon we were all dying for one of them to look our way. You'd get blokes spend half the shift pinching girls' bums and talking dirty to the new hands to try and embarrass them, then go home to their wives like as not and slag us off for being a bunch of tarts. If you'll excuse my language.'

'Sure. So you turned up bright-eyed and friendly, thinking you'd all be workmates together, and got chased around for your pains.'

'Makes me sound like a proper twit, that does.'

'I didn't mean to. I wasn't being sarcastic.'

'Makes a nice change.'

'Ada,' I protested, 'is that fair?'

'No.' She winked at me. 'But it makes me feel better. Because silly though it sounds, that's pretty much how it was. And of course, though I didn't know it, word started to go round that there was a new hand who was an easy touch. So every nasty piece of work in the factory started finding an excuse to come and pester me. By the time I'd finally worked out what was going on, they'd all made up their minds what sort of a girl I was. Just because I'd a friendly nature, I ask you,' she was indignant. 'Then I told them to b. off and leave me alone, there was one chap in particular that wouldn't take no. Said I'd led him on.' She scowled ferociously. 'Heard that one before, haven't you?'

'Many times.'

'Had to take a monkey wrench to him in the end.'

'Drastic measures.'

'Plainer than the King's English though.' She grinned in a satisfied way. 'Sometimes I think that's why I got on so well with John.'

'What was?' the digression had lost me. 'Your ability to duff blokes up with monkey wrenches?'

'No, you daft ha'p'orth. The fact that I didn't really know any better than not to be on my guard with him. Didn't mind what I was saying all the time for fear of what he'd make of it. Probably would've been a lot different if we'd met when I was a bit older.'

'Probably. But that's true of most of the people you ever meet, isn't it?'

'Maybe. Until you grow out of changing.'

'When's that happen?'

'You don't half ask some silly questions. Where was I?'

'Getting a bad reputation.'

'So I was.' She kicked off her house slippers and put her feet on the low table between us. 'Then Mary got to hear about it, of course.'

'Why of course?'

'Very sharp, Mary. Not much went by her on the shady side.'

'What did she do?'

'Give me a right rollicking for having let any of the men take liberties. Found out which ones were making the most trouble and sent them off with a flea in their ear. Got me moved to her section.

All in the space of a week.'

'How'd she manage?'

'There wasn't no stopping Mary when she was set on something. Bull at a gate wasn't in it. Lot of people were frightened of her.'

'Had you been good friends at school?'

'Not specially. We'd gone around together in the same gang. But she was the kind of girl your mum used to worry about you getting too pally with. Bit wild. And her family had a shocking bad name round our way. Then, of course, I didn't see her hardly at all after school, when I went into service.'

'So how come she took such an interest in you?'

'I don't know, she had a way of rescuing strays, maybe she would've done something for anyone being messed around like I was. But having been schoolmates helped.'

'She must have had her work cut out then.'

'She kept busy all right.' Ada wriggled her stockinged toes. 'Always getting into rows and ructions, usually for someone else's sake. Still, I can't say I wasn't glad when she decided to rescue me.'

'What was she like?'

'Mary?'

'Yes.'

'Short. Littler than me even. Very pale, like you could see through the top couple of layers of skin she had. Fiend's own temper when she lost her rag. And red hair, really bright. Dead curly it was she couldn't keep it under these kind of dishcloth caps we had to wear, always springing out from under. We used to tease her for that, you know what they say about red-headed people's temper.'

'Why was she on such a short fuse?'

Ada considered for a moment.

'Maybe she cared more than most. Not only about people, though she was loyal, to friends and that. But ideas. Over my head a lot of it was, to start off. And she was always going on about what was fair. Which I told her straight out was daft. One of the first thing you ever learn, my mum told me. Life's not fair. Specially not for our sort. Still, I must say, I never saw her fly off the handle without it was useful.'

'To whom?'

'To her. To get something that she was after and couldn't get by arguing, which she also liked to do a lot of. People who didn't know her that well thought she was all moods, but I always thought she

101

picked her times to throw a tantrum good and careful.'

'She sounds formidable.'

'If that means she got her own way a lot of the time, then she was. But she loved a joke, too. Had a real belly-laugh. Give you quite a shock to hear it, she looked so,' she rummaged for the word, 'church-going. Being small and quite pretty. Then she'd come out with this dirty old laugh of hers. Or the language. Shocking.' She smiled fondly.

'You've a very clear memory of her.'

'Not the sort you'd forget in a hurry. And after she'd got me working next to her, saved me from all that bother, I quite looked up to her for a while. You know how it is.'

'Why did you stop?'

'Well we got better friends. I didn't feel like she'd always win if we had an argument.'

'Did you argue a lot?'

'All the time. I loved it, hadn't had a decent argument with anyone since John joined the army. You know what sort I mean, not rows.'

'Yes, I know. What did you argue about?'

'Anything. She talked politics a lot. I'd never met another woman that did that till then. She wanted all sorts. Home rule and votes for women.'

'What was she doing helping out the war effort?'

'Same as most of us. Trying to make a living. And she had fewer choices than many. Wouldn't be in domestic service. Said it was degrading. She was pig-headed about what she called her principles.'

'Sounds surprising she got a job.'

'I used to think they was a bit silly letting her loose with all those bullets and bombs. Still, even if they'd known what she was saying they probably couldn't take it serious. Couldn't believe a woman'd have ideas of her own. Like the union. She was always on at them for the way they treated us. Didn't want us there at all. Once they saw they couldn't stop us being take on, they dug their toes in to try and stop us getting any of the better jobs. She even tried to go to their meetings.'

'Goodness.'

'Lucky they were all so frightened of her. The shop steward said she was mad, but really he was terrified she'd back him into a corner and start arguing at him.'

'She sounds very tough.'

'She was. And that's how I wanted to be. See, I'd always thought I was, when I was a kid. But I didn't know that to hold your own when you're around a lot of people who don't care about you, means you've got to know what you want and when someone's stopping you getting it.'

I looked at her a bit surprised. Ada didn't usually go in for that sort of philosophising. She blushed slightly and said, 'That's what Mary used to say at any rate.'

There was a pause. Ada looked embarrassed and slightly wary. I could see she thought she had given too much away. 'That's enough about me,' she said briskly. 'Don't know why I've been rabbiting on.'

'It's nice to have a chat,' I smiled innocuously.

'Hm.' She hauled herself out of the chair and fetched a pack of cards from the sideboard. 'Fancy a game?' She brandished them at me.

'What are you playing?'

'Cribbage.'

I agreed and she sat down again to deal. It turned out to be her best game. At first, I could tell, she was humouring my slowness, me not having played since I lived in the country and spent a lot of time in pubs with no pool table. But only for the first game or two, then she settled down to the enjoyment of some hard-won winning, once she'd seen I could take care of myself. She had a fierce concentration, and a quickness which left me struggling to keep up, as I tried to wrap my rusty brain round the old familiar number combinations.

She beat me well, but I wasn't disgraced. With a real look of satisfaction at the end of the last game, she said she'd enjoyed it, counting up the pennies she'd won off me.

'Always nice to find someone new who can play a half-way decent game of crib. Not so many kids know it. Not a young person's game really.' I took the compliment.

'I enjoyed it. Haven't played for years.'

'You never forget, do you? Like riding a bicycle. You soon get the hang of it again, though I thought you were going to be a walk-over, to start with. Mind you, I wouldn't fancy my chances on a bike. Not after fifty years or so.'

'I couldn't afford to play badly with a shark like you,' I teased her. She'd taken about thirty pence off me in an hour's play.

'Would you listen to the last of the big spenders here?' she asked the room theatrically.

I got up to make the tea, saying it was my turn. She didn't object, I was being counted as family, no ceremony stood upon. In her small neat kitchen, I found the tea in a plain china caddy. I'd long stopped expecting royal wedding souvenir ware. Ada showed me her collection of truly vile presents from her children, which she kept in a cupboard for when the donor was visiting and never otherwise used. I took the pot through and poured her a cup, leaving mine to stew a bit. She like her tea weak, like a southerner.

'Do you have a granddaughter?'

'Yes, why do you ask?'

'Oh, it's just that I think I may have seen her recently.'

'Don't see how you could, love. She's been in Australia these last six months. Not coming back till Christmas, either. If then.' She frowned down at her square-ended fingers, which were smoothing the material of her skirt over her knees.

'Oh.' I was puzzled. I'd been so sure the woman in the park had been related. 'She looked very like you. If you were sixty years younger, that is. This woman I saw.'

'Where did you see her?

'Regent's Park. By the lake, late one night.'

'Used to go there a lot,' she looked far away, 'me and John did. When we were courting.'

'Are you close to her? You granddaughter?'

'Best of that lot,' she smiled at me. 'You'd like her. Not mealy-mouthed, like her parents,' She sighed. 'Still, she's having a fine old time of it down there, by the sound of it. I don't see any great reason for her to rush back.' She walked over to the sideboard and picked up a postcard which hadn't been there last time I came. Bondi Beach, very lurid colours. Chosen, by the look of it, for its over-the-topness. She handed it to me. 'Got this last week. She's a good girl. Writes me a lot. More than to her own family. That gets up their nose.' She chuckled and sat down. I turned over the postcard and read, 'Weather is wonderful, wimmin are ditto. Wish you were here, you'd go great on a surfboard, love Shirley.'

'I can't leave that lying around,' Ada took the card back from me and pocketed it, 'or I'll have her dad noseying at it, next time he's around. And going on at me about how Shirley's wasting her life always being around a bunch of women, and when's she going to grow up and get married?' Her shoulders shook as she pictured the

104

scene.

'Is she a feminist?'

'Has been since she was at school. Precocious, you might say. But I never know what she's calling herself from one day to the next. Used to go on at me that I wasn't to say she was a women's libber. Now she tells me she's woman-centred.' She was still enjoying herself, while I struggled to get my surprise under control. 'So now I don't call her anything if I can help it, saves her having to put me right.'

'Oh,' I said weakly.

'I would have been a suffragette, you know.' She liked shattering my illusions that anything my generation knew was unique to us. 'Only it wasn't till after most of the fuss had died down that I ever got to meet any who were, well, like me. You know, from round here. Working girls.'

'When all the fuss had died down?' I watched her turn her inner eye back to the past, the way she did.

'There was some as had the vote, of course,' she sniffed, 'as a thank-you present for all being such good girls and not rocking the boat when there was a war on.'

'But you didn't?' My grasp of history was shaky.

'Not then. Too young, too poor, whatever.'

'Were you out setting fire to letter boxes and stuff?'

'Not me. I'd nothing against it, mind,' she gave me a sharp look, defying me to be shocked, 'I wasn't going around with those sort though.'

'But you would have done?'

'Yes. For sure.' She had set her jaw, looking out of the window now, her free hand pressed flat on the table, the knuckles whitening. 'It may not seem like much, getting to vote every now and then for a government that's always much of a muchness with whatever the other one was.'

'Unless you're not even allowed to do that?'

'Yes.' She looked at me and relaxed slightly. 'They kept telling us it didn't matter and it wouldn't make that much difference. But I always wanted to know, if it was so unimportant, why was they dead set on keeping us from it?'

'You got it eventually.'

'So we did.'

'And did it change much?'

'Maybe not. Me, I never had any time for politicians, so I didn't expect the miracles that some did. But,' she paused thinking, 'we'd wanted it. The vote, for what it was worth. And they'd not wanted to give it us, but we'd still ended up with it anyway. That changed something. More than having the odd woman in Parliament or being prime minister ever did.'

'I guess it had to be fought for. It seems a bit limited though. Like it's a shame it had to stop there.'

'What would you have done? If you'd been born then?'

I thought for a minute. About how things got to seem easy with the gloss of time. 'I guess I would have been out chucking bricks with the best of them.' I laughed at the idea of myself in a picture hat, with a rock in my handbag going out to smash up a minister's house.

'What's so funny?'

'Well, apart from anything else, I was heavily into non-violence until quite recently.'

'What's that supposed to mean?'

'I lived at a women's peace camp. We did everything non-violently. You know, letting ourselves be dragged around by the police to prove our moral superiority. That sort of thing.'

'Oh yes.' Her brow cleared. 'I never knew you were one of them peace women. You kept it very quiet.'

'I'm not now, really. I've stopped living there, and I don't go back much.'

'I always had a lot of time for them. The women at the camp, you know. Some of the things that get said, well it's enough to make you spit. But to tell you the truth . . .'

'Do please,' I interrupted her hesitation to hurt my feelings.

'Don't get me wrong, but all that stuff they do always seems a bit,' she looked for the word, 'good. If you know what I mean.'

'As in goody-goody?'

'I'm sure they're not like that, really. But it does come over as all sweet and nice. You know what I mean?'

'Yes,' I sighed. 'I do know what you mean. And, no, it wasn't like that. Isn't. But that was the sanitised version that the press gave the public when we were flavour of the month. After all, they couldn't come out and say it was good because it was all women, tough and raucous and rude and separatist, could they? So it all got prettied up for popular consumption.' I could see Ada wasn't entirely convinced. It was true about how we got presented in a deodorised form, not by our choice. The non-violence was our choice, though, and the moral superiority number.

'The funniest thing is,' I carried on, trying to explain, 'how identified with the suffragettes we were, you know a lot of the stuff was incredibly similar. The experience of being criminalised for your beliefs. The shock for middle-class women of being treated brutally, like an out-group by police and courts – men who'd never had to make it that explicit to them before. The way a little hard core kept doing things and going off to prison, within a much larger group who were supportive, but basically not into doing the same stuff themselves. The way I guess that smaller group got to have more and more trouble relating to those who didn't share their experience of brutalisation, got tighter and tighter bound to each other for their strengthening.'

'I can see that.'

'We would wear their colours. Assume that they'd be doing the same as us if they were around now.'

'Some would, maybe. A lot.'

'But the point is, we're claiming suffragettes, not just suffragettes but that radical, active core as our direct foremothers. And what they were about had nothing to do with non-violence. None of this going limp while your hair's pulled out by the roots. Sure, they let themselves be arrested, for the publicity, to prove a point. But when they got dragged off by the police, they kicked back.'

'You can't chuck a brick at an atom bomb.'

'I suppose not. I wish we'd learned a bit more from them. When I read their accounts of prison, for the cause, and how it wrecked them, and how the system could accept all that brutality without needing to change much, I only wish . . .'

'What?' she encouraged me.

'That we had learned the lesson that there's not usually a lot of point in making a martyr of yourself. Or that it might get some of what you want, support, public opinion, whatever. But the cost is likely to be too high.'

'Mm. Maybe. Though sometimes you don't get the choice.'

'Sure.'

'Me, I've never been a great one for doing things just for the satisfaction of being in the right. Not if that's all I got by it, apart from a load of pain and grief along the way.'

'You're a practical woman.'

'More than you, I think.'

'Sure.'

'What matters more, getting what you want, or being able to say you went about getting it the best way?'

'I would have said you couldn't separate the two. Until recently.'

'And now?'

'Now, I don't know. Maybe the means do justify the end.'

'But?' she sensed my reservation.

'I still don't see a violent answer to male violence on a nuclear level.'

'If you did, would you do it?'

'Yes.' I looked up from a healing graze on my knuckle, at which I'd been staring. 'I would.'

'That's something I suppose.'

'In fact, since I don't think I can save the world by whatever means,' a first-time admission, I noticed, 'I think next time any policeman twists my arm and starts dragging me towards the Christian enclosure in the arena, I'll kill the bastard. And sod moral superiority.'

Ada laughed.

# Twelve

I left, shortly afterwards. Too much taken in, too many lug-worms stirred up in the mud at the bottom of my uncomfortable mind-pond. Walking very quickly, hands deep in pockets, head hunched forward and down. The retractable neck of me with too much of another woman's world suddenly to cope with. Not wanting to go straight home, I carried on bouncing along, knees locked rigid, all the movement in knotted calf-muscles. Made my way to a playground, always good places for a think.

No attendant in this one, chasing me off. Or concerned parents looking at me askance because grown-ups aren't meant to be there without the excuse of a family. Passport to playgrounds. Otherwise, there must be something odd about you. The choice to be on your own, such an indication of strangeness. As the word implied, odd, not part of a pair or some safe round-numbered social grouping.

Not many children either. A couple of lads playing out some simple version of a television hero role on the long stockades of the adventure fort. The biggest of the two was playing the defender. The littler one was cast as the attacking forces. He would swarm up the sides of the fort while the hero made gunfire noises. When he got to the top, he was pushed off and the game started again. Hours of happy fun. When I was a kid – I sighed at how crusty my thoughts sounded – we had to imagine our forts. No well-designed mock-stockades, no adventure playground. Climbing frames set in concrete and the swings.

So why should I have to change my ways now? I went and sat on one of the old metal swings, looking frumpy and out of place among the elaborate mock-up space ships and mural-covered wooden walkways. The radical wall-painters had done the usual job of making youth look bog-eyed, oversized and soviet in execution. I sat and swung, working up a good angle of danger, feeling my back stretch and the ground rushing all around me in an arc, up to meet the skyline of tower blocks, then the endless pause, when the chain that holds the swing takes up its own slack, and every time you're sure it will break, or you're going right over the top, to crash into the compacted mud below. Then back down the way you came, stomach following with a lurch, seconds later.

Well, well. The words rocked back and forwards in time with the swing. She had an ability to unsettle, the ex-subject. Started out as a passive dispenser of oral history, and now, here she was, nudging me into revelations about myself that I wouldn't make to my best friend. I felt challenged by her. Not put on the spot, backed into a corner, prodded in the chest, but challenged.

I wound my arms round the chains of the swing and hung my head forward, feet tucked under me. Almost tipping forward, but not quite. She didn't demand much. That's what I wasn't used to. She didn't have a great urgency to see me recant or affirm anything about non-violence. Not one of the women I'd talked to in the last year had had that distance. Yet Ada still had her opinions on it all. Let me have glimpses of where we differed. Looked at my inconsistencies and smiled. Not threatened or reinforced by them. It was novel to me. All this room she gave me in which to explore what I really wanted. Not having to look over my shoulder all the time for the contradiction-catcher coming after me with her logic net.

Spanning the time I was a peace woman, a neat circle recalled my first and last time at the camp. It hadn't seemed neat at the time, and there was a daftness about finding an end point in a circle, but none the less. I rehearsed the story in my mind, as I would tell it to Ada.

The first time I went there, I almost said it aloud, I was so conscious of addressing her. The first time was winter. A big day. Tens of thousands of women there. Drawn there by the buzz that had been going around for weeks. As I had been. Not knowing too much about it, not knowing what to expect. Aware only that was where the women were heading. Not having to decide, drawn along by the momentum.

A freezing cold and beautiful December day. All the things that were to become habit, done then for the first time. The sights and places that were to be familiar as home, new then, and striking. The way the camp women stood strong, as though they were growing in that endless dark mud, filling me with a sense of identity, not thinking that anyone would ever look at me, amazed and say; she's so strong, so well rooted, see her stand as though she belongs in this inhospitable outdoors with no jacket on. A breed apart, it must be. Who knows the secret of the large thermal vest?

Never having been in the same place with so many women before. Everything new and magical, the singing, the sense of purpose, all the ritual and symbols. The fence-decorating and energy-focusing, the confrontation with the unseen forces of male evil, rather than (on that day) its insignificant uniformed representatives. I know it all sounds a bit wally, but honestly, in context, as it were, it all seemed fine and possible.

The next day, too, was a revelation. Doing actions. An affinity group with women I'd met at the bus stop. Blockading. The power of stopping the traffic, the illusion of controlling the road. Being removed by the less-filmed than the day before, and therefore rougher, police, but still feeling it was our power that was strengthened by events, their futility proved. The togetherness of us, as we sat in the road and defied hatred and violence and worried about nasty accidents. Dancing and singing to keep warm, sharing the contents of a thermos. And at the end of the day, exhausted, exultant, coming home with a minibus full of Scottish women who went miles out of their way to drop me off, still in the same state of tight-knit strength of feeling. Playing lesbian songs all the way home. You may think this is funny, I said aloud, but I'd never heard any before. No, never, in all those years of being what Shirley called woman-centred. Never having heard any raucous dykey singing. It opened up the vision of a very different world for me, I can tell you. I hummed those tunes all the way home, as I planned my abandonment of London life.

All my friends were pleased with me, who had not themselves been. Did you get arrested? they asked, for I was their proxy in this dangerous new departure of radicalism, defying the police, who normally we merely denounced at our conferences and meetings. Never actually coming across them, of course, unless we had cause to summon their good offices to our burglaries ('For the insurance', otherwise one wouldn't bother, naturally).

But I was gone already, lost to them. Spending only a few more weeks cancelling my old life, in my mind already staying under the wide sky beside the narrow fence. I don't know if the whole thing caught me at the right time, ripe for something like that – principled and absolute, romantic in design and practical in execution.

Combined appeal to strains of Catholicism and Calvinism. But I think I would have gone anyway. Let's say that it seemed the right thing to do at the time.

Not that there weren't things I left with regret. My urban self was dragged down there kicking and screaming, bewailing the loss of street cred. A set of ideas whose time had gone, they settled down to sit it out, like the unfashionable right in a period of technological boom. Knowing there would be a new scope for cynicism and self-interest at a later date. Knowing that it always comes back to that. Not suffering too much the anguish of opposition.

And there I fit, like so many other women. Turned up and clicked into place as though held by strong magnets. Finding a real women's space for the first time, after years of polite feminism, always prey to co-option in the let's-not-be-too-threatening-here world of giving them credit, they are trying, the poor lambs, mixed politics. Not having to compromise. Being able to make a virtue of rejecting men, instead of hiding or disguising it.

'Hasn't this turned into more of a women's thing,' our more searching visitors used to ask, 'than a peace thing?'

Doing a lot of world-saving as well, of course. An action a day, as we used to say. The post-prandial exercise, a bit of symbolism, a bit of vandalism. Always getting away with it when we chose, getting caught when we didn't.

When did it start to get to me? The first time I was surreptitiously punched by a squaddie, his back to the cameras? No, not then. Not either, the first dozen or so times I saw women carried off by their pressure points by men with that look in their eyes that spoke no longer of embarrassment at the job they had to do (as it once had, with them wishing themselves elsewhere), but now the look of common or garden sexual, sadistic, power-affirming pleasure. The sort you can see anywhere that men hurt women.

For a long time, I denied what I was seeing, denied the contradictions of my ideas of women's strength and the need to confront male violence always and everywhere with total refusal. No excuses or apologies.

They started getting verbal in their abuse later, as though that required more courage, more of a confrontation. After all, they don't have to see themselves, they can't help but hear.

'You're a waste of a white man's skin.' The words came back to me, hissed in desperate loathing through the fence by a soldier. Absolutely the worst thing he could think of to say. Total concentrated disgust and hatred. Fear too, but it's an abstract satisfaction, having what you always knew made evident in that way. 'Give us a blow job,' they would say, not sure themselves whether it was a threat or a plea.

Yes, I supposed, by the time I was allowing myself to see all this I was already on the way to leaving the camp. It was only a matter of waiting for my inability to stand any more of the abuse of these men without killing one of them, to win over my desire to carry on living with the women who mattered to me. The choice was clear, stay and accept the terms of the camp, the not-resisting violence (even if the main reason for being there had become the women, for you, not the peace). Or go. But there was no half-way. So eventually, of course, I left. Who hasn't spent enough of her life being a victim already?

Would that do? As an explanation? I wondered what Ada would make of it. Not for the first time, I asked myself why is the story of someone like Ada considered so secondary to the blood-and-guts doings of her menfolk? Even she regards it as right and proper that her world is less worthy of being written about than John's. What I do know about her life at that time, she's let out slowly and in small details, as though it were inconsequential. I should be writing about her, rid myself of this tiresome interest in why men do the stupid things they do. Who cares? Let them go off and slaughter each other. We can look after ourselves. Women treat each other as important. No time to lose.

# Thirteen

Maybe Ada was surprised to see me two days running, but she didn't show it, and welcomed me in warmly enough when I turned up on her doorstep the next morning. I'd put on a clean shirt for confidence and green socks for luck, not certain which spirits I was propitiating.

'You're back soon.'

'I didn't really feel like we got to the end of what we were talking about yesterday.'

She looked surprised, her eyebrows rising into a great mass of wrinkles on her forehead.

'Do you reckon to get to the end of everything you talk about, neat as that?' she said over her shoulder, walking into the sitting room. Ada always saw through my politeness. 'Must make life a bit like murder stories for you. Find out whodunnit and that's it. Nothing to go on with.'

'No, of course not. I wanted to carry on talking to you, that's all. I spent a lot of time after I left here yesterday thinking about non-violence and all that stuff. I wanted your opinion.' She gave me an unreadable look and turned back to the china washing which my arrival had interrupted. A bowl of soapy water on the table, her hands in bright pink rubber gloves and her wrapover pinny on.

'I'll go, if you like.'

'No, don't do that, love,' she was unfussed. 'Not on my account. You've only just got here.' She picked up a figure, shepherd girl, from the sideboard, firmly because her grip was unsure in the gloves. Blew the dust off and dipped the shepherdess head first into the plastic bowl on the table. 'But you won't mind me getting on? I'd never finish otherwise. Hate doing the china.'

'Of course not.'

Ada watched me over the rim of her glasses, which she had put on for the close work. I struggled to get myself out of thinking her into a role she didn't want: 'old woman'; 'good listener'; 'interesting source'. Whatever. She wasn't having any. Waited for me to relearn her as a person, not pushing me one way or another. Such patience, more demanding than the most upfront of 'don't treat me as' statements. And so calculated. It struck me that Ada could be very manipulative, when she wanted to. I met her steady look, she smiled slightly. The silence lengthened, only the gentle squeak of gloves on soapy china indicating that she wasn't permitting me to be too much of a disruption. Ada on her own terms, it would have to be. I sighed. Tussled into a corner of her will, again.

'Why don't you pop into the kitchen and make us both a cup of tea?' she said, sympathetically. End of round one. 'I don't know about you, but I'm gasping.'

Glad of the respite, I went next door and talked myself into the right frame of mind while I waited for the kettle to boil. Took a tray with the tea things back to the sitting room. Ritual offering. Set it down carefully on the floor, Ada taking up most of the table with her washing.

'Shall I dry?' There were a couple of clean cloths hanging folded on the back of one of the chairs.

'If you like. Mind the blue boy, though, his head's coming off.' I picked up the ornament in question, noticing the lines of years-old glue round his neck, ear to ear.

'He looks very smug for someone who's in danger of decapitation.'

'Poppy at the one-o'clock club brought it me back from a day trip to Boulogne,' she regarded the simpering youth with a critical eye. 'Maybe that's how those lot looked before they got hauled off to the guillotine.

'*A bas les aristos.*' I brandished him carefully over to the sideboard and put him down on it.

'What's that mean?'

'I don't know.' I tried for a translation and failed. 'My French was always pretty duff. I think it's something they yelled when they were rolling the upper-class twits into tumbrils and taking them off for the chop.'

'Sounds likely,' she sniffed, washing steadily on. Statuettes of big-eyed children and women in crinolines, commemorative plates and souvenir ashtrays. I found the careful work of drying and carrying the ornaments back to the sideboard or the cupboard in the kitchen soothing. Ada spoke only to tell me where each piece belonged, or to mention how she had acquired such an object. When we had worked our way through the lot, she peeled off her rubber gloves with a snap and carried the bowl of water through to the sink. I rescued the tea-tray from the floor and was pouring us each a cup when she returned, unwinding her apron to hang on the back of the door.

'That's better,' she took her cup gratefully and sank into a chair. 'Bugger of a job, that.'

'Why do you do it then?' I sat down as well, rummaging in the top pocket of my shirt for tobacco.

'They get so mucky.' She watched my manoeuvres. 'You got heart burn?'

'No, fishing for cigarette papers.'

'Not very ladylike. You should carry a handbag.'

'Oh yeah.'

'Maybe it would go a bit odd with the way you dress yourself,' she conceded.

'So why don't you just leave them mucky, if it's such a pain to wash them?'

'Because I never would have left it when there was anyone else around the house to see. My old mum used to throw fits about that, leaving the little things that didn't notice much undone. Said it was slovenly. Mind, I think she's right. Got me in the habit, though, when I was a girl. Anyways, if I wouldn't leave them all over dusty when there was anyone else here, I don't want to start doing it because I'm living alone. Letting myself go.'

'Fair enough. If it were me, I'd be glad of a rest, after years of clearing up for other people, I'd please myself and let it go.'

'You say that now,' she took a sip of tea, testing the temperature with her upper lip, 'but the way it looks to me, that's all the more reason I should keep the place nice for myself.'

'What, all those years doing it for other people, now it's your turn to enjoy it?'

'Yes. Not that all of it was for other people, like you say. Except when I was out on cleaning jobs. When Prince was around here, it was as much for me as for him that I'd do the tidying. More, I used to think he wouldn't notice if I never dusted from one month's end to another. "Leave that," he'd say, "bit of honest dirt never hurt no one. Let's go down the pub." Terrible, he was.' She smiled at the memory.

116

'Would you leave it?'

'No. I'd always have the best of both worlds. Hand him a duster and say we wasn't setting foot in the pub till the house was finished. So I'd get the cleaning done and get a drink in.'

'Cunning.'

'It was like a game, really, He'd never offer to help off his own bat.'

'Unmanly, was it?'

'I don't know that so much, though it's how he was brought up. With Prince I reckon it was laziness as much as anything. There's a lot you could say in his favour, never had a bad word for anyone. But he was bone idle.'

'Worse things you could be, I suppose.'

'True enough. John wasn't like that of course,' she was a shade over-casual, 'always a very neat man. And used to helping too, on account of having lived him and his mother, the two of them for so long.'

'Did you ever really get a chance to live together?'

'Not properly. We never had a place of our own while we were married. He was away most of the time, anyway, only got leave the once. So we were either at his mum's or mine, when he was over.'

'Must have been a pain.'

'I missed never having a home with him, I'll say that.' She looked at the wedding ring on her left hand. I wondered which marriage it was from. 'The rest of the time I was glad enough to stay put with my own family. Apart from the time when I took digs near the factory, to save travelling. I didn't care for being on me tod then.'

'Do you now?'

'Yes.' She was still looking at the gold band, twisting it slowly in the swollen flesh of her finger. 'I'm used to my own company now. Wouldn't want all the fuss and racket of living with a family again. Though the kids are always on at me to go and live with them. Think I need keeping an eye on,' she looked up and grinned at me, conspiratorially, 'say it would be nice for them, but I know. They think I'm too old to be responsible.'

'But you're happy as you are?' She had a very strong sense of personal territory.

'I won't say I haven't been lonely. Often.' She grimaced. 'But there's no doing anything about that. I'm content.' She looked around. 'This flat's not damp, like the old house. It's a good size for me. I've got company when I want it, and peace and quiet when I

117

don't. What more could you ask?'

'Not a lot.'

'So if they want me out of here,' she finished briskly, 'they're going to have to wait until I'm gaga, and carry me off when I'm not noticing. To the old folks home, or the hospital. Wherever they put you these days when you're no more use to anyone.' She saw me shudder at the bleakness in her voice. 'We all come to it, you know.'

'I know. I don't like the thought of being helpless.'

'Didn't say I was thrilled at the idea, did I?'

'No.'

'Hope I'll die before I lose me wits. Better that way.'

I was silent. She could face the process of ageing and death better than me.

'Cheer up. I'm good for a few years yet.'

I smiled at her. A vigorous old body, as my Scottish granny liked to describe herself.

'I'm sure you are,' but I still touched wood, unobtrusively, under the table.

She smiled at my superstition. 'Don't you worry about me.'

'All right.'

'Funny, isn't it,' she said, thoughtfully, 'how you're on your own when you're young and when you're old? It's only the bits in the middle gets so cluttered.'

'But you wouldn't have been alone when you were young if it hadn't been for the war, and John getting killed, would you?'

'Maybe not. But it seems like there's always some war or other for young women's husbands to go off to.'

'It must still seem strange that you hardly spent any time together when you were married.'

'It does,' she agreed.

'What was it like when John was home on leave?'

'At first,' she twisted the ring on her wedding ring finger, 'I was right up in the air about it. You know, I'd been looking forward to seeing him that much, and then there'd been a lot of delays with him getting over. And it was a big relief to see him in one piece.'

'And then?'

'It started getting through to me that he was holding back. I told you he didn't really want to talk to me about what it was like?' I nodded. 'That hurt. And the more I asked him what was up, why wasn't he talking to me, the more he said everything was fine.'

'Did you spend a lot of time together?'

'A fair bit. I was on nights just then, so I'd come home and catch a few hours sleep and we'd have most of the day. It was only for a week or so.'

'What was he like about you working?'

'A bit taken aback, I reckon. He'd heard all sorts of things about what a terrible lot the munitionettes were.'

'Munitionettes? Is that what you were called?'

'Silly, wasn't it? Maybe it sounded less serious than munition workers. Anyway, there was that, plus he wasn't used to me being with him and not having all my attention on him.'

'How was that?'

'I'd more things to worry about than just him. And I'd a job which wasn't a doddle, so I wasn't all over him worrying about what a hard time he was having. Not that I didn't care, but you could tell it wasn't what he'd been expecting.'

'How did you deal with it?'

'We didn't row, or anything. He thought I'd grown up a bit. Which makes me wonder whether he'd liked me at first because I was a bit what you'd call naive.'

'He probably worried that you wouldn't need him if you were getting more independent.'

'Maybe. Though he shouldn't have done. I daresay I'd changed, and what I wanted with him had probably changed too, but I didn't want out, or anything like that.'

'Did he want reassuring?'

'Yes. I think he knew by the time he went back that it wasn't him I'd grown out of. And he seemed to be getting to quite like the idea that I'd a lot of things going in my own right.'

'But he still didn't trust you enough to talk to you about the war?'

'Maybe he would've done, if we'd had a bit longer. It was like we had to get to know each other all over again. A week's not long to do that in, is it?'

'No.' We both sighed.

'He'd buried all that about the war away somewhere in him.'

'And didn't you feel like digging?'

'Not too much. I told you, I was hurt that he didn't trust me. Thought, "If he doesn't want to tell me, let him".'

'Understandable.'

'I was wrong. Should've made him see he could trust me. It might have made things a lot different for him.'

'And for you?'

119

'Yes.'

'You're still angry about it?'

'Sort of. When I think of all the things we could've shared that his pride kept to himself.' She shrugged. 'It seems like a waste.'

'Maybe he didn't know how to express himself?'

'Could be.' She leaned back and stared at the ceiling. 'I wouldn't have said that then. Thought John had more of a way with words than anyone I'd ever met. Didn't strike me he might not know how to say some things, even if he'd wanted.'

'You'd know now?'

'Course I would. Now.' She lowered her chin abruptly. 'I've been around enough men to know there's precious few can tell you anything about how they're feeling. Especially the ones that'll talk for hours about how the world ought to be run, and other people's lives. That sort of thing.'

'But you didn't know it then?'

'More's the pity.'

'Was John the first man you were involved with?'

'I've often thought it would have been better for the both of us if it hadn't been that way.'

'You don't blame yourself, do you?'

'Wouldn't be a lot of point in that, would there?'

We were both silent for a while.

I thought it might be time for me to go, and reached for my jacket.

'You're not off, are you?' Ada looked surprised.

'Thought you would have had enough of me for one day.'

'Don't be soft. Just because we got side-tracked doesn't mean I forgot you said you came round for a reason. I want to know what it was we never finished up talking about yesterday. Why you would have set fire to a letter-box seventy years ago, but not now?'

'Sort of.' I laughed a bit shakily at the rapid transition back to the danger area. 'You know, after I left here yesterday, I went off to the playground and sat on a swing for hours, trying to work out how I'd explain what I've done most of the last year.'

'Sounds uncomfortable.'

'Good places to think. And talk to yourself.'

'Do you do that? Out loud?'

'All the time.'

'Maybe it's you should be worrying about being carted off then, not me.'

120

'Well, playgrounds are the best places to do it, because everyone thinks you must be nuts anyway, if you're there and you're not a kid, or a mother.'

'You do get some funny people hanging round there, I will say.'

'It's like a licence to be eccentric. It's OK, people just avoid you. If you talk to yourself in the street you have to put up with them staring at you and wondering what's wrong. In kids' spaces they just try and pretend you're not there.'

'I'm glad you don't do it when you're round here, that's all I can say.'

'I don't need to, do I?' I smiled at her. 'It's only when I'm trying to work things out. And you always give me such a thorough grilling when I'm talking nonsense, I don't need to witter to myself about it.'

'I do?'

'Yes, you do. And very good for me it is.'

'So what were you chatting to yourself about yesterday? While all the poor kids ran away screaming with fright, thinking the bogey-woman had come to get them?'

I started to tell her, as well I could, the calmed-down version of the story about the camp and about non-violence; suffragettes; what doing right by your beliefs does to you as a person. All that stuff. I knew it was sounding disjointed, patches of narrative held together with threads of history, but she bore with it patiently, encouraging me with questions, egging me on with eye contact and smiles.

'The funny thing is,' I got to the point at which I had given up last night, 'the last day I was there, at the camp, I mean, was very similar to the first. In all the external circumstances. But it had a completely opposite effect on me. I still haven't worked out whether it was a change in me, or things outside me.'

'Or both?'

'Or both.' She got up sensing a break in the story.

'I'll put another brew on,' she said, 'and you tell me about it.'

While she moved around, fetching the pot through and straightening up the room, I sorted all the little building brick thoughts into a neat and pleasing heap. When she was ready, Ada returned to her chair, plumped herself down, elbows out, taking up all of her space.

'Well, I'm sitting comfortable,' she clasped her fingers in front of her stomach and crossed her ankles, 'so shall you begin?' She grinned at me, more of an expression inside her than the tired muscles of her face could keep up with.

'OK. Once upon a time there was this big day out at a peace camp, when Janet and Janet and some Johns, but mainly thirty thousand or so Janets went and held hands and sang songs and generally had a good time.'

'Was that the first time you went there?'

'Yes.'

'And what were the Johns doing in with all those Janets?'

'Worrying that they were being left out. You know what boys are like. So insecure.' She grunted.

'Anyway, the next day, some of the naughtier Janets stayed and broke some laws and had an even jollier time. Some of them left vowing to return as soon as possible to spend all their time surrounded by strong women, and stop worrying about their careers.'

'So you went to live there?'

'Quite a lot of us did.'

'But you didn't all live happily ever after?' she was indulging my whim.

'No. Perhaps that's because we haven't got to the end.'

'What happens next then?'

'Lots of adventures for the Janets. But time passes, until it's a year after that first day out in the country, which so many of our heroines found so inspiring. Almost exactly a year to the day.'

'Last winter?'

'Got it.'

'Go on, then.'

'Well, our particular Janet is there, of course, older and a bit more battered and generally fed up to the back teeth with being pushed around in the good cause that has brought everyone out in their thermal underwear again.'

'But she still went.'

'Couldn't miss it really. Big day out, lots of women there, sense of obligation, not wanting to be left out. All sorts of things.'

'And how was it different from the first time?' Ada was really quite good at this cross-examining business.

'In many ways, not at all. Same thousands of women milling around, looking pretty similar, singing the same songs. Same mud, same camera crews, same tail-back of coaches with posters in the windows jamming the Basingstoke road. More police helicopters, more barbed wire, more soldiers and watchtowers and floodlights and guns in evidence. More crackle of walkie-talkies filling up every bit of the airwaves, even the ones the Janets were trying to sing in. But a lot of the same looks on their faces. Untroubled.'

'And?'

'Like I said, our particular Janet was wandering around feeling rather jaded, and wondering why they all thought the nastiness would go away because they'd turned out in such numbers to be nice all round it, when they'd done the same thing last year and not changed it for the better.'

Ada tutted gently to herself. Not sure how to interpret the noise, I carried on.

'And, of course, Janet felt guilty for being so cynical and making comparisons with the way she always got taken to midnight mass when she went home for Christmas, a pleasant and colourful, but fairly pointless annual ritual.'

'Do you?' she interrupted, surprised

'Oh yes. Anyway, there's Janet, not feeling she belongs at all in a place that was her home, generally wishing she could be sat in front of a quiet fire with the *Observer*. but knowing she's got to grit her teeth and see it out.'

'Why?'

'She had a very confused sense of duty.'

'Daft bugger.' The chair creaked under the weight of one of Ada's silent laughing fits.

'Indeed.'

'What then?' She prodded me again to get to the point, knowing I was skirting it.

'Some of the Janets had decided to do a bit more practical damage to the base than sing it into submission. So they started to take the fence down.'

'And our Janet helped?'

'She did indeed. Well, how could she not? You don't turn your back on action.'

'You don't?'

'Not if you're unsure about your commitment. Choice is the prerogative of the certain.'

'Who would have minded if she'd walked away?'

'No one but her. Individual responsibility was sacred there, you see. But she was feeling guilty about being there, so she piled in.'

'Seems daft to me.'

'As you say. But she dived into the mêlée. Found a woman who hadn't done this sort of thing before getting rather beaten up by a policeman. Felt kind of responsible for the poor lamb.'

'As an old lag?'

'Yes. So Janet was jammed up against this horrid little policeman, punching him in the kidneys below the sight line of his colleagues. The crowd was so closely packed, all pressing up against the fence, you see, that no one could move through it.'

'The women were pushing at the fence?'

'Yes, pushing it down. It was actually falling down.'

'Not a very good fence.'

'No, and a lot of women. So there's this poor unsuspecting woman who came to do something to save the world huddled up to Janet on one side, trying to tell herself she doesn't find it all as distressing and frightening as she really does.'

'The one who was getting beaten up?'

'She's led herself to believe that she's meant to find this sort of thing inspiring, you see, not terrifying.'

'And on the other side?'

'Close packed, on the other side, this constable with whom Janet was having an out-of-sight fist-fight. An arrestable offence, if you like, but of course he couldn't do anything about it, because he couldn't move.'

'Then what?'

'That bit of the fence came down. Janet right up against it. Hundreds of women pushing her forwards. The policemen sees his chance, grabs Janet by the ear, throws her through a few rolls of barbed wire to the paratroopers who are waiting inside, like hounds at a coursing. Dying to get their hands on some of these women. A very heavy number.'

'Did they get you?'

'This Janet had just seen four of them falling on one of her friends, who'd got pushed through the wire next to her. Laying into her with such glee and very big boots. So this Janet turned and dived back into the crowd of women for all she was worth.'

'Did she get away?' Ada let me escape back to the third person, where I felt safer.

'The crowd of women, you see, had all got the idea that it was a good thing to get through the fence and confront the forces of darkness. They hadn't confronted the forces of darkness so often that they'd got thoroughly pissed off with it.'

'They stopped you getting out?'

'Every time Janet headed away from the fence, some helpful

124

woman would shove her back towards it saying, "We can get through if we all push hard enough".'

'Did the paras get you?'

'No. In the end our heroine gave up trying to reason with the women who pushed her from behind, or fight off the policeman who grabbed her from the front, got down on her hands and knees and crawled through the legs of the crowd to safety. Very undignified, but quite a relief.'

'Sounds a proper shambles.'

'It was.' I chewed the end of a match reflectively. 'And because there's no mechanism for anyone to have less than a wonderful inspiring time on a big day out like that, there were all these women left thinking that the kind of chaotic scrum they'd just been involved in was what you were meant to do there, and suffering from guilt that they didn't come away feeling good about it. Trying to convince themselves that they did feel good about it.'

'But you didn't feel guilty about running away?'

'No. Cured this Janet of guilt. When I got out of that particular bit of headbanging, there were all these women wandering about, blissfully unaware of the shoving and bruising going on at the fence. Having a nice peaceful symbolic day out with the kids. I left them to it.'

'And you haven't been back since?'

'Nope. That was it for me, with non-violence. When I stood in that crowd, the only thing I really regretted was that it was only my elbow and not a knife that I was sticking into the policeman's kidneys. If we're going to scrap with the bastards, we might as well do it thorough.'

'Or not at all?' she suggested.

'As you say. We hamstrung ourselves by getting into violent confrontations with men and telling ourselves that we are non-violent. So they could do what the hell they liked, while we tied ourselves with all these absurd rules designed to give us some kind of abstract moral half-nelson on them. Who needs it?'

Unexpectedly she rose, and walked round to where I was sitting, dropped both her hands on my shoulders, giving them something between a rub and a shake.

'We all have to change sometimes,' she said, 'no use upsetting yourself over what can't be helped.'

I leaned back slightly, feeling more comforted than I could say. She gave a last pat to my unwinding shoulders and stood back.

'I guess you're right.' I answered her without turning as she stood behind me.

'I know I'm right,' she said firmly.

# Fourteen

I made my excuses and left soon after that, needing time on my own to take in something new, dig it in and make myself feel sure of it. Feeling the barriers of age between me and Ada beginning to crumble. We agreed to have an outing soon, go for a drink or some such thing.

I wasn't looking where I was going as I came out of her block, and nearly bumped into a man standing in the narrow passage which let pedestrians back out on to the road. Him again, I thought, stepping to one side to avoid the collision.

'You again,' I said, for want of anything better to challenge him with. He made no answer. Looked at me, though, as if he were about to burst into tears, or more like he'd been crying for a long time and only recently stopped. Like a ghost who'd died of sadness. Same raincoat and stoop of tiredness, leaning against the wall of the passage. Even paler than the last time I'd seen him.

'Why do I keep seeing you? Are you following me?' I made my tone deliberately rough, because the situation seemed to demand it, but I didn't feel threatened by this strange person.

'No.' He focused his eyes on me with an effort. Took a step back out of the passageway on to the pavement behind. Craned his neck to look at the window of Ada's living room.

'How is she?' His voice was faint and he wheezed slightly. If he'd been older, I would have thought he had emphysema.

'Who?' I wasn't giving anything away, in case he was a run-of-the-mill weirdo, casing what he thought was a defenceless old woman living on her own.

'Ada.'

'You know Ada?'

'Yes.' He sounded tired and distressed. Defeated. 'I used to.'

'You family?'

'No.' He paused, seeming to consider it. 'No, I wouldn't say that.'

'What then?'

'Someone who used to know her.'

'Why don't you go up and see her then?'

'I don't want to bother her. She hasn't seen me for a while,' he looked imploringly, not quite straight at me, but as though he wanted me to help him out. Let him stew, I thought. 'There'd be a lot of explaining, you see.'

'No, I can't say I do.'

'I shouldn't have stopped you.'

'No.' I stepped forward out of the passageway, he stood aside to let me past.

'I wanted to know how she's doing, that's all.' He was still wanting something, his voice had a little desperate edge to it.

'She's fine.'

'I shouldn't have asked.'

'You're weird, mate.' I started walking away. He looked startled, had trouble understanding what I meant. He took a couple of steps beside me to keep up, then fell behind. Last I saw of him, as I turned the corner, he was standing in the road, looking after me, but his eyes always drawn back to Ada's window. Picture of uncertainty.

How could anyone look so hopeless, I wondered, as though he'd given up on being alive, and still walk around in two socks? Strange though he was, this apparition was losing the power to disturb me. I was getting quite used to the sight of him popping up all over the place and the more I saw of him, the less I thought he was really there.

'Either you've lost all your marbles, or he has,' I said to the world in general. A woman coming out of a shop as I passed gave me a strange look. I guess I know which option she would have voted for.

I put the strange man out of my thoughts and started to whistle. It was a fine day, cool and fresh. I felt full of life, for some reason, bouncing along strong and energetic. I felt good that some barrier between me and Ada, stopping us from calling ourselves friends, was undermined. I looked forward to going out for a drink with her. A regular, non-territorial, easy-going outing.

In the meantime I relaxed some of my anxieties about her and her boundaries. One afternoon, jumble hunting took me to Ada's local church hall. Filled with this new-found ease and confidence, I decided to pop in and see her. Ada eyed the bulging carrier bags with suspicion, as I dumped my booty on the floor and sank into my accustomed chair.

'What you got there?'

'Been to a jumble sale.'

'Clothes, is it?'

'My autumn collection.' I pulled out a pair of sturdy cast-off trousers and held them up for her inspection. 'What do you think?'

'How much?' she looked critical.

'Ten pence. A snip.'

'They're like the first ones I ever had. Not so thick.'

'When was that?' I'd never seen Ada out of her sensible skirts and dresses.

'When I was a munitions worker.'

'I thought you wore long skirts and overall things then?'

'First off, I did.' She turned and started rummaging in the cupboard part of the sideboard. 'And a bleeding silly way to dress for that work it was.' She dragged an old album out of the depths of the cupboard and straightened up.

'But then you got into trousers?'

'Mary did first.' She saw my face and laughed.

'Of course.'

'Why of course?'

'Oh, I get that impression of Mary. From what you've said. That if anyone was going to flout conventions, she'd be well in the lead.'

'I never said that.'

'But you did give the impression that she was pretty adventurous. Strong-minded and all that.'

'Stroppy, I suppose you mean?'

'I wasn't going to say it.'

'Well, you'd be right. But the trousers were a good idea. Not doing it for the sake of shocking. Though, it's true, she was never one to worry about what people thought. Still, we were at the Woolwich Arsenal by then, and a lot of the girls were wearing them. It was a bigger place.'

'And that made a difference?'

'Seemed to. Here,' she hefted the album on to the table and opened it near the beginning. 'Take a look at this.'

It was a pen-and-ink sketch of three women sitting on a low wall. Two of them were balanced against each other back to back, one reading a paper, the other eating an apple. A little apart, the third woman was sprawled, watching the others, her short legs caught in mid-swing. All of them wore trousers and shirts with the sleeves rolled up.

'Who's she?' I pointed to the woman reading the paper.

'Doris.' Ada looked surprised. 'You know who the other two are?'

'That's you, isn't it?' I pointed to the apple-eater.

'I should be flattered,' she grinned. 'To've changed so little in all this time.'

'The shape of your head doesn't change. And that must be Mary. Looking like she's up to no good.'

'Full of devilment,' Ada agreed. 'Sharp aren't you?'

'Who did the drawing?'

'Daisy. She was good with things like that. Said she was going off to art school after the war. We always said to her "why wait? This war could go on for ten years", but she wanted to stick it out till the end.'

'Maybe she needed the money.'

'Not her. Old man was a doctor or something. Thought she was doing her duty.' She sniffed. 'Still, it's a nice picture. And you can see what we're wearing.'

'It's a lovely picture.' I put the album down carefully. 'What were you doing?'

'Larking about. It must've been summer, then we'd sit out with our sarnies, though the canteen wasn't so bad. Me and Mary, Agnes and Doris. Aggie's not there in the picture, she was Doris's best mate. A whole gang of us. And Daisy used to tag along. She was all right, really.'

'How come you changed jobs?'

'It was after John died.' There was a bleak pause.

'Yes?'

'I was working up the first factory still. Got news he'd been killed.'

'The telegram they sent you?'

'That's it. Came just before I was going off to work. Still went and all, can you believe that?' She pulled a handkerchief out of her pocket and blew her nose sharply. 'No, I don't suppose you can imagine really. But I didn't stop at all, not even to have a proper cry. Went into work like that, like I was asleep. Like that for days.'

'It must have been a shock.' I rubbed the back of her hand tentatively. 'It's no wonder you felt numb.'

'That's how it was.' She gave my hand a slight squeeze and pulled herself up straight, sitting back in her chair. 'Some ways knowing it might happen made it worse.'

'A sort of suspense?'

'Yes. A shock that wasn't a shock, if you see what I mean.'

'I do.'

'Anyway, so there I was, going into work with less sign of life than one of the machines we were using. And you know, it all seemed a bit pointless.'

'War work?'

'Any work. I'd used to think how it would be when John came home, and maybe I'd have a bit put by from the wages and we could start thinking about getting somewhere of our own. All that.'

'Didn't the fact that you were making munitions have anything to do with it?'

'I can't say it did, not if I'm being honest. Not then. Later, after the war, I started thinking about how it was, with me churning out bullets like there was no tomorrow, trying to take my mind off things, when it was some poor bugger of a German they'd be used on, leaving a widow wondering how she was going to manage, like as not. Funny that.'

'One of life's little ironies.'

'I wouldn't do it again,' she bristled defensively.

'Didn't suppose you would,' I soothed.

'Anyway,' she got back to her interrupted thread, 'not feeling anything much wore off, and the factory started to get me down, though I didn't know why. Not having anyone to talk to there.'

'What about Mary?' I was puzzled.

'She'd left.'

'How come?'

She tugged at her earlobe and thought. 'Better pay at the other place. Plus the shifts were only eight hours, instead of the twelve we were doing. And she reckoned she was beating her head on a brick wall, where we were, on about our rights and conditions and that. Wasn't anyone taking no notice of her. So as soon as you didn't need a release any more, she was off.'

'What's a release?'

'Like a certificate you had to get if you left the job. Saying the factory didn't need you any more. If you didn't get one, you couldn't start another job like it for six weeks. So you didn't leave, can't live on nothing for a month and odd.'

'That's outrageous.'

'That's the way it was,' she smiled at my shock, 'But they got rid of them, in the end, then they had to let Mary go.'

'You must have missed her.'

'There wasn't really anyone else, you see.'

'But you got a job at Woolwich?'

'After a bit. Well, there was no point staying local for John's leaves, was there? Not any more. And after a few weeks, it felt like I'd go barmy doing the same things all the time like a zombie.'

'Was it hard for you to leave?'

She shook her head. 'Easy. Mary sent a postcard, saying they were hiring in her section, and she could put in a word for me. So I packed up all me worldlies, went down there, got a job and a place in a manky hostel, and there you are.'

'Sounds easy.'

'Well, all me worldlies did fit in one bag, which helped.'

'Did the change do you any good?'

'Give me something to think about other than, you know.'

'Yes.' I nodded sympathetically.

'And the work, it wasn't easy. But it was different. In the danger area. Nice and quiet.'

'Sounds very sinister.'

'It's where they put together the business bits of shells. I was in a shed with Mary, doing detonators. Nice it was. Nice little wooden shed. And a sight more air and light than the last place. And not the noise, either.'

'You make it sound like a real treat.'

'Don't take the mickey. It didn't have to be much good to be better than the job before. It was dangerous, though, but I never got blown up, so I'm not fussed. What used to get up my nose was the way they searched you going into the sheds.'

'Why?'

'Make sure you'd nothing on you that'd strike a spark. Jewellery and such. But it always got me down. Like being in prison.'

'I bet.'

'Ended up driving a hoist,' she brightened up. 'Right up in the air, running on rails under the roof. Lifting the shells about. Great big ones.'

'Did Mary move to that too?'

Ada snorted. 'Course she did. Her doing, wasn't it? Always deciding on things and dragging me along of them, she was.'

'You don't sound like you minded.'

'I was younger then,' she smiled. 'Got a lot more pig-headed nowadays.'

'Don't I know it.' I got up and reached for my coat and bags of tat. 'Better be getting on, I suppose.'

'You still on for a drink sometime?'

'I'm game if you are. Sometime next week?'

'All right by me. See you, then.'

'Sure.' I let myself out, smiling. Ada's company cheered me up no end.

On my way home I passed the end of a street whose name rang a bell. Why? I'd never been up there. Than I remembered Bert, when he'd told me his address. In that street. Poor Bert, convinced that he alone held the key to my researches, whatever he thought they were. Certain that I would be beating a path to his door as soon as he'd come round to drop heavy hints about that mysterious legacy of John's.

I passed the end of the street still whistling, pitying the old man for not being able to bear the feeling of exclusion. I stopped and turned back. I was in a good mood. No harm in checking it out.

Struggling to remember the house number which he'd told me, I found my way to Bert's front door and knocked loudly. The door was opened on a security chain, and through the gap Bert's voice, asking my name and business. An old sentry never dies, they just get anti-burglar devices and live in modern flats with doors you could kick off at the hinges, if you wanted, and leave the burglar chain still securely attached to the plywood and frame.

'It's me. Jo. I've come to pick up that stuff of John Gower's. You remember, you said I could call round for it.'

There was no answer, but the door was pulled to, and the chain slid out of its slot. Bert opened the door wide and motioned for me to come in.

'I'd given up on you,' he said, a trifle huffily. His back was stiff with dignity as he led the way into his front room. 'Thought you wasn't going to come round.'

'I've been pretty busy.' I didn't put much effort into my excuses, observing the forms. Bert sniffed.

'I've still not made up me mind for definite that John would've wanted you to have it.' Did he think he was going to make me beg?

'Suit yourself, Bert. You know what's in this diary, or whatever it is. I've told you that I'll take care of it, and respect whatever privacy you think your promise to John involves. But you've got to decide whether you're going to give it to me or not. To be honest, I'm not sure I'll be able to use whatever it is, until I've had a chance to see it. Can't make any promises about that.'

Bert looked disconcerted by this approach. I was hoping that the temptation to shame my gracelessness would win out over the pleasure of telling me I couldn't see the diary, but either way, I wanted a quick answer.

'I don't know,' Bert grumbled to himself. 'I don't know what's best to do.'

'Well, I don't want to push you one way or the other.' I had deliberately not sat down, keeping Bert standing too. In front of his cold hearth, very symbolic. The room was small and cluttered, noticeably dingier than Ada's. Not squalid, but everything looked as though it was on the edge of going musty. There was a faint smell of damp and frying onions coming in through the air-brick.

'I don't know,' said Bert again, this time talking to me more than to himself. He surreptitiously stuck one finger into the heel of his bedroom slipper, trying to pull it on properly. He must have shuffled his feet into them to come and answer the door. Maybe some of his grumpiness and confusion was due to his having been asleep when I called.

'Did I wake you up? Sorry.' His eyes snapped with irritation. He thought I took sleeping in the daytime as a sign of weakness and senility. I couldn't reassure him without making it worse. I sighed at how touchy people give you points to score off them even when you're not playing.

'I'll go and get the diary,' he said suddenly. Maybe he thought that was the quickest way to get my disruptive presence out of his house. He left the room, shuffling, having failed to get his slippers firmly on by his further manoeuvring of heel against hearth stone. He radiated humiliated anger that he was walking like an old man, but he was too stiff to stop and pull his slippers on properly. I turned and looked out of the window to give him ease.

While he was gone, I looked at the wallpaper, which was at least twenty years old and had a bold floral pattern clashing with the busy diagonal stripes of the carpet. A green girl print hung on the wall opposite the window, and a few family photos stood on a low table beside the one sturdy armchair. Mostly Bert in middle age, rigid and formal with large and small groups of two-dimensional proper citizens. Hearing him returning I straightened up from examining the pictures and stood in the middle of the floor, staring out of the window as he had left me.

'Here you are.' He held out to me a small, very battered notebook. Bound in what had once been black cloth, I guessed, but was now greenish with age. I stretched out my hand to take the book, but Bert didn't immediately relinquish it.

'You'll mind what I told you?'

'Of course I will.'

'I don't want you doing anything to upset Ada.'

'Of course not.' I soothed him, not saying that I thought Ada was a damn sight tougher than he was capable of understanding and certainly didn't need the protection of his chivalrous notions.

'And you're to take care of it, and bring it back next week at the latest.'

'OK. I can probably let you have it back sooner, if you like. I'll read through it and take any notes.'

He nodded. 'So long as you take the time to read it proper.'

'All right, I'll be off then.'

'Right.' He was relieved. 'I'd ask you to stay for a cuppa, but I've got to be going out myself.'

'Sure.' He was ushering me towards the front door, both of us keen to bring the uncomfortable meeting to a close.

'I'll see you.' I stood, one foot over the threshold.

'Right-oh.' He shut the door and I walked quickly away, the diary tucked into my pocket.

# Fifteen

It wouldn't be true to say that I rushed home, barely able to wait before starting to read the diary. I got back to the flat, made myself a coffee, went through to the front room, kicked off my shoes and stared out of the window for a while, taking in the day.

I took the book out of my pocket eventually and looked at it. No one much-read page at which it fell open. In fact, it didn't look as though Bert had touched it in years. Didn't need to, I supposed. I bent back the cover to look at the first page. There was a quiet sound of long-dried glue cracking in the spine, and a small stream of dust fell on to my hand.

The writing I recognised from the letters. Small and neat, a clerk's hand, a ledger enterer's copperplate. Few loops or embellishments. Emotionally controlled. Flicking through, the first neat pages, black ink and even hand. Later on, pencil so faded it was barely legible, and the look of words written in a hurry, leaning on an unstable surface. Here and there, the washed out stains of long dried grime and what looked like gun oil. Some of the pages had been torn out in places later on, whole passages were scored out. By John?

Back to the beginning to read it through properly. The first entry dated from early in 1916. I wondered if he had kept diaries for the other years of the war and, if so, what had become of them. Must ask Bert. When he started writing, John had obviously just finished his first (and only) leave from the front. Had the little cloth bound volume been a Christmas present?

Jan. 16th, Leave train, Victoria [the first entry read]. Hour late setting off. Glad I told Ada not to wait at the station, as I could not have thought of anything to say after goodbye, and expecting the train to pull out every minute, and then you're still there and have to say goodbye all over. Finally got off, although the delay meant we had to rush on to the boat. Then that was late sailing, so we might as well have saved our hurry.

Crossing rougher than coming over. Had a game of pontoon with some of Sherwood Foresters who were next to us in the line last summer. Won sixpence.

17th. Étaples. Getting back to 'Eetaps' worse than Aldershot, worse than the first time we were here. There is snow on the bull-ring and we are cold all the time except when they have got us doubling about in full kit. Makes me wish I'd never put in for leave. Having to stop off here before they send us back up. As though ten days of having it soft would make us forget how to be soldiers.

18th. Twisted left wrist very bad during bayonet drill. Swollen up like a balloon. Our Sgt/instructor has said that he will have no shirking and any man taking sick parade, he will make life not worth living for.

19th. Wrist very sore, still very big. Sick parade. God Medicine and Duty. MO made it plain he thought I was lead-swinging. Same for all who paraded, including one old regular who could hardly stand with malaria, which he has from serving in the tropics. But it was 'M+D' all round and back to the bull-ring with a rollicking from your NCO for trying to pull a skive. MO has put on a linament which smells like it was filched from the horse lines.

20th. On the bull-ring there were about four battalions-worth of men, it looked like, with nothing but men running; men marching and men standing still and the snow and the sand-dunes to be seen. The bleakest place in the world, I thought.

There were no more entries for the rest of the stay at Étaples, a training camp notorious for the savagery of its instructors and the mindlessness of its drill. But not so different from any other bit of the army, I supposed. I thought John was pretty restrained about the whole affair.

There was a break of a few weeks in the diary, covering the end of the training period and the journey to rejoin his unit, who were 'resting'.

18th. We are in the reserve trenches waiting to go up and relieve a battalion of the Coldstreams. It is to be the same spot, almost to a yard, that we had last autumn. We have marched up here a bit brisk, on account of the cold and are having to kick our heels now until the proper time for the handover, for our pains. We have a very punctilious new subaltern who worries a lot and looks at his watch every five minutes. Finally get up to the front line well after midnight. Bitter cold. The old lot are not sorry to be going, the trenches here are the worst-drained I've been in, and there is a good two feet of mud and slush on the bottom. The Coldstreams have had a rough time of it. They said that there are now Prussians opposite, who are very keen, and their snipers well posted and active. With that they wished us the joy of it and took themselves off. Cheerful bastards.

19th. On wiring party. I hate working with that stuff. It always does me more damage than any German I have met. Have gashed my face a bit, where Nobby let the end of a roll spring back on me in the darkness.

20th. Snow, or freezing rain. Letters from home came up with the rations. Seems like a year since I was there, not a few weeks. Ada writes she hopes I can be back soon, although there is no chance of that unless I get a Blighty. Does she want me wounded? She knows that is the only way I'll get home again now. Funny to think of hoping your old man will get a bit of him lopped off, maybe, but not too much. I've stopped hoping for a good wound, or the end of the war, or whatever it was I used to think about when we first came out here. Now maybe, a soft sector is about as much as I can think about, and we've never had one of those yet, so there's not much point.

21st. Bert and Nobby Clarke caught out in no man's land. They'd gone out to get Capt. Turner's body in, or bury it. He was shot last night and couldn't be brought back then. The gerries crept up on them while they were at it and Nobby, thinking they must be some of ours as they swan past, whispers 'Come over here and give a hand, you idle buggers'. I don't know who was more surprised, because the party must have been lost, and hadn't seen our two. How they didn't manage to get themselves shot, I don't know, but they came hurtling over the parapet like ferrets down a drainpipe and haven't stopped shaking since. Bert has polished off a week's rum-ration, which he'd been saving for an emergency, and is now slumped on the fire step, just as though he were home on a Saturday night and out of the ale-house a bit tiddly. I am trying to keep him out of sight of the Lt.

22nd. Bert very sorry for himself today. Says that is definitely the last time he lets himself be volunteered for anything. Thought he was for it, last night. I say I got to that idea a long time ago, and will not be doing anything for the rest of this war unless I get ordered. Not like when we first came over, dead keen and still wet behind the ears. Bert says he can remember when I was a regular fire-eater, and used to tear about looking like one of Kitchener's recruiting posters. I remember that time, when I would have thought that getting this gong, which they pinned on me a few months ago, was quite something. He knows that I could as easily have been torn off a strip for the cock-up we made of that day, as given a medal, but that's the way it turned out. Proper shambles.

23rd. Stanley got a bit of shrapnel in the eye. While we were carrying him down to the dressing station, got a real sharp twinge in my wrist that was sprained at Eetaps. Think it might be setting in rheumatic, never having had a chance to mend proper, and always being in the cold and wet.

25th. Snowed.

26th. Lt. Harrison called me into his dugout this morning. I think he must have been listening to that chat I had with Bert the other night on the fire-step about not volunteering for anything, and keeping our heads down and our noses out of the way of trouble. He gave me a little speech about my attitude, and the importance of men who had been out for a while, and had shown themselves courageous to be setting an example to the younger troops, etc. He thought I might have been unsettled by having gone home on leave, says he wouldn't let any of the men back to Blighty, if he could help it, for they always seem to come back with only half their wits and their heart not in it. I told him I was still very keen, etc. and that I wasn't pining for home (which was true enough, in a way) and that when I was over there I didn't really feel I belonged, and that this soldiering was all I knew how to do any more. He nodded away and said, yes, he knew how I felt, although he has only been out three months himself, and will not have to wait a year for his first home leave, like I did. He was embarrassed by it all, I guessed. He is younger than me, and not a bad bloke. Still keen as mustard and takes himself too serious, but it'll wear off, if he lives that long. I was worried that he was going to give me some pigging detail or a raid to go on to pep me up again, but he finished his speech and offered me a fag. All very man to man.

27th. Rained all day.

I stopped to draw the curtains and rub my aching neck. What was written now was mostly in pencil, on paper that had been damp and dried out again many times by the look of it, so the surface of the page was warped into ridges and hummocks, with the words climbing up the sides of irregularities and vanishing into dips of the weave.

I turned on the desk lamp and pulled it down to shine directly on John's diary as it lay on the table. Resting my forehead against the warm edge of the light shade, I read on. Skipped through a few more entries in the trenches, mostly about the foul weather and food ditto, because of supply problems. A rest period behind the lines, a ten-day run of domestic details; of delousing and inspections; church parades and a couple of visits to the village estaminet. Then it was back up to the front, same place, same round of sisyphean duties.

13th. Here we are again. The old place hasn't improved with keeping. Our reliefs are very keen and went out to show gerry who was master of no man's land every night. Consequently there are a lot of them lying about not far from the parapet, stinking up the place and waiting for some poor sods to go out and shovel them into the nearest shell-hole.

14th. We have been told that we will be here for a while now, as everyone is getting ready for some show or other, and there will not be anyone to take over from us nice and quick like happened last time.

15th. Heavy artillery barrage at dawn.

16th. As yesterday, shelling all morning. Part of the trench was stove in ten yards along from our patch. We have dug Nobby out half suffocated, but were too late for Wills and Mayhew.

17th. A lot of heavy stuff coming over, so we all guess that they (gerry) will be following soon. Our wire is not much damaged, although the trenches are very battered, and we spend all our time shoring them up, which is hard when we are short of timber and the earth is so wet it won't be banked, but just slides to the bottom of the trench however fast you dig it out.

18th. Infantry attack.

21st. Their push running out of steam hereabouts.

22nd. Quieter today. German attack did not get very far with us, as they couldn't get through the wire. We have taken a lot of casualties from the shelling, one whole platoon was standing in the way of a trench mortar which landed round the corner from us.

23rd. They seem to have given up for the day. Clearing up.

24th. Lt. Harrison's replacement (he was blown up by a stick-grenade on Monday) has arrived and told us that we are all a bunch of gutless wonders, and if he'd been here last week we would have been out there beating off the Boche with a bit of good old hand-to-hand fighting, instead of cowering in our dugouts and waiting for the artillery and machine-gunners to do our jobs for us. Etc. etc. I do not think this man is going to be very well liked.

25th. Two journeys to casualty clearing with shrapnel cases. Ground still liquid, in places impassable. Dropped the second bloke off his stretcher four times, with us being tired and losing our footing on the boards like ducks on a frozen pond. He was well soaked by the time we got him there.

26th. Clearing up. Blowing hard all day.

27th. Lt. Sutton called for volunteers for a bombing party tomorrow, to take out a machine-gun gerry had got set up in a shell-hole half-way between the lines. No volunteers. Sgt. Wallis has been ordered to detail six men from the platoon. Lt. Sutton will lead the raid himself.

28th. 'Volunteered' for bombing party by Wallis, the bastard. Sutton was taking us straight at the crater, in their sight lines. I told him we should work our way round the side, where there is a bit of a dip in the land and we might get some cover. He was all for going straight at them, with the result that they spotted us when we were still twenty yards away and have shot half the party with not a bomb thrown. Those of us that weren't hit got out pretty sharpish. Now Lt. Sutton, who seemed very upset by the whole business, has it in for me, thinking that I am a clever bastard, and windy with it. He does not like to be seen in the wrong.

April 1st. Bert and Chalky and me had a little party on account of having been here a year, and us all that's left of the company as then was. Chalky had got some vin rouge in his canteen, and Bert had a bit of grog by, as ever. I chipped in with a tin of cigs which have been sent out from home, and we had not too bad a night of it, though none of us know what we might be celebrating. Not being alive, that would seem like pushing our luck a bit, and we are all getting superstitious.

On late sentry-go, after the others had finished off the wine and turned in. Leaning on the sandbags, writing this by moonlight and keeping half an ear out for the other lot. A year and it seems like centuries. I think I must have believed that the war was necessary then. Even that it might be a good thing for me, in some way, to test myself or something. It is hard to think back. Now, I reckon, I still believe it would be a bad thing if Germany was to overrun Europe, but I can't see that what we've got instead is so much better. I can't seem to care, that's all. I just know that there are a lot of Germans over there who are trying to kill me, and probably don't worry about why, too much, and if I don't get them, they'll get me. That's the way of it. Not enough light now to write any more.

2nd. Thickish head. Bert pulls my leg for mooning about writing nonsense, when the whole of the Kaiser's army could have been coming over the top without me noticing. He had been out in the night to relieve himself and seen me writing up my notebook. Chuck him off the duckboard for his cheek.

3rd. Wet. Very blowy.

4th. Have new chilblains on hands and foot. Also toothache. Figgis offers to pull it for me. I refuse.

5th. Nothing doing.

6th. Ration party. Carrying all day.

7th. Mother's birthday. Have forgotten to write to her in time. Started letter, can't think of any news.


He stopped there, and there was nothing entered for the next week or so. The writing had been erratic, as though he had snatched time to write, resting the book on his knee, or shaky boxes. Then, with the next entry, a change to a firm and regular pattern.


16th. Guardroom, Battalion depot. Brought in yesterday. Charged with cowardice in the face of the enemy.

17th. Day three. Adjutant has told one of the redcaps, who has told me, that they are going to have a field general court martial the day after tomorrow, if the major that is due to preside gets back to the depot by then. They are pretty slack in this guardroom, they searched me when I was brought in, but only made me turn out my pockets, so I have kept this notebook. It would be quite easy to do a bunk, but there doesn't seem much point, as all behind the lines is crawling with MPs. I can't work up the necessary to even think about doing it, this all doesn't feel real.

18th. A young lieutenant has just been. He is to act as my 'friend' at the FGCM which looks set for tomorrow. This Lt. will present my case, and says he was a lawyer in civvy street, although he has never done a court martial before. I asked him, trying not to say it so he could take it as insolence, not to use any of his lawyer stuff on the court, as I can't think of anything that would get up the noses of a bunch of old regular officers quicker than thinking some kid with a temporary commission was coming smart at them.

He said not to worry, there wasn't a great deal he would be doing anyway, least said and all that. Maybe asking a few questions. I said there was not a lot of point in even that, as it is my word against Lt. Sutton's, and I know who they're going to believe.

19th. The court martial was in an upstairs room of the big old house that the battalion staff have taken over. I was marched in with an escort, and it was face the front, caps off. The major, who is president of the court, I know by sight, a very grizzled, short man in his forties, who looks a bit yellow around the gills on account of all the time he has spent in India getting fevers. Next to him, at the long table, covered with a cloth that looks as though they have brought it up from the farm dining room, very nicely embroidered and fine linen, a captain who I do not know, with his arm in a sling and looking pretty battered. Also at the table are two other captains, one is Capt. Marsh from C company, who I know is all right, and the other is a stranger, with no chin and a very small upper lip, not covered by a moustache he is trying to grow. A sandy little man and weak-looking.

There is a bit of shuffling about, and my name and particulars and the details of the charge are read out, and the president asks how I want to plead. He looked as though he thought 'Not guilty' was a bit of cheek, the others showed nothing in their faces. The major was the only one who looked me in the eye throughout, the others mostly were staring at papers on the table in front of them, or taking glances at me when I wasn't looking in their direction.

When the prosecutor had said a bit about what he was going to say, they brought in Lt. Sutton, looking very smart and dependable, and I could see he had taken some care with turn-out. To listen to him you wouldn't know him for the weak and stiff-necked bully he really is. He came across very calm and reasonable, though with not two thoughts in his head, which is just how the other officers liked it.

He said how we had been taking part in an attack on the enemy's front lines on the morning of the 13th. We had gone out through our wire and he had ordered me to stay beside him as we crossed no man's land, as I was meant to be acting as his runner.

143

He told how the advance had run into some heavy machine-gun fire, and had been badly broken up. He had been slightly wounded and we had taken cover in a smallish shell-hole, with a couple of the other chaps from our company, one of them quite badly hurt with a bullet in his guts.

Up to this bit, he was telling the truth, although I thought he laid it on a bit with his wound, which was only a scratch on his leg from some nearly spent shrapnel. He had even walked in with a limp, trying to look like a man who is determined not to draw attention to his suffering.

He told how we had found a couple of German snipers posted in the shell-hole, and very surprised they were when we all tumbled in on top of them. He had shot one, and I had seen off the other. It was a real messy scrap, with neither of us using our rifles, since I landed almost on his head when we dived into the hole. It was dead muddy, so we were wrestling away, only at maybe a quarter the speed we'd normally move. None of the others could take a shot at one without hitting both. I strangled him eventually, although it was hard to get a grip, we were both so muddy, my hands kept slipping.

Well, we stayed in that hole for a while, with the machine-gunners sending off a burst right on the lip of the crater every time we showed any sign of life. They had us well pinned down, maybe two hundred yards from the gerry line, a little bit further than that from our own.

I had time to think all about that day while Sutton was giving his evidence, because they did everything slow enough for the president to write it down, which he did looking as though he would be happier with a riding crop in his fist than a pen.

Chalky died in the afternoon, which was a good thing all round. He wouldn't have made it anyway, with half his guts out, and we'd no more morphia to give him, so he was better off dead. On top of which, the noise he'd been making had really got on everyone's nerves. You couldn't get away from it. I was sorry for the pain he was in, but I wished he'd shut up and was glad when he died. A couple of times, I thought Lt. Sutton was going to go and finish him off, the screaming was making him shake all over.

So then it was just me and Bert and him. Bert was posted off the other side of the shell-hole. Sutton was pressed up flat against the side of the crater a few feet from me, pretending to be keeping a look-out, but really pressing himself into the mud in the way you do when you want to make yourself feel small and safe.

144

I thought about the time I spent there, with the body of the bloke I'd throttled lying where he fell. About my age, I guessed, something similar to look at, dark hair and not so very big. It had never bothered me before, to kill a man who would have got me otherwise. I was always just grateful that I could take care of myself, a bit proud of it, I suppose. Even after I'd realised that the war itself was more or less a big con.

But now, as I stood and watched his body sinking into the mud, I couldn't get the feeling that it was worth much, being able to kill someone else, even if he was trying to do for you. I kept asking myself what's the point, and the more I thought, 'You'd be dead if you hadn't', the less of an answer it seemed. He wouldn't have tried to kill me, if I hadn't tried to kill him, if he hadn't tried to kill me. It went round in my head. When it came to it, even to save yourself, there was no point to killing. I'd strangled him so I could live a few more hours in a mud sump, then start for home and get shot in a few yards, as like or not. Or if not today, some other day, soon.

Sutton was getting to the point of his story, so I concentrated on what he was saying again.

'As darkness fell,' he told the court, 'I decided that the time was right to attempt to break out of the position which we had been holding during the day.' Holding sounded better than hiding in. 'There was an enemy machine-gun position, in a depression of the ground roughly fifty yards from our place, some way in advance of their forward line. I decided that in order to make safer our return to our own lines, we would have to silence this gun first, as the night might not be of sufficient darkness to enable us to retire unobserved by them. I therefore ordered Privates Gower and Cranley to engage the enemy by rifle fire, while I left the cover of the shell-hole and worked my way round to one side of the machine-gun emplacement, in order to despatch them with the use of Mills bombs.'

You lying bastard, I thought, and not a tremor in your voice. I looked at him, as he faced straight ahead, his back rigid and his hands clasped behind him.

'Was this order carried out?' The president of the court prompted. Why did they bother having a prosecutor?

'No, sir, it was not,' Sutton got going again. 'Private Cranley who was on the far side of the hole, moved into position preparatory to opening fire. Private Gower, however, approached me and said that he would not expose himself to the risk of being shot by putting his head above the edge of the crater in order to fire upon the enemy.

He insisted that we retire quietly to the rear, without making any attempt upon the enemy machine-gun position, or in any way drawing attention to ourselves. I ordered him to get into position and be ready to fire, but he refused again.'

Didn't he look the very picture of a serious young officer, standing there so neat and clean? Me, I'd been hauled straight out of the line, with the mud of that damn shell-hole still on me, for all I'd been able to smarten myself up in the guardroom. He told the court that in the light of my refusal to fight he'd had to abandon the planned attack for insufficient fire-cover, and ordered a silent return to our own lines, which had gone unnoticed by the enemy. They wrote it all down.

'Upon regaining our own trenches, I had the prisoner placed under close arrest.'

And that was pretty much it, from Lt. Sutton. They asked a few simple questions, making sure there was no possibility that the order could have been misheard or misunderstood, not that it would have made any difference. My 'friend' was asked if he had any questions for Sutton.

'No questions, sir,' he bobbed up to speak, then sat down again in a hurry.

They didn't call Bert, which I was glad of, because he couldn't have helped me, not having been in earshot, and it would have broken his heart to be a prosecution witness against me. So the next thing was it was up to me to tell my version, with everyone there knowing that it wasn't going to be believed. You could smell disbelief in that room, along with the furniture polish and last night's cigar smoke. I nearly didn't bother saying anything at all. Why should I let them be comfortable with the thought that there's any justice in what they're doing? Why not just refuse to have anything to do with it, say, 'If you want to put me in front of a firing squad, you go ahead, but don't expect me to pretend I think it's all fair and proper above board and that. Sir.'

But it riled me to see Sutton standing there so smug, knowing he was going to get away with it. So I took the oath, although I don't believe in all that, and looked at him and thought 'right, this is for you, mate'.

I told them how, when it had started to get dark, he'd ordered me and Bert to open up on the machine-gun, like he said. He was convinced that they would see us if we went out the back. Like a kid scared of the dark, he'd got to thinking that they couldn't fail to see him once he was moving about out there.

Maybe they would see us go off, I told him, but maybe they wouldn't. One thing for sure, if me and Bert popped up and started shooting at them, we'd get our heads blown off in seconds. They had the gun trained on the edge of the crater all day, it'd only need one burst. And, I knew for sure that Sutton didn't want us making a diversion so he could have a crack at bombing the gun. He had so much wind up he could hardly stand without the help of a mud-bank. It was written all over his face that he thought he'd be able to get off back to safety unnoticed while me and Bert were blazing away, creating a handy little diversion for him to leg it in.

Not only did I not feel like getting shot to bits to help save his skin, I also thought it was a daft idea, the only way we'd get out was if we all took it quietly. Once gerry knew there was something up, they'd send up flares and anyone who was moving about in no man's land would get picked off.

He didn't deny that he was planning to get out and leave us to cover his back. Didn't say anything about it. Just called me all the names he could think of for refusing to make myself a sitting duck for him. Said I didn't understand, there was no hope for sneaking away, but if the gerries were busy, they wouldn't notice him legging it about. He didn't say which direction he'd be going in, mind. He was getting hysterical all right, almost screaming at me about how I was spoiling it for him. I worried about the noise he was making, so I told him to shut it, or they'd know something was up and be waiting for us. He calmed down a bit eventually and said, all right, we'd try crawling out without getting spotted, but he knew they'd see us, and he was going to die and it was all my fault and he'd get me for it, which didn't make that much sense, but I let it pass. He was snivelling a bit, and I wasn't sure if we'd get him out of the hole, which didn't bother me too much, but at least he was quieter.

It had clouded over, which was lucky for us, and we managed to worm our way down to the dip in front of our own lines where we could stand up and run like hell to our trenches, pulling up to make sure we didn't get shot by our own sentries. We got in and Sutton had me arrested, though it was all he could do to get the order out, he was that near collapsing. And here we are.

They were livid. I could see the four faces the other side of the table swelling with anger, like they only had one neck between them. They kept interrupting with questions like 'Are you calling Lt. Sutton a liar?' and 'Are you saying the officer was in a state of cowardice?' It was obvious that was what I was saying, but they made me say it again, I guess it made it look worse for me, but I was past caring by then.

They closed the court while the four officers considered their verdict. I was marched out. It didn't take long before they called for everyone to be brought back in, and the president was clearing his throat and saying that the court had no findings to announce, and calling for evidence about my character. That threw me for a minute, until I remembered what the lieutenant who was defending me had said. The only verdict a FGCM can say is not guilty. If you're guilty their recommendation had to go all the way up to the area Commander-in-Chief before the verdict and the sentence can be confirmed. So they read out some reports from my company commander and the colonel, saying I was a good soldier and had been decorated, all the usual stuff, although the colonel probably didn't know me from Adam and had the adjutant to write it from records. Then they asked if me or the 'prisoner's friend' had anything to say in mitigation of sentence. He got up and muttered something about my previous gallantry, and length of service, but you could see his heart wasn't in it. I hadn't told him what I was going to say about Sutton, and after all, he was one of them too.

And that was it. The court closed again, while they considered the sentence, which there wasn't any doubt in my mind would be for shooting. I was taken off back to the guardroom, where I am sitting now writing this. The orderly has told me that I'll probably be removed to Divisional HQ. I still can't believe all that happened this morning was real, though. It felt like a bad dream.

The orderly is a decent bloke, and has warned me that I will be given a harder time of it at Division. So I am going to give this notebook to him, as he has promised to get it to Bert somehow, or if Bert has gone west in the last few days, to take care of it. He knows that I don't want it getting sent back to Ada. She musn't know about this.

# Sixteen

It was late when I finished reading. Too late, I guessed, to rush round to Bert, hammer on his door and say 'Is that what happened? Was he put in front of a firing squad? When and where, and were you there?' First thing tomorrow, it would have to be.

I stood up and stretched, weighed the small notebook in my hand for a minute, thoughtfully, then put it away in one of the desk drawers. There was nothing more to be got out of that. I would have to talk to Bert again. Dammit, that man had been stringing me along. He could have told me all this straight out weeks ago. Well, I suppose it had been worth humouring him.

My head ached with the effort of concentration, and the hours of peering at the faded handwriting, trying to decipher the more unruly bits. I rubbed my neck and swung my shoulders, but it didn't help much. The bottle of asprin in the bathroom yielded only a trickle of white crumbs on to my outstretched palm. Why could I never remember to get some more before I needed them? Upstairs to scrounge a couple from Dympna.

On my way back down, I checked the letter rack in the hall and found an envelope addressed to me, Beryl's writing. I hadn't seen it earlier. I stuffed it into my pocket and decided to give the pain-killers a chance to work before I read it. Washed them down with a can of beer, also borrowed from her upstairs, sat down again and waited for things to sort themselves out. If I'd had a TV, I would have watched a pulpy old film on it. Instead I lay in front of the gas fire and looked at the ceiling, trying hard not to worry at the missing bit of this dying of John's. It's all so nearly there, wrapped up neatly and waiting for me, not too many more mysteries that can be sprung by this, what was going to be simple, character. Surely?

Stop it, forget it, it's work and you've finished. Clock off, you'll find out the rest tomorrow. My skull had stopped throbbing, so I rummaged along the radio dial for some undemanding music and remembered the letter from Beryl. Fished it out of my pocket and slit the envelope. Read her news, polite and cheerful, carefully non-commital. She'd met up with a bunch of women who were getting a show together, down there at her dance workshop. She was joining in, so she'd stay in Devon for a few weeks. Then there was some possibility of working in Holland. Unlikely, anyway, that she'd be back in London for a while.

Through the casual self-deprecating charm, and the total absorption in what she was doing, disguised as entertaining snippets of description of the little ways of the women who she was with, came the message. Attention Elsewhere, loud and clear. A 'dear Jo' letter, in effect.

I can't say I was desolated, and nothing was made explicitly hurtful for me to weep and wail and chew the carpet over. We'd had so much distance between us recently.

It had been fun. I started composing epitaphs for the relationship. A thin slice of uncomplicated delight, sandwiched between two doorsteps of doubt and absence. The chunk of worry seemed disproportionately large compared to the time we'd actually managed to get it together, but I put that down to bad management. Energy-inefficient, as young go-aheads would say.

Well, there's a turn-up, I muttered to my favourite rubber plant. Bereft of lover and simple canon-foddery end of the play's subject, all in one day. Whatever next? Superstitiously, I unasked that, in case there was a sudden volcanic eruption in W10 to teach me not to ask silly questions.

I wanted to get very drunk and feel sorry for myself, but I didn't have the resources, liquid or emotional. I reread her letter. No big deal there, no scope for hair tearing and sack-cloth wearing. She didn't even say that we were ex-lovers. She didn't need to; when you're waving a hanky from the deck of a ship bound for another planet at someone who's decided to stay home and watch the mice grow their winter coats, there's a lot that doesn't require spelling out. I lay down again and let the implications settle on my chest.

I fixed her in my memory. Instant canonisation of the things I would choose to carry around as references of who I had known. Selected features of character and appearance, there was only room for a handful in my people-file memory store.

There's no point getting maudlin. I picked myself up off the floor and went to look for my old teddy. And so to bed.

I woke with a jolt, and my teeth clenched, at half seven. My body was telling me I hadn't had a good night's relaxing sleep, but I was too tired to listen. I tried to persuade brain to stop her warming up crackles and interference, but she wasn't responding to manual override, so I gave in and got up.

No milk. Bleary-eyed out into the sharp morning air to chase the milk-person up and down Ladbroke Grove. Following the trail of delivered-to doorsteps, always prevented from whipping a pint off one by the thought of what it's going to do to some other poor bastard starting the day tea-less. Not that I'm particularly law-abiding.

The air was clear and crisp, start of autumn chill and delightful. My favourite time of year, and I usually slept through the best of it. I was running intermittently to keep warm, and because it was a cleanish sort of a morning with my lungs enjoying being awake, for once.

I'd covered a mile already, and not caught up with the milk float. Serious workers were starting to stream out of their homes, making automatically for the tube, eyes glazed and gummy. Washing into the tail end of night-shifts whistling, in the other direction.

I found a shop that was open before I caught up with the phantom deliverer. Went in for a pint and got hit on the nose by the smell of fresh ground coffee. Irresistible at that hour, so I bought some. Never knew the shop existed, I couldn't have passed that smell and not noticed. Instant abroad. My nose could get me into trouble with my bank manager.

With two things to carry, I couldn't stick my hands in my pockets, so I hurried along, with my knuckles tingling indignantly at being exposed, unaccustomed as they were, to the cold air.

I picked up a paper from the stand outside the station and bounced home. Put the coffee on to brew and glowed with smugness. Now that Beryl's out of town, maybe I can go back to the gym in peace and quiet. A healthy mind in a celibate body. Or something like that. I grappled with the Latin of it for a minute while the coffee pot burbled and spat on the stove, but I couldn't cope with the genders and endings this early in the day.

As soon as it was a half-way decent hour to be paying visits, I took myself off round to Bert's. Hammered on the door and hoped he didn't have a sacred lie-in, because I wanted to get to the end of this long spun-out story now.

Without too much delay, the door was opened, on its chain as before. The side of Bert's head and one of his eyes appeared in the narrow opening.

'Oh, it's you.' A touch of sourness in his voice.

'Yes.'

'You've finished the diary?' Still he made no move to open the door. We were both craning our necks round an unnatural angle to speak with each other.

'Would you mind if I came in? I want to talk to you.'

He said nothing, but shut the door and took the chain off. When he'd got it open again, he stood on his threshold looking at me.

'You've brought it with you?' He looked as though he expected me to come bearing the diary in a gilded casket before me.

'Yes.' I patted my pocket vaguely, knowing I'd put it in my jacket somewhere. Bert sniffed lugubriously.

You'd best come in.' He shuffled off down the hall, I followed. We went into the sitting room, same as before. It was cold still, with the recently-lit fire smoking obstinately, chilly coal in the damp air. Giving out more dust than heat.

'Sit down, I'll get this bugger going.' He turned to the fire, leant a poker against the front of it and spread a sheet of newspaper over that to get an updraught. I perched on the hard ladderback chair by the window. When the fire had taken, Bert carefully folded the paper and put it back beside the coal-scuttle. Either finicky, or not one for a daily read.

'Didn't take you so long then, did it?' He turned away from the grate and sat down in the armchair. He's settling in for a gloat, I thought, seeing him pull his shoulders round himself like his old cardigan, and some of the sparkle come back into his eyes.

'No. I finished it off in one go. Last night.'

'Thought you'd be back round here pretty sharpish when you'd read it.' There was satisfaction in his tone. He'd expected me to behave so, and here I was. Some illusion of control, perhaps? I kept my patience.

'Obviously, I want to know what happened.'

'Didn't think you was much interested in his diary, not when I first told you about it.' He smiled at me. More in triumph than malice, but still enjoying himself. All right, you old bastard, I said to myself, you've scored your point, let's get on with it.

'I didn't realise the sort of thing it was going to be. There was no way I could until I saw it. You must admit, it's not what one would expect.'

'You want to know about what happened after the court martial?'

'Yes.'

'What I said about not telling Ada still stands, you know. You promised.'

'Yes, I know.' I leaned back in my chair as far as was possible and tried to look as relaxed as I could. Take the point out of the wind-up.

Bert's features relaxed, a mirror of my own. He stopped playing the cantankerous old man for all he was worth and apparently decided to get back to normal, turned on the sprightly manner and impish charm. At least, that's what I assume to be normal, because that's how he was when I first met him. With Ada he was always like that. Maybe it's a big act for her sake and he really is a miserable old sod by nature. He cleared his throat with a deafening cough, making room for conversation.

'I was there, you know.'

'When he was killed?'

'That's right.'

'Will you tell me about it?''

'John stopped writing because they were going to take him off to Division.' He tilted his head in my direction to check I'd got that far. I nodded. 'They always did that, and he must have reckoned slipping the diary to the guardroom orderly before they moved him was the best bet he had for getting it to me safe. Or at least making sure it didn't get sent home with his other papers. To Ada.'

'But they didn't shoot him straight away?'

'No. Maybe he could have kept the book a bit longer, although they still might have taken it off him at Division, and there's no saying he would have got it back.'

'How come you saw him again?'

'They always brought a bloke back to his own battalion, that was due for a firing party. Dunno why, maybe they thought it would make us all more leary of doing the same ourselves, seeing one of our mates shot in cold blood for whatever it was. And of course, it meant the firing party would have to be found from his own lot, so they'd know the man they were doing for. Terrible that, I always thought. I don't know that I could have shot one of me own pals. Well, there's a lot that said they wouldn't if it came to it, but I wouldn't put any money on them refusing when they were ordered. It wasn't like that.'

'So John was brought back to your battalion?'

'That's right. A couple of weeks after he'd been court martialled. We'd been in the thick of it. Don't know how I managed to keep a whole skin, all that was going on. And not a lot of time to wonder what was happening to John, if you know what I mean.'

'Sure. I can understand that.'

'It didn't seem like any of us had a cat in hell's chance of being alive at the end of that little lot. So knowing John'd be shot like enough didn't come as that much to worry about.'

'No.'

'Anyways, we were so cut up, they had to pull us out for a bit, to get our breath back like. And while we were off back of the lines, sorting ourselves out, John's brought up by a couple of redcaps and handed over to our own guardroom.'

'You saw him arrive?'

'It wasn't exactly kept secret. I didn't get to say anything to him, mind, they had him under close guard, but I sort of waved as they was marching him past to the guard room, and he smiled back. Cool fish, that bloke was, didn't turn a hair.'

'What happened then?'

'He'd been in the guardroom a couple of days, and we were all dreading being marched out to hear his sentence read, and then have to go through the business of finding a firing party and topping him. But there was a lot of officers toing and froing, that couple of days. Trying to find a way out of it. To spare the disgrace, you see. Bad for the regiment, firing squads. It was like saying they couldn't keep control of their own men.'

'Was there any possible way out? I thought the sentence was final?'

Bert scratched the side of his nose and looked puzzled. 'I'm not too sure how it worked, but as far as I could ever make out, John's case hadn't got to very top of the brass hat tree, when he was brought back. There was still the final say-so to be given on whether or not the sentence got confirmed. Though there wasn't much chance that it wouldn't be. But we'd thought at first that it was all settled, you know, they'd brought him back for the execution, and that was it.'

'But that hadn't happened?'

'Not then.' He'd completely forgotten his grumpiness in the telling of the story, whose complexities still exercised him after all this time. 'What they'd done was turn him over into the custody of his own unit pending the final sentence.'

'You sound like you're quoting that from somewhere.'

'What?' He was momentarily at a loss. 'Oh, yes, maybe I am. The adjutant's clerk was a mate of ours, and he took a dekko at all the bumph that was flying about. That's how we got to know they'd decided to return him to his unit.'

'Did that mean he got let out to go and fight some more? While they made up their minds to shoot him, if he survived?'

'That's it. Sounds daft, doesn't it?'

'Yes.'

'I think they used to do that quite a bit. Especially if the charge was cowardice. Like, you've got nothing to lose, and maybe if you put up a good show while you're in the trenches and they're still thinking about what to do, they might let you off.'

'Did it ever happen?'

'I don't know.' He tugged at his cauliflower left ear. 'Not that I know of. But I don't reckon it was anything more than a way out for them.'

'A way out of the disgrace of an execution in the family?'

'Yes. You see, they wanted to avoid that. And they'd take some lad who knew he was for it, and stick him back in the fighting and say, now's your chance mate, you make a good show of this and we'll maybe let you off. So he's dashing about all over the shop trying to show he's not a coward and what happens?'

'He gets killed pretty quickly?'

'Course he does. Stands to reason. Put yourself in the way of trouble out there and it's a pound gets a penny you've copped it inside a week.'

'Which saves the powers that be the embarrassment of having to do the dirty work themselves.'

'And the poor sod goes down as "killed in action" with no one outside the regiment any the wiser.'

'Neat.'

'Not half.'

'Is that what they decided to do with John?'

'Yes, well we was going back into it, and I can tell you everyone was cheesed off good and proper, reckoned we'd done more than our bit in that lot already. But the evening before, we're all sorting out our kit and getting ready for the trains, when up pops John and says he's coming with us and they've told him that if he does well he might just get away with ten years' hard labour instead of a shooting.'

155

'Did he believe it?'

'Not him. He was no fool. He'd as good as called Sutton a lying windy bastard, and there was no way they could let him off after that. Even with a long stretch of rock-breaking, it would have looked like they thought he might have a point. And that wouldn't do, would it?'

'Not for them, I suppose.'

'No.'

'How was John?'

'Changed a bit.' He thought about it. 'I'm not sure. You know, when he first strolled out of the guardroom, we were all that pleased to see him I thought, he's just his old self. Never was a very showy chap. Hard to tell what he was thinking. Bit distant. But lively, if you take my meaning.'

'I think so.'

'That's what had gone. After a bit, when the fuss had died down, and all the lads had stopped slapping him on the back, there was me and him with a chance to talk. I thought, well it's like something's gone out of him. The spark if you like. For all he used to say about the war, that bloke would come alive in a scrap. Funny, really. He hated it, but he was a dead good squaddie. Anyway, there wasn't that any more. He didn't seem to give a toss about much. Not that he was slovenly, or anything, not like some blokes you'd see, who were past caring. It was like he'd said to himself, "I'm going to die, so let's not make a big fuss about it." No fight left in him.'

'It seems natural enough, under the circumstances.'

'Granted it looks that way to you.' He searched for the words to explain himself. 'But if you'd known him like I did, it would have come as a real shock. That change in him.'

'Was he so full of life before?'

'Well, it was like I said. He wasn't a loudmouth, or particular showy or anything. It was like you got the feeling that he thought there was more for him than what most of us had to look forward to. Aside from the army. Sort of a going places attitude, they'd call it now.'

'Not just living for the day?'

'That's right. It was rare enough, I can tell you, because that's all there was to live for, out there. And that was if you were lucky. Most of us never looked no further than our next bit of kip, or fag, or detail. Whatever.'

'Not John?'

'I'm not saying it right. Sounds like he wasn't the same as the rest of us. Well, he was and he wasn't. He didn't have any soft ideas about his chances, but he seemed to have more going on in his head than most. It's hard to explain. He knew he might get killed any time he was out there, and it would interfere with other things he wanted to get on with a lot. Inconvenience him, you might say.'

I laughed at the choice of phrase, and he joined me with a reluctant grin, when he thought about what he'd said.

'I told you it sounded daft. And I've never had to try and tell this before. But anyway, that was gone, after he came back from the court-martial. Didn't care for being good in a scrap any more, didn't matter whether he lived or died any more than the next man.'

'What happened when you returned to the fighting?'

'It was a fine old muddle we got back to. There was battalions down to company strength all thrown together higgledy-piggledy. No one knew from one day to the next where they was properly supposed to be, or what they were meant to be doing. After we'd chased around like blue-arsed flies for a couple of days, we fetched up at the bottom of a valley, on the edge of our old sector. Ten miles, maybe, from where we'd been most of the winter.'

'Were the Germans attacking?'

'God knows what was going on. I think it started with one of ours. What they probably called a Spring offensive, though if that was the staff's idea of Spring, all I can say is they should have tried living out in it.'

'The weather was still bad?' How inconsequential that sounded.

'Fair to middling dreadful. Anyway, by the time we're talking of, there was no way of telling who was on the offensive, or what. It was each little bit of the line for itself. They didn't seem to know what to do at all, kept sending us out in the same old way, we'd get maybe as far as the other lot's front line trench, maybe not that far even. Then we'd have to turn round and come back again.'

'Business as usual.' I tried not to let the bitterness that was missing in his tone creep into mine, but he heard it anyway and gave me an understanding smile.

'That's right. And I can see you think we were pretty stupid to go along with it.'

'No, I don't think that. I don't suppose you had much choice.'

'We had a choice, all right. It was the one John made. Tell the bastards what they can do with their stupid orders and traditions and discipline. Tell them you're not playing any more. Mind, he was one of the brightest blokes I ever knew, and proud too, and it still took him over a year to get to the point where he did that. Decided not to go along with them any more.'

'Not much of a choice though. When you think that they still had him on their terms. He might have decided not to play, but they were still making the rules.'

'No.' He was emphatic. 'From the minute he told Sutton where to go, John was making his own decisions. For the first time in a year.'

I must have looked sceptical, because Bert put more emphasis on what he was saying than he'd used all morning.

'I know they had him there,' he made a pinching gesture with thumb and forefinger, 'but the last week or so he was, what can I say? He was a free man.' He nodded to himself. 'That's it.'

Not knowing what to make of this at all, I tried to keep my face neutral. Bert sat back, surprised at himself. He wants me to believe, I thought, that John didn't die for nothing, desperately wants me to believe it. But is that the way that John would have seen it? The whole point of what I'd read in that battered old diary now sitting on the table beside us, was that he knew he would die for nothing, that we all did, always. Death is the most pointless thing of all. He knew that, and made choices that still led him straight to it. Well, when the bear's going to get you anyway, the least you can do is pick your own species. Grizzly or polar, sir?

'I'll get us a drink,' Bert went out. Still embarrassed at his own vehemence. Gone out to marshal his argumentative reinforcements. He came back with a couple of cans of ale, and though it was still early, I could see the point. While I was peeling the ring off mine he fetched two glasses, sticky and clouded with age, and handed me one.

'Thanks.' I poured out the light frothy stuff and took a sip. I pressed on. 'How did he die in the end?'

Bert looked at me over the rim of his glass, calculating whether I was going to press him for an answer now. He wanted to carry on justifying his friend. I could have told him there was no need, if only I'd known how. Eventually he sighed, put his drink down, half drained, and wiped his mouth with the back of his hand.

'You seen the telegram Ada got?' he asked, roundaboutly.

'From the War Office?'

'That's the one.'

'Saying he was killed in action?'

'That's it.'

158

'Was he?'

'What it says, doesn't it? And that's the way of it.'

'I thought they might have sent that anyway. You know, to spare the family's feelings.'

'No, they always told them, when a bloke'd been shot by us lot.'

'So there was no firing squad?'

'No.'

No execution at dawn, no blindfolding and bonds and target pinned over his heart. I felt relieved, I don't know why.

'So what did happen?'

'We were going forward,' he picked up his can off the table, refilled his glass, took a drink and settled into telling the story. 'Me and him and what was left of the battalion, trudging across no man's land with orders to take the German first line trenches and wait for reinforcements to come up and leapfrog us to take the supports.' He snorted. 'That was the story. Load of cobblers. We went over in the second wave, John and me. Scrambled out of the trench and started crossing the gap in line abreast. That lasted about ten yards, like always, then we got broken up, mixed in with the first wave.'

'Was John left to his own devices?'

'Maybe the CSM was keeping an eye on him. I don't know. There wasn't any place for him to go, out there. If you wanted to run away it had to be either forwards, where you was meant to be headed anyway, or back to your own trench, which was full of men waiting to come over. So I don't suppose they bothered about him doing a bunk.'

'So you were crossing no man's land?'

'Yes. Well, we'd got about half-way across. It was misty. You couldn't see clearly more than fifteen yards. Made it hard to judge distances and that. I walked into an old blown off tree-stump and winded myself. John stopped and picked me up. Cracked some joke about how I was always walking into things. I was too, very clumsy as a lad, you know.' I finished my beer and tried to see the ungainly, slightly roguish young man in his old frame and skin which hadn't shrunk to fit its wearer.

'They started shelling us, as we was coming across. We were close packed enough out there that they didn't need to see us clearly for targets. I'd just about got me breath back from that blessed tree, when a shell bursts behind us and flattens me again. I picked myself up out of the mud, checks I've got all me working parts and has a look for John. No sign of him.'

'Was he blown up?'

'No, the shell wasn't that close. I could hear his voice, anyway, from a little in front of me. So I cast around a bit and finds him lying in the bottom of a crater. He's been blown in there, you see,' he demonstrated with a hand movement, 'by the force of the shell-burst.'

'Was he hurt?'

'Didn't look it. There wasn't any blood on him or nothing. Bit concussed, he must have been, though. It was a fair old wallop.'

'Did you try and get him out?'

'Well at first, I wasn't that fussed. I thought at least he'd be out the way of the snipers and machine-gunners down there. They was getting a bit busy now, with the mist lifting. I got over the edge of this shell-hole, for cover. But I couldn't get down to where John was, you see, because apart from this little kind of ledge it was, where the lip had crumbled, that I was sat on, the sides went straight down.' He used his hands for illustration again, pointing stiffly.

'Was it deep?'

'Deep enough. Fifteen, twenty feet, maybe, down to where John was lying. It was an old one. You got a lot of them in that part. The crater'd been there since last winter or well before that. More than one shell would have fallen on the spot by the look of it.'

'What was John doing?'

'Lying stretched out, at first, when I got there. Looking pretty sick.'

'But conscious?'

'Oh yes. Well, he called out, didn't he? Wouldn't have found him otherwise.'

'Was there no way you could reach him?'

'I tried stretching down off the ledge to him, but the sides were vicious. Slippery, you see, and great slabs of mud coming away under the slime that was on the surface. So he told me to pack it in, or I'd be down on top of him and both of us would be stuck. Told me to find some rope.'

'Could you?'

'Well, there's not exactly handy coils of life-saving gear lying about on the battlefield. But there is all sorts of junk. And you can always scavenge a bit, if you use your nous.'

'Did you find any rope?'

'No rope. I wasn't expecting it. Where the shell had fallen, that

160

had knocked me and John over, there was some of our blokes lying around, or what was left of them. So I thought for a minute, then had the belts off them. Their cross-belts would have been better, not so thick, but it's a bugger to get off a corpse when he's lying on his back with a haversack on. So I got about six or seven belts and the odd bit of webbing and strung them all together as best I could. Nipped back into the shell-hole and stretched out on the ledge, reached all these belts and tackle down to John. He sort of crawled across to under the ledge and made a grab for them, but we could both see there wasn't enough length to it.'

'What did you do?'

'Went out again to scout round for some more. There was plenty of bodies around, but just where we were there'd been some heavy shells, so I had to go off quite a way to find any that was whole enough to still have their kit intact.'

'Were you gone long?'

'Maybe twenty minutes. Half an hour. I don't know, you lose your sense of time when it's like that. And there was whizz-bangs going off all over, while I was crawling about out there. I'd no idea how our lot were doing, but I guessed we were stuck in front of their wire as usual. Anyway, I made it back to where John was.'

'He was still lying at the bottom of the shell-hole?'

'No.' Bert's face clouded. 'Not exactly. You see, when I tried to get a line down to him that first time, he'd stood up, under the kind of ledge thing that I'd been on. Before that, he'd been lying or crawling, which was all right.'

'And standing wasn't?'

'The bottom of the crater, it was a sump. Liquid mud. God knows how deep. And there was like a crust, that had part dried out. When he'd been lying on it, he'd had his weight spread. But as soon as he stood up, he broke through it. Started sinking into the gluey stuff underneath.'

'Was he stuck?'

'He could move. When I got back he was thrashing about trying to get a handhold on the side walls. But that was a non-starter, they were like glass.'

'What did you do?'

'I shouted down to him to keep still, for a kick-off.'

'Did he?'

'He swore something frightful. Said if I thought he was going to stand around all day up to his waist in filthy muck while I did me

161

fancy work, he'd I don't know what. But he stopped rolling around, while I'm trying to string these belts together. Not easy, I can tell you, most of them was dead slippery, with mud and blood and whatnot. Anyway, I got some sort of length together, and threw it down to John. Of course, while I'd been doing that, he'd sunk a bit deeper into the mud.'

'Did it reach this time?'

'It was long enough. He was up to his chest in the muck by now, and had some bother getting his arms free to catch hold of it. But we managed. After a bit he got one end, and I started hauling on the other. Careful, like, because I knew the knots wouldn't take any sudden strain.'

'And?' He'd stopped, for breath, for courage.

'Five hours, I was, trying to haul him out of that sump. I couldn't get no purchase, you see, up on this ledge thing. And every time, we'd have him half-way out, maybe free to his knees, then one of us would lose hold of the rope, and he'd fall back even further in. He was covered in the stuff, hands and all and couldn't get a proper grip. Both of us knackered, and a couple of times he nearly had me off the shelf and in there with him. In the end he said, chuck it, you're not going to do it mate. I wouldn't let go, kept on trying. But he waited till I was exhausted after one heave and kind of twitched the belts out of my hand. Threw them across the far side of the hole, where neither of us could get at them. Said he didn't see the point of me falling in on top of him, which is all that was going to happen if we carried on. Said he wouldn't have me crowding him and to find a better hole of me own.' Bert's voice cracked noticeably. 'It was an old joke that, you, know. And he said I wasn't to think I'd dropped the rope, or anything, because he'd for sure pulled it out of my hand, because he knew I was too stupid and stubborn to give up on a bad job when I saw one.' He stopped, his voice shaking, and blew his nose. I looked away, leaving him to his sorrow.

'What happened then?' I asked eventually, gently as I could.

'He drowned.'

Neither of us said anything for a while. Bert looked into the past in silence and smoked a cigarette, then began again as though there had been no pause.

'I stopped by him, of course. Till dark. That's how long it took. Another few hours. We didn't talk much. He was trying to cheer me up. Should've been the other way round, I know, but John was always stronger than me. And all the time he was sinking into it.

162

When it was up to his chin, I thought he was going to ask me to put a bullet through his head to spare him the drowning. It would have broke me heart if he had, because I don't think I could have done it, even to save him that. He must have known, well, he knew me well enough to guess. So he never asked me. But when he was up to here,' he tapped his chin with his knuckles, 'he said 'right-oh, Bert,' and started struggling like crazy. Knew he couldn't get out, of course, he was making himself go down quicker. Get it over with. Then his face went under and that was the end.'

Another long silence. Bert looked out of the window and I turned the other way again, as he blew his nose again and rubbed his sleeve against the corner of his eye.

'And was that better or worse than the firing squad?' I said, half to myself.

Bert brought his gaze back to me, seemed glad of the question.

'For John? Better. Not what I'd choose, mind. But dying's dying, and it's strange to think of picking between ways of doing it. But it mattered to him, to make choices. Once he got to feeling being dead wasn't such a big deal. I don't think choosing how he died mattered so much to him as doing what felt right. Choosing about how he'd live, if you like.'

I knew what he meant. Seeing the old man preoccupied with his dead friend, I got up quietly and left.

# Seventeen

Fresh air. Lots of it, I need. I came out of there taking great gritty lungfuls of damp reality. Let's get back to the 1980s, shall we?

Of all the stupid things. Drowning in a pool of mud. I was quite cross. It would have been neater to have been executed, blander to have been blown up. But dead's dead, and what matter how? Dammit, I thought, walking fast and angry, fists shoved in pockets, shoulders hunched, I wasn't buying that old line again. A good life matters more than a good death. I gave up moral superiority for Lent. Damned if I'd have this legacy of 'better free and drowned in a mud hole than submit to their rules' lark thrust upon me.

'You have your choices, mate,' I said to his ghost, wherever it was. But life is full of compromises, if you stop making them even for a moment, you pay for it.

'Have you exorcised your fascination with this pointless war then?' I asked myself sternly. No answer. And hadn't I started out with some quaint idea about understanding the motives of those who made it possible, by their participation? I felt no nearer that now than I had months ago. Lots more about the how, nothing on the why. Such a foolish notion – if only you could grasp why they did it, perhaps it would be preventable for the future. Not a prayer. For all my in-depth acquaintance-getting with this dead typical First War facilitator, I knew I would never understand why. Who wants to anyway, comprehend why men do the stupid things they do? I'm not a sociologist.

I got home and went straight over to the desk. Sitting there, awaiting my continued commitment, such of this strange project as I'd managed to write. Half a play. Sheaves of notes. Odd thoughts jotted on scraps of paper and a file full of envelope-backs. Trains of thought to follow and factoids to catch. Sketches of character and chronologies of events. I took the whole shooting-match into my arms and walked out into the garden. Resigned.

The woman next door was having another of her illegal garden bonfires. Bless her unmodel-citizenly heart. The respectable curtains opposite twitched in silent fury. The neighbourhood tone-lowerer stood unbowed by the smouldering heap of leaves and broken up furniture. One of the smaller children tottered up with a cardboard box full of rubbish half his own size and tipped it on the fire. Nearly fell in after it, but the woman didn't bat an eyelid, scooped the child out of the way by the scruff of its T-shirt and pushed him back in the direction of the house.

I leaned on the fence, close by the burning. She flicked a glance across at me, but didn't speak. Checking me out for a tirade about the washing going black and sooty on the line, I guessed.

'Mind if I put this on?' I nodded at the stack of papers clutched against my chest.

'Go ahead.' I leaned further over the fence and dropped the papers smack on the top of the bonfire. They settled quietly down and began to smoulder, curling brown at the bottom edges. A couple of sheets drifted off on to the singed grass. Without a word, the woman stooped to pick them up, placing them back on the fire without looking at them.

We stood in a peaceful silence watching the smoke rising. Soon the paper caught properly and burned in cheerful flames. The pages blackened, what was written on them still legible, in negative. As the breeze caught them and started floating A4 cinders around the garden, the woman broke up an old orange box at her feet and dumped it on the top of the fire to stop the burnt paper blowing off. The last of the play vanished under the freshly burning wood.

'What was it?'

'Something that didn't work out.'

'I've seen you writing. Sat at the front window. Is that what you were doing?' she pointed at the embers with a stick.

'Some of the time.'

'Lot of hard work gone to waste.'

'That's the way of it.'

'Isn't it just.' She smiled at me, sympathetically enough. 'What'll you do now?'

'Oh, I don't know. I hadn't thought about it.'

'Start something else?'

'Probably. Not right away.'

165

'Give yourself a break, love. You always look so serious.'

'Do I?' I was surprised she should have noticed, so preoccupied she seemed herself.

'I can see you sitting frowning at that typewriter every day.'

'Hm. Not over this any more, I won't be' I caught one of the flying bits of carbonised effort and crushed it in my hand, letting the fine black powder run out between my fingers.

'But there'll be something else?'

'I guess so.'

'Rather you than me.'

'Thanks for the use of your fire.'

'Any time' she said, with exaggerated politeness. Then laughed. Not sure how to take it, I sketched her a multi-purpose smile and went into the house.

# Eighteen

A Grand Gesture a day keeps the future at bay. I tap-danced across the hall and wondered what to do next. Go get a job in a Wimpy bar? Become a tax inspector? Crack a bottle of scotch and get good and stinking? Something was called for.

Go and see Ada. My old mate Ada. Tell her the great work's been scrapped and all those hours of diligent prying gone up in smoke. Her invaluable contribution to the researches of a rank and file social realist raining down in little specks of black ash on an ungrateful suburb.

We'd had a date half fixed anyway, and I could take her down the pub. Give me some Dutch courage and I'd tell her that I'd chucked it. Would she mind? Should she care? Not take it as a personal insult, I hoped. How protective did she feel about the dear departed's memory? Blowed if I knew.

I neatened myself up a bit. Who do you take the most care for? Not a buddy, who takes you as you are on condition you make no judgements of her, truce of habit. Not a lover, who doesn't need to see you, really, with her own idea of what you are so clearly before her. A potential lover, maybe, who still assesses? Or a friend like Ada, close enough to see you, separate enough to register the fact of your scruffiness.

I set off whistling. Covered half the distance to Ada's at a skip. Slowed down when I turned the corner of her road. Wary eyes out. And there he was. Pale, damp and anxious-looking. The thin man with the moustache and a slight case of the shakes. Hanging about outside Ada's block again. Waiting for me, I had no doubt. I walked up to him. Let's get this out of the way.

He had stepped out into my path, as if to make sure I didn't hurry by. No chance, buster, I'm seeing you off.

I stopped, two-square, facing him. His jaw worked a bit, but he didn't manage to get any words out. 'What do you want?'

'You're going to see Ada?' he said lamely.

'Of course.'

'What are you going to say to her?'

'That's my business.'

'I want. . .' he didn't finish. His hands clutched at each other, cracking the knuckles soundlessly.

'Why don't you go and see her yourself and tell her what you want?' He looked at me with a complex mix of fear and dislike and a desire for pity, but made no answer. 'Is it because you can't?'

Silence. This was getting a bit one-sided, but I carried on. 'No, I guess you can't really. It's just me you're bothering like this.' He stood there, shoulders hunched, pushed back by my annoyance, although he didn't move. 'That night in the park. I saw you then. You couldn't be real for her. You don't know Ada, do you?' No answer, a sad look. 'Not as she is. You can't talk to her as she was then, years ago. No such woman exists any more.'

'I can't,' he started, stumbled over something painful, stopped. Tried again. 'I don't want her to know.'

'You take yourself too seriously,' I said, brutally. And what an understatement.

'It's for her,' he sounded surprised, resentful. 'I want to protect her.'

'Bullshit.'

'You don't understand.' He was seething.

'I don't think it's got a lot to do with her. It's your idea of what you owe to yourself that's brought you here. The strength of your own self-image.'

'No.'

'Why else? Where do you get off on this thinking you know best what she should and shouldn't hear? You're as bad as Bert.'

'I'm trying to do what's right,' he swayed before my eyes.

'Sanctimonious nonsense.'

'Don't tell her.'

'Listen, mate,' I was getting angry myself now, 'you may have some trouble with this concept, but I'm a radical feminist and I'm not taking orders from any damn man. Living or otherwise. So you can take your doomy spectral utterances and stick them.'

He said nothing. Fading fast.

'And I don't care if you've struggled seventy years across the ether to deliver your pious injunctions. I'll tell Ada any bloody thing I want. Now shove off.'

I stepped past him, ignoring the frustrated flapping gesture he made with his hands.

'And I don't want to see you again.'

There was a sigh, like a closing lift door, and when I looked over my shoulder, he was gone.

# Nineteen

I was still feeling a little wobbly from the encounter when I knocked on Ada's door. If she'd notice my strained expression, and made some conventional quip about me looking as though I'd seen a ghost, I think she'd have had me rolling on the doormat laughing hysterically. Luckily she didn't.

'How do you fancy popping out for a swift half?'

'I'm game. Why don't you come in while I get my coat on? Is it cold out?' she called from the bedroom, where she'd gone to get her things.

'No.' I lounged in the doorway of her room, watching her rummage in a tall old wardrobe. First time I'd seen in here. 'Not too bad.'

She took a light-weight woollen coat off a hanger and put it on. Pale green with large, old fashioned buttons. She picked out a scarf and wrapped it round her, tucking the ends under her collar.

'That should do.'

'You'll be warm enough,' I agreed.

'Soon be time to look out all my winter things.'

'A few weeks yet.' I was answering at random. As I stood aside to let her past, I caught sight of the photograph which stood on the bedside table. John, without a doubt. In uniform. Old fish face, little moustache and centre parting, pale and worried-looking even then. I stared at the photo and crossed my fingers behind my back. Ada followed my gaze.

'I never got round to showing you John's photo, did I?'

'No.' I turned and walked towards the front door. 'Shall we be going?'

Ada looked slightly surprised, but made no comment. She fetched her handbag from the kitchen and joined me on my way out.

170

'Where to?'

'Your choice.' I waited for her to check the locks, yale and mortice. 'Whatever your favourite pub is. Which is your local?'

'Not that one.' She nodded over the balcony at the early sixties block of shops and flats opposite. There was a plastic tavern tacked on to the end of the row. Instant community. 'Let's go down the road a bit.'

Ada walked not too fast and not too slow, with a stride about the same length as mine. We fell easily into step. She dug her heels in the same way I did, slap, firmly down on the uneven paving stones, toes turned out. Her old leather lace-ups and my tatty trainers, same size by the look of it. We swopped notes on chiropodists, her bunions, my in-grown toenail. I didn't pay much attention to where we were going, until Ada stopped and said, 'This is my local, or at least the one I use most often.' I looked up and realised that we were at the pub I had come to that distant summer day I first bumped into Beryl. While I stood and wondered at life's little ironies, Ada was already half-way to the bar in the public.

'What'll you have?' her voice cut through my dithering. I pulled myself together for the umpteenth time that morning and joined her at the bar.

'Pint of bitter, please.'

She nodded to the waiting barman, 'And a bottle of stout.' She pulled a worn leather purse out of her handbag and started counting out the right money.

'I'll get them.' I stuck my hand in my back pocket for some cash, suddenly realising that dragging Ada out for a midday drink might be a strain on her pension.

'You can get the next one,' she finished counting out the price of the drinks unperturbed. 'Unless you were just planning to have the one?' She gave me a sideways grin, wicked. I relaxed.

'Not me. I've got quite a thirst on for some reason.'

'Me too, and for no reason at all. But who needs one?' She picked up her drink and walked over to a table in the corner. I followed.

'And I don't suppose you're any better off than me,' she murmured incidentally, settling herself, placing her coat and scarf on an empty chair, setting her handbag on the table before her. She poured half of the bottle with the ease of long practice and raised her glass.

'Good luck.'

'Here's to it.' I joined her, put my glass down, stretched and got

171

my feet neatly folded on to the wrought-iron hat-rest under the round Victorian table.

'Smoke?' She shook a cigarette out of the packet for me to take. The old-fashioned sort, unrepentantly tar-sodden. I took it gratefully, watched her bounce the untipped end on the back of her hand to flatten down the shreds.

'These things are supposed to take years off your life.' I tapped the health warning on the packet in front of me.

'Pah,' she snorted. 'Don't believe a word of it. And if it was true, it'd mean I should've lived to be a hundred and thirty odd, without I'd smoked. Who wants to hang around that long?'

'It might be quite interesting.'

'No. Three score and ten's your natural. Any longer is a bonus, far as I'm concerned. And there's not many can make their wits last that long as it is.'

'Maybe you're right. I still think it would be quite interesting to live through so many generations.'

'You're stuck in the past, girl. That's your trouble.' I was shocked, though she only spoke lightly. 'When you get to see as much history as I've done, on the hoof as it were, you realise it's not much cop.'

'I suppose not. But you never think of it as history at the time, do you? Not when it's happening.'

'No,' Ada agreed, 'it's the wisdom of hindsight mostly. Though sometimes you know what you're going through's a bit special.'

'Like what?'

'Well,' she took a sip of her drink. 'Like the wars. Both of them. And like getting the vote. You all knew things like that were going to be history. Taught to the kids in school years after. Especially when the newsreels started. I could just see people sitting down to watch them twenty years on and thinking 'Oh, that's history,' not like it was real people doing it. You know, all those 'Allies open the second front' ones.'

'Tarantara. Yes, I know the sort. One eye on posterity when they made them.'

'But most of your life's ordinary. Even if it didn't seem like it at the time. Most people looking back wouldn't think much happened. Beats me why you're so interested in it all.'

'Because things did change. Even if they've been buried since. Like when you and all those other women started doing men's jobs during the First War. That was a pretty drastic change.'

'We thought so at the time,' she agreed.

'It was,' I insisted. 'Even if when life got back to 'normal' they all started pretending you'd never done those things.'

'Did seem like everyone forgot pretty quick,' she nodded, 'even us as had been doing the work. Relief it was all over, I suppose.'

'Did you all get turfed out when the war ended?'

'Not so much call for bombs when there's no war on.'

'Tell that to the White House,' I muttered. Ada ignored the remark.

'They turfed us out, all right. Couldn't get rid of us quick enough, when it was done, and such blokes as was left coming home wanting jobs again.'

'Thank you and goodbye?'

'Not so much of the thank you, as I remember. It was sort of taken for granted that we'd all be going back to our homes. I ask you. As if there was more than a few of us had our old men coming back.'

'I suppose there had to be some excuse for not bothering what happened to you.'

'The papers were full of it. That women back to the home stuff. Like we'd been let out for four years on some kind of a treat to play in the nice factories,' she screwed up her face in disgust.

'So off you went. Back home?'

'There was a lot of talk. About our rights and that. They demobbed all the men, they could at least've done the same for us. But nothing come of it. No one was listening, it was like everyone went a bit bonkers at the end.'

'Did you go back to your mum's?'

'Nowhere else, was there?' she shrugged.

'What about your friends? Did you still see them?'

'Aggie's family lived not far off ours, though I'd not known her before. We still knocked about together. The others were all over the place.'

'And Mary?'

'She'd a husband come back more or less in bits. They got a flat in Bow, and she was looking after him till he finally gone off. Meant I hardly saw her for the best part of a year. Plus I didn't have the fare to go 'cross town anyway.'

'But you saw her again after that?' I pressed.

'I'd started going about a bit again. To meetings, sometimes. Women's meetings, you know.'

'Yes?'

'Aggie took me to one just near. Lot of us, there was, that'd been doing war work, and dumped when they didn't need us no more. Left with nothing.'

'Is that what the meeting was about?'

'Yes, anyway, I got involved one way and another, and that's how I run into Mary again. She was always up agitating for something.'

'She was politically active?'

'I should say. She was a bolshevik.' Ada produced this announcement with an air.

'Really?'

'Only reason she didn't hoof off to Russia was she thought the same'd be happening over here any minute. Mind, a lot did.'

'Think it?'

'Yes. She used to go around with a lot of people who never talked about much besides the revolution. Bit impractical, some of them.'

'How did you meet them?'

'She talked me into going along to some of their things,' she smiled, 'even though I didn't see eye-to-eye with her.'

'Why's that?'

'Oh Mary, if you knew what she was like,' Ada smiled and waved her hands expansively. 'You could see why she'd go for that sort of thing. Nothing by halves for her. Lot of enthusiasm. And she made some lovely speeches, I must say.'

'But basically, you disagreed.'

'Well, she thought that if you got the revolution, then women would get a fair deal. So she didn't have so much time for stuff like changing laws, and getting up deputations about pensions and dole and that. She thought it'd all be taken care of once we were living in soviets.'

'And you didn't?'

'Always been practical, me.' She grinned.

'But you still liked her?'

'I did. But I could see that her ideas and my ideas were different. And I thought mine were better.'

'That's progress, I suppose.'

'I reckon. It was easy to get dazzled by her talking. Like being run over, it was. But I preferred it when we got so I could trust my own way of thinking all the time with her.'

'Did she mind?'

'No, she never said. I think she got a bit impatient with me, being a reformist and that. But I told you, she loved to have someone to argue with.'

'So you kept on seeing each other?'

'On and off. Trouble is, being in the revolution took up a lot of her time. So we'd sometimes spend an hour together between meetings of hers. That was nice, but she was a bit what you might call preoccupied.'

'I know,' I sighed. 'I've got friends like that.'

'Went to Canada in the end. Sort of washed her hands of us. After the strike, it was.'

'The General Strike?'

'Yes. Thought England was a bit slow on the uptake, or something. Told me I should go too, but I was married to Prince, by then, and he wasn't keen to shift.'

'Did you keep in touch?'

Ada shrugged slightly. 'We wrote at first. Quite often. She used to write these great long letters, all excited about the new place and things she was doing. Made me feel a bit boring, not having much news myself. Just family stuff, really.'

'That's bound to happen, isn't it?'

'I don't know. Anyway, she got more taken up with things over there. Politics and that. She'd a job as well. So she didn't write so often.'

'But you missed her?'

'Yes,' she bent over the cigarette she was lighting. 'It was only after she'd been gone a year or so that it properly sank in that I wasn't ever likely to see her again. That was terrible, when I realised that. For all we'd gone our different ways after the war, she'd always still been there, if you know what I mean. Like we could have got right close again any time.'

'Did she realise it too?'

'Must've done. All of a sudden, after her first Christmas out there, she stopped writing about how I'd like Canada and she knew I'd find a good life there. Like she'd realised we were both staying where we were.'

'A sort of cut-off.'

'Whatever. We were in each other's past. Nothing new happened between us. Though I still thought of her as my best mate even when I hadn't seen her for ten years.'

'Did you ever meet up again?'

'No.' Ada twisted her wedding ring absently. 'She never came

175

back. Died over there. 1970, it was.'

'I'm sorry.'

'So was I.'

'She sounded like a very interesting woman. I would have like to have met her.'

Ada relaxed and smiled. 'She would have gone a bundle on you. Very keen on history, Mary was. You could've sat down and asked her questions about the past till the cows came home.'

'Do you really think I'm obsessed with the past?'

'No, love, I was only teasing. One swallow doesn't make a summer.'

'Pardon?'

'Because you've been doing one thing' she waved airily, 'this play, or whatever, that's history, doesn't mean that's what you've got your nose in all the time, does it?'

'No.'

'You do write modern things, don't you?'

'Oh yes. In fact, this was the first, um, historical project I ever did.' I was stumbling and a bit formal, like I get when I'm not sure of myself. 'Thought it would make a nice change from dissecting the contemporary lifestyle of me and my kind.'

'Oh yes? And what's that then?'

'What's what?'

'What you just said. The whojamawhatsit of you and your kind.'

'Oh, you know,' I shrugged.

'No,' she said reasonably. 'What's so special about your lot? Whoever they are.'

'You know in the thirties, when they used to have clubs like socialist cyclists, or neo-facist glee singers, or humanist bowls players?'

'I know what you mean. What's it got to do with you?'

'Well it would have a cluster of descriptions like that. My kind,' I took a gulp of beer and a deep breath, 'lesbian feminist vegetarian cat-owning young self-propelled dole-drawing ramblers. Or something. Though I don't own a cat. Being allergic.'

'Oh.' No hints in her tone. I didn't look at her, busy arranging a pile of burnt matchsticks into a neat pattern.

'Or separatists for short.'

'Separate from what?'

'Men. Patriarchy.' There was a small silence. We both picked up our glasses at the same moment, so British. I caught her eye, and we

176

laughed at ourselves for our embarrassment.

'Each to his own. Or her own.' And that was Ada's last comment on the unplanned pronouncement. She drained her glass, pushed it across the table towards me, giving me a get out from my awkwardness. 'Your shout.'

'Same again?'

'That's right. Mackie for me.'

I went and got the drinks, and by the time I returned from the bar, all was back to normal. Must be something about this pub. Some soul-baring agent in the beer, perhaps.

'Did you ever go and see Bert?' The change of subject was easy and unforced.

'Yes, as it happens. I didn't know you knew he wanted to see me though.'

'He thought I didn't,' she made a noise, half snort, half laugh. 'Hopping about like a budgie in a bird-bath, he was, last time the two of you were round together. I knew he was up to something. Bert's always like that when he thinks he's being crafty. Big kid, really.'

'Yes, he wanted me to go and talk to him alone.'

'About John?'

'Sort of,' I hedged. 'He wanted to tell me his, you know, Bert's version of events.'

'Oh yes?' she was non-committal, inviting me further. I wasn't sure how to go on.

'He was very fond of John.'

'They were like that,' she agreed, with a gesture of inseparability.

'I think he feels a bit lost. Being the only survivor of a group of friends who were all wiped out when they were young.'

'Maybe he does. I always told him he should think himself lucky to have come out of it at all. Didn't seem properly grateful for his chances to me.'

'I suppose what looks like a lucky break to everyone else can seem like a bum deal to you.'

'People do have some funny ideas,' she nodded. 'Like when John was killed there were some as said I was lucky, he'd died so well. What's that supposed to mean, I ask you?'

'I don't know. How do you die well?'

'What they were getting at was I should be grateful he was killed in action, you know. Him with his medal, a brave man and all that, killed straight out, nice and clean, no hanging about for months

177

with all his bits missing, or stuck in one of those mental hospitals out of his mind. Not died of puking up his guts in Gallipoli, like the Parry boy.' She crinkled her face sourly. 'Never got off the ship, he didn't. Went all the way there to die of the runs.'

'What's the difference?'

'That's what I used to say.' She slapped the edge of the table. 'What does it matter? He's gone, it makes no odds how.'

'I suppose they were trying to be kind.'

'Yes.' She looked at me with her head on one side, like she did when she was thinking. 'I was meant to feel better that I could keep a picture of him in my head, like he was still in his prime. Nothing messy and lingering about the way he went. One day there, all whole and heroic and the next day,' she clapped her hands together, 'voomph. Gone. But still perfect.'

'But you didn't need that picture?'

'Bloody right. I remember what I remember of him. Didn't need no nice sharp ending to keep him perfect in my mind. Well he wasn't perfect, was he?'

'Who is?'

'No one. And it never mattered to me that he was a good brave soldier. I always thought that was a daft thing for a grown man to be doing. Told him so, as well.'

'But you were still thought lucky?'

'Compared to some. They wanted me to put my memory in a little velvet box along with his medal, and take it out for a polish every now and then.'

'Who's they?'

'Family. Neighbours,' she shrugged. 'They were all looking for ways to kid themselves that what was going on made any kind of sense.'

'But not you?'

'I knew it didn't.'

'So it wouldn't actually make any difference to you if John had died in some other way?' I asked, trying to sound as hypothetical as hell, looking at the air above her head.

'No,' she said sharply, 'it wouldn't. I told you that.'

'It's possible that he didn't, of course.'

'Mm.'

'You didn't get very much information at the time, did you?' No comment. She was playing a game of some sort with me, but I didn't know what. Should I tell her about the diary? She was making me

178

do all the work.

'Did you ever talk to Bert about it?'

'No,' she shrugged again. 'He clammed up when I asked him. The only time I asked him. But I know when he thinks he's being clever. Gets that look on his face.'

'The budgerigar one?'

'That's it,' she smiled. 'Thinks he's as sharp as all get out, does Bert. Either that, or he takes me for a fool.'

'But you know something? More than what you've been told?'

'Yes.' Afternoon sunlight filtered through the smoke shone in my eyes for a moment so I couldn't read her expression.

'I think you're playing games with me, Ada.'

'I don't know what you mean.'

'You're not telling me something you know.'

'Can't tell you everything I know about everything.' her tone was injured innocence. 'We'd be stuck here all week. I've learned a thing or two in my time.'

'You know what I mean.'

'You started it.'

'OK, let's call it quits,' somebody fed the juke-box, and I had to raise my voice against the sudden blast of music. 'Did you know Bert had John's last diary?'

'Yes.'

'You've seen it?'

'Yes.' I was staggered.

'When? How?'

'Years ago.' She leaned closer to me across the table so she wouldn't have to shout. Her breath was sweet with ale and her eyes gleamed through the smoke. 'Right after the war. Bert had the pneumonia and got packed off to hospital. His sister let me into his room to have a nosey around. She was a mate of mine.'

'Why did you think there'd be anything to look for?'

'Bert gets terrible smug when he's something to keep secret. Makes him feel responsible. So I knew he was keeping something from me. And I'd given John that little book for Christmas, when he was on leave. He had this habit of writing things down, long as I'd known him. So I reckoned it was a fair bet that he'd kept a diary of some sort, though private soldiers weren't supposed to. And Bert was the obvious bloke to have it, if anyone did, them being such mates.'

'So you found it?'

'Of course. Under his mattress, just where you'd expect it to be.'

'And you read it, obviously?'

'Yes.'

'And then what?'

'Put it back and made no mention. Bert came out of hospital none the wiser.'

'And has spent all these years thinking he's protecting you from the awful knowledge?'

'Bert's a fool.' She leaned her elbows on the table to rest her back. 'But he means well, and he's been a good friend to me, all these years. If he's happier thinking I don't know, then what's the harm in pretending?'

'What did you think? When you read it?'

She sat back a bit, lit another cigarette. Looked at the ceiling and shrugged.

'Were you upset?'

'I was sad.' She leaned forward again, re-engaging me. 'For him. Sad that he had to go through all that. It seemed a waste.'

'But not surprised?'

'That he was that way of thinking?' I nodded. 'No, I had some idea. We'd been very close, before he went off.' She stopped herself. 'That's sounds funny, you'd say of course we were close, being married. But I mean, like we knew what each other was thinking, and there's not a lot can say that.'

'I know what you mean.'

'So it wasn't no surprise to find out the kind of trouble he'd got himself in, with his attitude. I could have seen it coming. But he'd stopped talking to me about stuff like that by then.'

'Trying to protect you?'

'Bloody silly. I don't need protecting. Didn't then.'

'I see that.'

'He should have known it, too. He did know it, before he went over there. Got so wrapped up in it, I suppose, he thought I wouldn't be able to understand.'

'It's a man's life.'

'They get like that about their games.' She laced her fingers in front of her and stared at the swollen knuckles. 'What can you do?'

'I don't know.'

'I could have given him some comfort, maybe, if he'd had the sense to tell me what was going on.'

'Maybe he thought it would make it worse, since there was no

180

way out?'

'Stiff-necked. Pride, he'd too much of that for his own good.'

'So you wouldn't have minded if he'd been shot by a firing squad?'

'Of course I'd've minded. What do you take me for?'

'Sorry. I put it badly. I mean you wouldn't have thought any the less of him?'

'No. Don't seem no worse to me than being killed in action. Still the same man it was happening too. But I can see why he preferred it the other way.'

'There's no doubt he wanted to protect you from what he thought would hurt you. If you knew he'd been court-martialled and all that.'

'Most likely by then he'd started to forget who I was,' she sighed. 'Or he'd have known that wouldn't make any difference to me.'

'Forget?'

'He was carrying around this idea of me in his head all the time he was out there. A year maybe, when he only saw me for a few days. And they all got proper sentimental. Not like us who stopped over here. The women. Stayed in touch with reality. So his idea of me ends up being more real than I am.'

'Larger than life and twice as perfect?'

'Maybe. I couldn't say. But I know we all forget very quick. Even someone you love, you can't remember how they look and sound. Let alone how they think.'

'Forgetting's not a problem unless you try and pretend it's not happening.'

'That's right.'

'Let's have another drink.'

'You'll have to get them though. I've gone through a week's beer money already.'

'That's OK.' I stood up and scooped the glasses off the table. 'I told you I feel like getting over the odds.'

'Don't mind if I join you.'

'I'll see to it.' I went to the bar. She waited till I got back, then asking me to watch her handbag for her, went off to the ladies.

I stretched and stared out of the window at life going on and by, its top half at least, above the ornamental frosting of the glass. By the time Ada came back, I had put some distance between myself and the rawness of what she had been saying, and so, by her look, had she.

181

Without sitting down again she said, 'Fancy a game of dommies?' and I laughed at the normality of it and agreed. She went to the bar and fetched the set.

'Crib, now dominoes. Whatever next?'

'Do you good, nice quiet game. Stops you brooding.' Her speech was very slightly slurred. My head was getting that old cotton-woolly feeling. Pleasant.

'I think you're assimilating me into your peer group Ada.' I picked up my hand, arranged it in front of me, like half a Stonehenge. 'I'll be pensionable by next week at this rate.'

'Sometimes, girl, I don't know what you're talking about.' She was concentrating. 'And that's God's honest truth. Are you going to play?'

'Sorry. I was just wittering.'

We played for a while in silence, against the background of pub-talk rumbling and the juke-box and shouts from the darts board. She was beating me hands down, so I made an effort. Not that I cared if she won, but I know Ada, she's no savourer of an easy victory.

'Again?' she asked. Her inflection reminded me of Latin lessons. Suffix something or other, expects the answer yes. Through a haze of beer fumes I chased the word round my reluctant brain, but never quite caught up with it.

'You want another game?' she said again with heavy patience.

'Yes. Sure.' I grinned at her. We played. I was lucky, had good doms, managed to win that one.

'Best of three?' She barely waited for my answer, her thick knotted fingers sorting the pieces with fierce dexterity.

'Sure.' One to settle the series, and she saw me off, no shock result. She had a lot of gusto in her game style. Slapped the pieces down with firmness and panache. Like her card play. 'Your game.' I picked up the glasses with a glance at her for assent. She grinned at me, released tension of her concentration.

'I shouldn't let you.'

'Go on. If you want one. I'm having another.'

'That's two I owe you.'

'Forget it. I'm feeling irresponsible.' We drank some more and the haze got thicker inside my head to match the rising blanket of blown-out smoke that was filling up the bar as the mid-day session drew to a close. Ada's face swam before me, square and strongly-marked, flushed a delicate shade of pink. A line of sweat

182

fringed the top of her forehead, the air in the pub was close.

'What're we celebrating?' She rested her chin on her hands, elbows on the table, and took the weight off her smile.

'It must be Thursday.'

'I used to get paid Thursdays. Years ago. Used to push out the boat a bit then too.'

'That's funny I got paid on Thursdays. When I was little. I thought they only did that in the north.'

'How little? You're not such a great lump now.'

I held out my hand, palm down, about four feet off the ground. Indicating that it had been a long time ago.

'Child labour,' she muttered.

'S'right.'

'How old were you, when you had your first job?'

'Fifteen. Sixteen, maybe.' I racked my brain, but it wasn't up to sums. 'There was a heatwave though. In an ammonia factory.'

'Ha!' Ada was triumphant. 'Call that child labour? I'd been out working three years by the time I was that age.' She sat back heavily in her chair and looked pleased with herself. I made a conceding gesture, tilting my head to one side and retrieving it with an effort. It seemed to weigh more all of a sudden.

'I'd rather write plays than pack ammonia,' she announced judiciously.

'So would I. Not that I've much choice in the matter.'

'No?'

'No.' There was something niggling away in my mind. Something I had to tell Ada. What was it? So many revelations in one day.

'How is the play?' she asked. That was it. I had to tell her about the bonfire. I coughed, gave myself a shake, chewed a match.

'I can't do it.'

'What d'you mean?' she settled her forearms on the table and leaned forward to stare up into my face. 'Why can't you do it?'

'I just can't. It wasn't working out.'

'I thought you'd done quite a bit of it.' She wrinkled her brow ferociously. Puzzled, not angry, I hoped.

'Yes, I had.'

'And you've given up on it? Just like that?'

''Fraid so.'

'Seems like a waste of effort. Couldn't you've finished it off? Since you done so much. Seems a shame not to finish.'

'I've started, so I'll finish? Mm. But it wasn't going anywhere. I'd started it for the wrong reasons. With an idea that had changed in me by the time I'd got half-way through. I was changing while I wrote, you see.'

'So all your –' she struggled for the word, 'research. That's gone for nothing.'

'No. Not for nothing. You can't waste knowing something. But what I found out from you and Bert and John,' I waved at the outside world, 'all that. I can't use in the sort of thing I thought I was doing when I started out. If you see what I mean.'

'Not sure that I do,' she grumbled.

'It got too personal,' I tried again. 'I got too involved in individuals. It wouldn't have done for a thing about the whys and wherefores of war and peace.'

'Wasn't there a book went by that name?' Ada had stopped being cross with me. Thank the goddess.

'There was. And if I was doing a lesbian feminist rewrite of Tolstoy, don't you think that's reason enough for going down the pub instead?'

'Maybe so.'

'Posterity will thank us. For a narrow escape.'

'Here's to your next thing.' She raised her glass. 'And I hope it lives long and happy.' I drank with her.

'You don't mind then? That you won't see the story of your chap on the boards?'

'Wouldn't have gone to see it, me. Not unless it'd been on the telly. I don't mind. I know what I knows.'

'Why did you come round? The first time?'

'Always been one for something new. Thought it might be interesting. Glad I met you, though. Play or no play.' I was pleased, touched.

'And I'm glad I met you,' we beamed at each other in expansive good-will. 'Play or no play.'

'That's all right then.'

'Here's to us.'

'To us.'

'Mind you,' I tried to concentrate on the serious things I had to say, but they were slipping fast, 'I've learned a lot. Doing this.'

'That's good,' Ada said vaguely, looking around her as the pub started to empty.

'Bound to come in handy some day.'

'Bound to.'

'It's chucking-out time, isn't it?'

'Looks like it.'

'We're going to be the last left.'

'Maybe we'll get a lock-in. Used to have 'em here all the time when I was younger,' she looked hopefully at the landlord, but he was clearing the bar with more energy than tact. 'New man,' she said in disgust. 'Lil, who had this place between the wars never used to chase us out like that. Fact she never used to close at all, far as I can remember.'

'Maybe we'd better be off.'

'Better had.'

'Allyoop.' I struggled to my feet, walked unsteadily round the table and gave Ada a hand on with her coat. Together we rolled out on to the street, blinking in the natural light, fresh air striking strangely on our tar-coated tongues.

'I'll see you home if you like.'

'Don't mind if you do.' I felt her weight as she tucked her hand through my arm for support. 'I could do with a bit of propping up.'

'Me too. That's why I'm walking you home. If I had to set off on my own, I'd probably fall over.'

'Funny how it gets to your legs, drinking mid-day.'

'Mm.' I was concentrating on weaving a path through the crush of schoolkids coming out of the swimming baths.

'I always reckoned it took twice as much to get me tiddly of an evening.'

'Me too.' My head was clearing a bit. It was comforting to bumble along, Ada's solid well-wrapped person leaning on me. We must have looked like a music-hall turn.

'I haven't been out on the bevvy for,' she waved her arm, nearly sweeping half a third form into the gutter, trying to indicate an enormous amount of time, 'oh, for donkey's.'

'Does you good.'

'There's life in the old girl yet.'

We got back to her flat without walking into any lamp-posts, which I was quite proud of. Ada flopped into her armchair, unbuttoning her coat, but not quite getting around to taking it off. I went into the kitchen and put the kettle on.

'Coffee?' I called to her.

'S'pose we ought,' was her answer. I took it to mean yes. Made two cups, strong but not shocking, and took them through.

'Ta, love.'

185

'Drastic measures.'

'You can always stop here and have a bit of a snooze, if you can't make it home yet.'

'I'll be all right.' We sat in silence for a while. My ears were ringing, and I felt the start of a thick head warming up. Better get going. I gulped down the last of the coffee, bitter and gritty, and stood up.

'I'd best be off.'

'If you're sure.'

'I'll be fine. It's only round the corner, anyway.'

'Go and get your head down.'

'Yes. Will you?'

'I think I might have a little lie down,' she nodded graciously.

'Seems like a good idea.'

'What did you learn?' she said unexpectedly.

'Pardon?'

'You said, back there in the pub, that you'd learned a lot. Doing this, stuff about John. You know.'

'Oh yes.' I collected my thoughts. 'Different things. Some about other people. Some about myself. Motives and all that. You know.'

'What?'

'Well, there was John, model soldier, good in a fight, realising that there wasn't any point for him in the violence he was engaged in.'

'Yes?'

'And there was me, if you like, woman of peace writing about man of war, and having realised there was no point in non-violence for me. Seemed funny.'

'You reckon?'

'Yeah.'

'Life is, though.'

'What?'

'Funny.'

'You're right there. I've got to scoot.'

'Mind how you go.'

'Will do.'

'Give us a hand up out of this chair before you go. It clings like a bloody octopus when you've had a few.' I stretched out my hand, clasped hers, pulled her to her feet.

'You're a pal,' she said, 'even if you do take yourself too serious sometimes.'

186

'Thanks,' I grinned at her. 'I'm thinking of giving it up some day.'

'Why wait?'

'Us introverts you know. Slow to change and all that.'

She held the door open for me. I stepped out on to the landing.

'High time you got started then.'

'Maybe tomorrow. Don't bully me.'

She laughed and gave me a friendly pat on the shoulder.

'Take care.'

'And you.'

'And pop round again soon, won't you?'

'Sure.' I gave her a quick hug, left her smiling and set off for home.